# PLAY THE PART

*Because some mistakes
are worth making twice*

# NAOMI LOUD

FIRST EDITION

Cover Design: Cat at TRC Designs

Editing: Louise Johnson, Literary Maiden Editing

Proofreading: Shanireads

www.naomiloud.com

# AUTHOR'S NOTE

This book is *messy*. If you do not like OWD or OMD, this book might not be for you. These are two flawed individuals just trying to figure it out. I love them with all my heart.

Although Play the Part is a contemporary romance, it deals with heavy subject matter and may contain triggering situations such as: prison environment, cheating (not the main couple), other woman drama, other man drama, PTSD, feeling of abandonment, childhood neglect, absent mother, deceased father, panic attack (on page), anxiety, witnessing a suicide (quick mention), gaslighting (not between the main couple), alcohol & drug addiction (not on page, secondary character), implied cheating (but don't you worry, bestie).

*To my muse, Meghan. They say you should write with only one person in mind. You're my person.*

# 1

# HUXLEY

I'm all alone.

My body is shaking.

*I'm alone. I'm so fucking alone.*

I curl my fingers into a tight fist, nails biting into my sweaty palms, willing myself not to shake. I can't show weakness. I can't show emotion.

*I'm alone, so fucking alone.*

*Alone, alone, alone, alone—*

"Step up, state your name and age," a stern voice dictates.

Snapping my head up to face Officer Berty on my left, I choke down my beating heart before quickly walking up to the bench on shaky legs where he's waiting for me. The intake room is full of men just like me, waiting for their turn. But the silence is stifling.

"Huxley McKenna." My voice cracks, I don't bother clearing my throat, and push through. "Eighteen."

Officer Berty glares down at me from the height of his booted feet, his face freshly shaven with ruddy cheeks and a severe brow.

I want to puke.

I want to scream.

I want to bash my fists against my head and wail.

"One article of clothing at a time. Got it?" His lips curl with every word.

He hates me. He hates everyone here.

My mouth is so dry I can barely lick my lips, but I give a quick little sniff and nod silently.

"Shirt first," Officer Berty orders.

As I pull my shirt off, the first hit of the cold air on my heated skin solidifies my fate.

I'm a prisoner.

Scum of the earth.

I'm nothing but a failure.

I hand Officer Berty my shirt.

Then come the shoes.

"Bang them together," he barks.

I do as he said.

"Socks next. Turn them inside out."

The floor is dirty, grit digs into my naked soles as I bite into my cheek, knowing what will eventually come next.

I take my jeans off.

Shake them.

"Boxers."

Such an innocuous word. But here. In this room. My forehead breaks out in a cold sweat.

I stick my fingers under the elastic but hesitate.

*Don't show weakness.*

I push them down my legs and turn them inside out as instructed before handing my underwear to Officer Berty.

I'm now naked in a room full of strangers.

Stripped bare and hopeless.

"Stretch out your arms. Let me see your palms."

Officer Berty's glare stays clinical, but it scorches my skin nonetheless. His gaze sears into my soul and carves gashes into my naked body.

My mind slips somewhere far away while my body obeys his orders. His words become one long, mashed-up sentence. I barely register a thing.

*Openyourmouthwidestickoutyourtongueliftupyourtoplippull-downyourbottomlipliftyourarmsintheairbendyourrightearbendy-ourleftearfingersthroughhair.*

"Lift your piece."

I snap back to full awareness.

He means my dick. Shame burns like gasoline through my veins.

With cold fingers, I follow the order.

"Lift your sack." This time, I hear disgust in his tone.

I'm sure he wants to be here just as much as I do. But I'd switch positions with him in a heartbeat if it meant I could walk out of this room a free man.

He orders me to turn around.

Lift my right foot.

Lift my left.

Bend over.

"Spread your cheeks."

I thought I already knew what self-loathing felt like. Thought I knew it intimately. But no feeling will ever compare to this very moment. Nothing will ever match the intensity of my revulsion—my rage.

For myself. For the system that failed me. For the parents that brought me into this miserable life. For the same parents who gave me nothing.

*You're no better than her now.*

Just like my mother.

Locked up and worthless.

I pretend there aren't multiple sets of eyes on me and pin my gaze to the ground as I spread my ass cheeks.

"Cough."

I cough.

"Alright, get dressed," Officer Berty snaps.

A wave of relief washes over me as I hurriedly stand up, grab my clothes, and get dressed as fast as possible. He points to the end of the hallway and tells me to face the wall and not speak.

My feet lift up and down, but I feel like a puppet on a string, as if most of me isn't even here.

A few men are already standing in line. I step up next to them.

We ignore each other.

Face the wall.

*Think about what you've done.*

# 2

# HUXLEY

*Five Years Later*

My skin feels too tight. My clothes too itchy.

I pick at a hangnail and chew on my thumb as I try to drown out the noise, but nothing I do helps. Everything is too loud. Too bright. Too much.

I'm at my brother Ozzy's engagement party. He's been with his girl for six years now, but he said he wanted me out of prison before getting married.

That should have made me feel good.

It doesn't.

All it does is remind me that I spent almost half of my twenties in prison and made him wait to marry the love of his life. For a stupid fucking decision I made when I was seventeen. I was the getaway driver in a liquor store robbery gone wrong. The car was stolen, so they eventually got me for Grand Theft Auto.

Ozzy should have forgotten about me.

Everyone else has.

I study him from where I'm sitting. He seems happy. Like *really* happy. Eyes bright, shoulders relaxed. He's dancing with James, his fiancée, and his friends on the small makeshift dance floor they made by pushing some of the dining room tables against the wall near the kitchen. They closed their friend Itzel's restaurant just for their engagement party.

It's meant to be intimate.

Still, there are too many people here for my taste.

I've been out for a couple of months now. But it still feels like there's a rope around my neck, choking me. Ozzy told me that therapy would probably help. I told him to fuck off. The feeling is especially acute when I'm around practical strangers and can't drink alcohol to numb the edges.

*Fucking probation.*

I abruptly stand up and head for the back door.

At least I'm still allowed nicotine.

---

THE BACK DOOR SWINGS OPEN, letting the music spill out along with Connie, James' best friend from LA.

"Oh!" she blurts when she realizes who's outside with her.

I already feel like a fucking pariah, but the look she gives me just solidifies the feeling.

I look away, pushing the smoke from my lungs out into the night sky.

*They can all fuck off.*

I pretend to ignore her, toying with my tongue ring for something to do, but I can sense every small move she makes. A skill I picked up in prison. Amongst others.

With the quiet scuffs of her heels on the asphalt, she seems to deliberate, but eventually, she says, "I just needed some air."

Her giggle is disingenuous, but I look back at her anyhow.

The light above the door bounces off the red in her hair. It almost looks gold from this angle.

"And maybe a small drag of that?" Her hazel eyes sparkle like we're sharing a secret as she brings her index finger and her thumb close together before pointing to my cigarette. "I never really smoke, but I just had a couple of glasses of wine and—"

"I don't care."

I'm pressed against the brick wall and make no effort to lean any closer, but still hold my arm out toward her so she can grab my cigarette. Connie scoffs, slightly vexed, but still takes it out of my hand. She takes a drag, her eyes fixed on me.

"Haven't seen you since Jamie's first Christmas with Ozzy."

*God ... Is this chick for real?*

I drag my tongue over my teeth and look down at the ground before lifting my gaze to the sky. "I've been busy."

This time, her laugh is real. "You're quite the charmer."

My attention lands back on her as she takes another drag of my cigarette. She's propped an elbow onto her opposite palm, the cigarette dangling from dainty fingers. Her eyes are narrowed, head cocked to the side, clearly assessing me.

A shiver tickles my nape.

"How old are you now, anyway?"

My first reflex is to bite out an annoyed, "*Why do you care?*" But I let the words simmer on my tongue and instead say, "Twenty-three," then add quickly, "Twenty-four in October."

I internally cringe. I sound like a fucking kid counting their age in halves and quarters trying to sound older. It's especially mortifying knowing that she must be around the same age as James, who is twenty-eight. I try to offset the feeling by barking for her to give me back my cigarette.

She quirks a smile. Unbothered by my aggressive outburst. The silence floats around us before she steps a little closer to me and hands me back my smoke.

She doesn't step back, and her body so close to mine makes my skin start to itch again. She's almost my height with her heels, her hazel eyes lifting upwards ever so slightly to meet my gaze. Shooting me another coy smile, she slides a finger over my forearm.

"Nice tattoo."

My skin breaks out into goosebumps, and I look down at where the pad of her finger is slowly pulling away from my arm. She's pointing at a shitty stick-and-poke tattoo of an eight-ball my bunkmate gave me two years ago.

The tattoo is anything but *nice*.

The realization that she might be flirting with me hits me square in the jaw. I suddenly feel cornered between the wall and the dumpster next to me. I croak out a *Thanks* and avoid her gaze, hoping she'll take a step back soon.

She lingers for a few seconds longer, watching me smoke.

"Anyway," she says as she turns around. My eyes drop to her ass in her tight green pants. They fly back up before she looks at me over her shoulder. She shoots me a wink. "See you back in there."

---

EVERYTHING IS STILL TOO LOUD, too bright, too much.

But ever since the shared cigarette with Connie a few hours ago, I haven't been able to keep my eyes off of her. I've memorized every toned curve on her lithe body from head to toe, and it's made everything else a little more bearable.

I keep convincing myself that I've made everything up, but then I catch her staring at me from across the room, and it feels like there's a fist squeezing my lungs into a tight ball.

I'm sitting at a table with my younger sister Sophia and baby brother Charlie. They're the only other sober people here since they're both underage—nineteen and thirteen, respectively.

Ozzy became their legal guardian three years ago when our dad died of liver failure.

None of us were shocked. He was an alcoholic and a piece of shit. Technically, our mother is still alive. I hear she's out of prison, but no one has heard from her in years.

Sophia is listening to another one of Charlie's weird tangents about the Vietnam War, which he's been hyperfixated on since he watched *Full Metal Jacket* last year. I pretend to listen as I track Connie's whereabouts around the restaurant.

"Wait, where you going?" Charlie squawks when he sees me stand up. "I haven't gotten to the best part yet!"

"I'll live." I give him a condescending pat on the head, my eyes still on Connie, and his teeth narrowly miss my hand.

I see Ozzy near the bar with James and avoid their line of sight, not wanting to be pulled into a conversation. As inconspicuously as I can, I move to stand near the swinging kitchen doors, Connie just a few feet away.

She's facing me, talking to someone whose name I didn't bother remembering. Her eyes flick to me, then back to her friend. I try not to feel awkward just standing there, leaning against a table as casually as possible while my heart is racing.

*I'm such a fucking idiot.*

I'm about to bolt when I see Connie move away from her friend and slowly strut my way. I notice her quick glance toward James as if double-checking that we're not being watched. My stomach twists into a knot at the implication.

"Hey," she says softly.

"Hey," I croak back, swiping a hand over my buzzed head before rubbing the back of my neck.

She studies me for a second, the music drowning us in bass, before curling a finger around the belt loop of my jeans and giving it a short tug. It's quick, and her hand is off me just as fast, but I feel like I'm toppling over the edge of reason.

She smiles, her tongue pushing into her cheek.

"Follow me?"

My throat tightens, and I lose the ability to speak.

I swallow hard, my gaze locked with hers, and nod.

# 3

# CONNIE

*Fourteen Months Later*

I can feel my blood pressure rising the longer I stare at it. My hands clench harder around the few items of groceries I have propped against my chest as I wait in line at the checkout.

I stare at it some more.

Burn a hole right through it.

*I'm going to scream. I swear I will.*

It's finally my turn in line. I unceremoniously chuck everything on the conveyor belt and grab the tabloid magazine with as much ire as possible, slamming it beside the organic bananas. I add a pack of orange Tic Tacs to my purchases as an afterthought. The cashier rings up my items, her eyes dipping to the tabloid magazine before setting it to the other side.

"Oliver Campisi," she chirps in her best Venice Beach vocal fry. "I've loved him since I was sixteen and saw him in *Eternal Hearts*." She smiles. "That'll be $35.60."

My blood boils, as I forcefully shove everything into my tote bag, including *fucking* Oliver Campisi from *Eternal Hearts*. I tap my card with venomous haste and finally make eye contact with the cashier. My smile is lethally saccharine.

"Just so you know — Oliver Campisi is a piece of shit nepo baby who can't act to save his life."—I shove my tote bag on my shoulder—"Oh!" I say a bit brighter. "Not to mention his raging mommy issues."

My little mic drop moment barely gets a reaction. The cashier stares at me blankly. I want to screech like a banshee but instead snatch the receipt out of her hand and storm out.

———

I CAN'T EVEN WAIT till I get home, the magazine burning a hole in my tote bag. I find a bench facing the ocean and pull the damn thing out. I reread the headline as if it's not permanently seared into my psyche.

*Trouble in paradise? Hollywood heartthrob Oliver Campisi caught sharing stolen kisses with* The Enigma *co-star Harriett Lemmy.*

"Fucking egotistical loser," I grumble under my breath as I flip the pages to find the article. "Two-timing narcissistic cokehead."

Nothing about this is *news* to me. I discovered Oliver was cheating on me two days ago from a *concerned friend* who I think took more pleasure in telling me the juicy piece of gossip than actually coming from a place of genuine friendship.

Oliver and I had been dating for almost a year. And I can't deny that being Campisi's girlfriend did help put me on the map as an actress. Nothing major, a few guest spots here and there, but it was far more than what I had been able to land on my own in the six years of living in LA.

I'm not naive. I know everything in Hollywood is transactional, but a hopeful part of me still believed that maybe Oliver and I had a genuine connection.

I was sorely and categorically *wrong*.

I skim the article, the glossy pages crinkling under the force of my hard grip.

*Seen cozying up at Joie … Giggling like teenagers … Left arm in arm after midnight.*

The tabloid fails to mention that it wasn't *just* Harriett Lemmy.

There were others … *many* others.

I'm mortified. I look around me, suddenly paranoid that someone will recognize who I am. I don't know what's more embarrassing: Being cheated on by Oliver Campisi or caught reading a tabloid magazine about it in broad daylight.

Still, it doesn't prevent me from letting the surge of rage overtake me. I spring up from the bench as I rip up the pages of the magazine like a scorned lover—because I am—before balling it up and dunking it into the nearby trash can.

My phone buzzes in the back pocket of my jean shorts, and I fish it out. My heart drops into the pit of my stomach.

*It's Oliver.*

I've been ignoring his texts and calls ever since the news broke. I nearly hurl my phone into the ocean to get away from him. I give my phone the middle finger and let out a small screech between clenched teeth before blocking his number.

---

I'M ROTTING in bed when Jamie, my best friend, calls. She lives back east in our hometown, Marsford Bay. It's a video call, and I deliberate not answering considering my current state, but do so anyway.

"Hi, babe." My voice cracks, and I want to disappear into my silk pillows.

Jamie takes a second to answer. "Have you been crying?" Her tone is soft and gentle, and … that's it, I'm withering away from embarrassment.

"No." I look away from the screen. "Maybe."

I look back just in time to see her cant her head in concern. Genuine concern. Because it's Jamie. My favorite person in the entire world. She already knows about Oliver. Anyone with a beating heart and access to the internet must know by now.

"I miss you." My bottom lip starts to tremble. Tears blur my vision, and I wipe them away with a groan.

"Oh, Connie …" she says tenderly, "I miss you too. So much. Ugh, I wish I could hug you right now."

I shrug. "Whatever. It's fine. I'm fine." I wipe away another wayward tear, vexed that my tear ducts are betraying me like this.

"Why don't you come down and visit?" Jamie offers, "You could come for Thanksgiving? We're hosting this year, and Ozzy already has a whole menu planned." She laughs warmly, and my already bruised heart pinches with envy at the love she shares with her fiancé.

Pure. Unconditional. Everlasting.

But the feeling is quickly swept under the rug when she mentions a family gathering. Especially knowing that Ozzy's younger brother will most likely be there.

I cringe and push the foggy memory away. It's a quick reflex, a well-honed muscle because I've been suppressing that *specific* memory for over a year now.

"I don't know … maybe." My response is half-hearted at best. "I might be busy."

"Please! You haven't visited since the engagement party, while I've been to LA *twice* since." Her blue eyes sparkle through the screen, full of love and hope. Then, almost like an afterthought, she adds, "It's like you're avoiding Marsford Bay or something."

Her comment is light-hearted and not meant to mean as much as it does.

*Marsford Bay isn't what I've been avoiding …*

"I'll think about it."

Jamie celebrates my noncommittal response as if my bags are already packed, and we hang up the call not long after. I flop onto my back, my phone resting on my chest, and stare at the ceiling. My thoughts are muddled, clambering on top of one another, and I watch them flash behind my mind's eye like a strobe of neon lights.

I hate to admit how much this breakup hurts. I feel like someone hollowed me out with a rusty spoon. Nothing in my life is working out like I had hoped, and it's getting harder and harder not to feel sorry for myself. The familiar itch to escape all my problems and pretend nothing is wrong rears its weary head. Maybe a visit back home is exactly what I need.

# 4

# CONNIE

Jamie's house is tucked inside a quiet street in Benfield, a trendy neighborhood popular with young families and restaurateurs. Jamie and Ozzy are—*technically*—both.

They own a small, yet very popular, sandwich shop just a few blocks away called Enter Sandwich, an obvious ode to the Metallica song. As for being a young family, they might not have children of their own, but Jamie has treated Ozzy's siblings as family ever since they got together almost seven years ago. It was around the same time that Jamie cut her parents out of her life.

Perfect, albeit bittersweet, timing.

Guilt spears through me at the thought of her connection to Ozzy's siblings ...

*God, what the hell was I thinking?*

I climb the few steps up to her small porch and ring the doorbell. The grey door is adorned with a large autumnal wreath, and I don't need to ask to know Jamie crafted it herself.

My heart is in my throat while I wait to be greeted. I try to shake the nerves off, looking skyward and inhaling slowly.

"*Get a grip. Who cares,*" I mutter to myself.

My small puffs of cold air taunt me as if complicit with my anxious thoughts.

I'm not sure what exactly I'm referring to. My *very* public humiliation or the fact that I'm about to see Huxley for the first time since ... well since—

"Connie!" A wave of relief washes over me when Sophia, Ozzy's sister, opens the door. "Finally, someone interesting to talk to," she says with a roll of her green eyes, flashing me a mischievous smile.

Walking in, I bring her into my arms after closing the door behind me. "Ugh, Sophia," I grumble into her short, blonde hair. "Please tell me there's alcohol in this house."

Sophia was just a teen when I first met her, but we clicked immediately. She's the little sister I never had, and I made a point to keep in contact throughout the years.

Sophia snickers. "Of course there is." Then, adding much louder over her shoulder, "Even though I'm *still* not allowed to have a glass of wine even when it's *literally* Thanksgiving, and I'll be twenty-one in two months."

We share a private laugh, and I give her a wink, wordlessly promising her that I'll sneak her a glass when no one is looking.

The house is already lively, a crowd of Jamie's Marsford Bay friends milling about the living room, plates of hors d'oeuvres set up on a table near the already lit-up Christmas tree.

Sophia takes my coat, revealing my yellow Miu Miu blouse and knitted skirt underneath. I step into the living room, suddenly feeling awkward. I wave at a few familiar faces, hoping I'm imagining the pity I see on their faces. I toy with my gold ring, not knowing what to do with my hands.

*Kill me.*

Thankfully, Jamie appears out from the kitchen, looking like an ethereal fairy with her crown-braided pink hair and gossamer dress.

"You're here!"

Tears immediately well up in her eyes as she clutches me into her arms.

"Oh my god, stop," I say, chuckling warmly and hugging her back. "Such a Cancer, crying for literally anything."

She pulls away and dabs the corner of her eye. "I'm *sorry* if I'm happy to see my best friend," she replies with mock vexation. Looking over my shoulder, she adds, "Where are your bags?"

A twang of guilt crawls up my throat. "Oh — uh, I stopped by the hotel first." I try to keep my response as casual as possible, but I know what reaction is coming.

"Hotel? But I told you that you could stay here." The disappointment in her voice makes my teeth ache. "We have plenty of room now that Sophia and Huxley moved out."

The mention of his name has me scanning the room anxiously but there's no sign of him yet.

"I know ..." I say softly, rubbing her shoulder tenderly as I meet her gaze. "It was just easier this way." I pause. "Is everyone here?"

*Oh my god, you're being so obvious.*

Luckily, I haven't lost any of my acting skills since I landed, and Jamie doesn't pick up on any of my ulterior motives.

"I think so," she says, looking around as if assessing her guests, then points her thumb behind her. "Ozzy is in the kitchen with Itzel and Huxley. Alec couldn't make it."

My heart skips a beat, but I swallow down my nerves.

"Great," I say, slapping on a fake smile. "Let me go say hi — is there wine in the kitchen?"

Jamie smiles and nods, then ushers me through the living room and into the kitchen. My legs turn slightly wobbly, and I have no other sane choice but to brace myself for the inevitable.

Huxley's back is to us when we walk in. I'd pick out his

close-cropped blue hair anywhere. He's always been a little taller than his older brother, and by what I've seen—and *felt*—of his build, he spent his whole stint in prison lifting weights.

My nerves are so frazzled that something suddenly takes over me. Like a switch, I slip into the Connie that oozes confidence. The version of me that is unbothered and is the life of the party. Itzel, who was the head chef when Jamie and Ozzy worked at Orso, sees me first. She's not cooking but always seems to be more at ease in the kitchen.

"Look who I found!" Jamie announces happily.

I focus on Itzel's welcoming smile, but my entire body picks up on Huxley freezing just a distance away. I swallow hard and give Itzel a quick hug before beelining for the open bottle of wine on the kitchen island. Luckily, there are a few clean wine glasses beside it, so I don't need to forage for one.

Now fully locked into my smooth and casual persona, I pour myself a glass. "Hi, guys," I say with a cheeky grin. "Miss me?"

Ozzy is standing over the stove, busy stirring some kind of sauce and sauteeing mushrooms in a pan with a deft flick of the wrist. He flashes me a smile from over his shoulder, but he's soon distracted by Huxley abruptly walking out of the kitchen, not once looking my way.

Jamie's smile fades. "What got into him?" she says to no one in particular.

My stomach adds another knot to the already twisted mess, but I push out a forced laugh and take a large gulp of my wine.

Turning to face us, Ozzy blows a brown curl out of his eye as he wipes his hands on the white rag flung over his shoulder. His gaze flicks to Jamie, and they quickly share a wordless conversation before he turns his attention back to me. His blue eyes crinkle as he smiles.

"Hungry?"

# 5

# HUXLEY

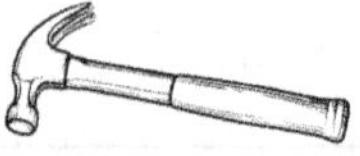

I wanted to leave.

I even made it all the way outside, but my feet never left the porch. I told myself I was only staying because Sophia was my ride back home. We live together now. I smoked two cigarettes back to back, muttering complaints into the cold night before I stepped back in.

Now, we're all gathered around the dining room table, and I'm trying to choke down some mashed potatoes while Connie is sitting a few chairs opposite me.

The yellow of her blouse brings out the gold in her red hair, and I fight the urge to stab a fork into my eye at even noticing such a detail.

I shouldn't care.

I *don't* care.

She hasn't tried to address me since she first walked into the kitchen, and I haven't said a word to anyone since we sat down to eat. Luckily for me, it's not completely out of character.

I've been out of prison for sixteen months now, but people still walk on eggshells around me—especially Ozzy's friends. At least that means they leave me alone most of the time. But I'd rather not be here to begin with.

It all feels so fake. Especially when Ozzy tries to play the patriarch of the family.

Give me a fucking break.

Dishes full of food that *still* taste too rich for me are passed around, everyone chattering excitedly about how good everything looks.

Sophia, who is sitting to my right, elbows me in the ribs.

My head snaps to my side.

"The hell was that for?" I grit out.

"You look like you're planning to murder someone," she says from the side of her mouth.

"Maybe I am."

Sophia is one of the few who hasn't treated me any differently since I've been out. She disregards my comment and, with both hands, gestures for me to smile like a stage mom prompting her kid on stage.

I glare even harder, but she simply presses her lips together and looks away, unbothered.

"So Connie," I hear Michelle, one of James' friends, say from somewhere to my left. I grow still, listening in without looking over. "How long are you staying in town for? Just for Thanksgiving?"

I'm burning a hole into my plate, pushing some veggies around while I wait for Connie to answer.

"Actually, I was thinking of staying until January."

James chimes in, her voice pitched high in excitement. "You are?"

Sudden dread at the news turns into a lump in my throat, and I finally look up.

Connie's attention is on James sitting beside her while she toys with her wine glass. "Yeah, I figured, why not?" She shrugs. "It's not as if I have much waiting for me back in LA."

The table falls unusually quiet. I might not be online much, but even I know why everyone is suddenly acting weird.

Connie's cheeks turn slightly rosy. She laughs, trying to break the tension, and looks around the table breezily, although her gaze never finds mine.

"It's okay, guys," she finally says with a dry chuckle. "You can ask me about it. I don't mind."

There's a loaded second where everyone at the table seems to deliberate until Michelle launches into a barrage of questions about Oliver Campisi and Connie's glitzy Hollywood life. She answers them all with humor and a smile, the energy around the table easing back into casual conversation.

The mention of her ex pisses me off, but I pretend not to be remotely affected while I wrestle with the goading fact that she'll now be around *a lot* more often. Worse is that she's been ignoring me since the engagement party; she just disappeared, never to be heard from again, and she's still ignoring me now.

I slowly lose my appetite.

I'VE BEEN LYING in bed, in the pitch black of my room, staring at my ceiling for over an hour.

Sophia and I came back from Ozzy's a while ago. It must be close to two a.m. by now. She wanted us to watch *Die Hard* together, but I opted for sitting in silence in my bedroom instead. Even I know my attitude was especially sour tonight, but Sophia didn't push it.

"Your loss," she said.

As if watching *Die Hard* for the thousandth time since we were kids would be a life-altering event or something. The TV turned off some time ago, so she must have gone to bed.

But I'm wide awake.

I pat for my phone next to me. Squinting at the brightness, I turn it down, my screen cracked in multiple places, but still functional. I broke it on one of my first days at the construction site this summer. Never bothered fixing it.

I tap on the Instagram icon. I'm not active on the app, it's my old account from before I went to prison. I almost deleted the entire thing when I first got out. There was something excruciatingly nostalgic about seeing my life frozen in time like that. Perpetually eighteen with his whole life in front of him. But I never did delete it. Maybe I like the pain it offers.

I pull up Connie's page. I don't follow her, but she's the first handle that pops up in my search bar. I've stared at her pictures and videos countless times over the past year. It's embarrassing. I would deny all of it if she ever found out.

I've convinced myself that the reason I haven't been able to forget about her is simple. She was just my first taste of normal after getting out of prison. It's not like I didn't get laid during those five years, but ... situations were different then.

Connie's hands on my skin felt like freedom that night.

*Fucking idiot.*

It was nothing but a quick fuck over a bathroom sink.

We didn't even talk afterward. She just fixed herself up and left me standing there. I felt fucking stupid. The next time I heard her name, she was dating that pretty boy from LA.

Been feeling stupid ever since.

I scroll down her feed and find my favorite picture of her. I don't even know why I like it so much. It's just a picture of her holding a margarita and smiling at the camera. I'd rather not think about who took the picture.

Instead, I stare at the crinkle of skin near her eyes. The small dimple on her right cheek. The small heart tattoo on her middle finger. I shift my position in bed, lying further back into the mattress and palm my dick. I keep staring at her picture, my cock growing hard under my grip, and deliberate just tugging one out. I tsk loudly, annoyed with myself, and pull my hand away. Closing the app, I open my text messages and find my conversation thread with Selina.

You up?

**6**

## CONNIE

"Do your parents know you're in town?"

Jamie waits for me to answer from across the restaurant table.

I've been home for almost a week now.

"Yeah." I take a sip of my Paper Plane before continuing. "But they're in the south of France vacationing with the twins."

Jamie and I come from the same background. Upper class and bougie. But Jamie chose to walk away from it all, whereas I still rely on my trust fund.

"I can't believe they're eighteen now," Jamie says with a chuckle as she signals the server for another round.

My parents divorced when I was young, and my mother remarried and had the twins, Edward and Matthew, when I was eleven. I love my brothers, but we've never been that close.

I laugh. "Don't remind me, I already feel ancient."

There's a small lull in the conversation as Jamie sips her Malbec. I watch her smile fade, eyebrows slowly dipping in concern.

*Great.*

I already know where this is going.

"So, have you talked to him?"

She doesn't have to say his name for me to know she's talking about *Oliver*. I look away, idly watching the other tables before finding her gaze again. The ache still smarts even though I've been desperate to ignore it. Maybe if I don't pay it any attention, it will go away.

"I blocked him. What's more to say?" I answer simply, playing with a few breadcrumbs on the white linen of our table.

"And that's it?" Jamie has that *If you don't start crying, I'll start crying for you* look in her eyes. "You don't want any closure?"

"Not everyone needs to pour their heart out to have closure, babe."

I mean it as a tease, but there's a sliver of irritation that still filters through.

"But Connie." Her look only intensifies.

I laugh, trying to break the tension. "Can we not? I don't want to talk about this on my birthday."

I turned twenty-nine today.

I woke up spiraling into an existential crisis about the passage of time, then promptly went to a spin class and cycled until I forgot how to think. I might have shed a tear or two in the dark of the spin studio, but there were no witnesses, and it was most likely sweat now that I'm thinking about it.

Jamie gives her head and shoulders a small shake as if snapping herself out of it.

"Yeah, you're right. Sorry — sorry." She flashes me a watery smile. "I just worry about you."

I reach over and snatch a fry from her plate.

"You don't have to worry about me." I wink conspiratorially as I take a bite of the cold fry, smiling as I chew. I make a small circular wave with my hand and swallow my bite before answering. "Everything happens for a reason and all that, right?"

She matches my smile and nods, but I can tell she doesn't really believe my laissez-faire attitude. She drops the subject nonetheless, and we finish our drinks in levity.

---

BY THE LINE already forming outside, Eden is packed for a Wednesday. It used to be my favorite club when I still lived here, hidden inside an industrial-looking building in the Garment District.

Jamie has to open the sandwich shop early tomorrow, so she left after dinner. Luckily, I'm a Sagittarius with a wide array of friends ready to party at the drop of a hat. And my birthday is an especially good excuse to party. Perfect night to drink and have fun. And who knows, maybe find someone to end the night with.

I see my friends Malik and Amy waiting for me outside and speed up my walk to meet up with them. We used to go to prep school together. Malik now works in finance but splits his time between here and Senegal, where his mom still lives. Malik might be the most beautiful man I've ever seen in my twenty-nine years. I always told him he should pursue a modeling career, but he never listened. Amy on the other hand, with her straight black hair and thick striking eyebrows, *did* become a model—an Instagram model—and lives in Dubai most of the year.

"Happy birthday, honey!" Amy leans in to kiss me on both cheeks. "God, can you believe how old we are now?" she comments with a laugh.

I turn to Malik next, who wishes me a quick happy birthday over my shoulder as we hug.

"Are we even going to know anyone in there anymore?" I reply with mirth when we both pull away.

"I know most of the staff," Malik says matter-of-factly.

Amy and I fall silent, looking over to Malik, impeccably dressed in a midnight blue Brioni suit, busy texting on his phone.

His dark eyes flick up. "What?" he says innocently. "I bring a lot of clients here."

"Right," I tease. "Clients."

Skipping the line thanks to Malik, we leave our coats at coatcheck and make our way to the table he reserved for us, a chilled bottle of Belvedere on ice already waiting there.

"You really *do* know the staff here." I blow him a kiss, and he sends me a coy wink as we settle around the booth.

As predicted, the club is busy. The place is huge, all one floor with tons of space to dance around the circular bar near the VIP tables where we sit. The music is loud, and the lights are low. It's perfect.

I grab three empty shot glasses and pour us a round.

"To me," I declare with a flirty smile, holding out my shot glass high up in the air.

Amy scoots closer to the edge of the booth, facing me. It makes her black silk dress ride up higher, revealing more of her thigh-high boots. "To the most perfect girl and the most perfect night!" Amy shouts over the music, holding out her shot just the same.

We toss back the alcohol, the vodka burning nicely down my throat.

I settle into the booth with a pleased sigh while I absent-mindedly watch Amy make us a round of Belvedere sodas.

There's a prickle at my nape, and I suddenly feel like I'm being watched. I dismiss the feeling but scan the room anyway, assessing the rowdy crowd while I try to find a good spot to dance later. My gaze eventually lands on the booth two tables away from ours.

I freeze, my heart jumping up my throat.

Huxley is staring straight at me. Or *glaring* would actually be more accurate. Eyebrows creased, green eyes severe and penetrating.

"Here," Amy chirps, handing me a drink.

I look back to our table and smile distractedly; I thank her and take the vodka soda out of her hand. Like a magnet, my attention falls quickly back on Huxley, barely listening to whatever Malik is trying to say over the loud bass.

*What the fuck is he doing here?*

It strikes me as uncharacteristic for Huxley to be at a club. Well, not that I know anything about him, but he'd look a lot less out of place in a grungy music venue where all the bathroom stalls are covered in graffiti.

There's a girl sitting on his lap, she's barely twenty-one by the look of her. She's laughing with the others sharing their booth while her arms are slung over Huxley's neck.

He isn't paying her any attention, his jaw tense while his eyes are still narrowed on me as he plays with a strand of her brown hair, slowly twirling it around his finger. I ignore the ridiculous pang of jealousy I get from watching him like this.

Having had enough of our little staring contest, I break eye contact and look away, bracing myself to shut him out for the rest of the night.

7

# HUXLEY

I can't believe Selina dragged me to this fucking place. I stick out like a sore thumb, and the only reason the bouncer let me in dressed in my tattered jeans and combat boots is because Selina works bottle service here on the weekends.

When I asked her why on earth she'd want to go out to the club she works at on her day off, she looked at me as if I were insane. I guess I don't understand the service industry since it seemed obvious to her. She never did give me an answer. Not that I really cared in the first place.

Selina and I met a few months back when I worked a construction job near her condo complex. She'd walk by the site almost daily and stare at me as she passed by. It took me a while to realize she might be into me—around the same time she walked straight up to me when I was on my lunch break and gave me her number.

My work crew gave me shit for weeks after that. I almost threw her number away out of spite. Told myself I wasn't looking for any distractions, but I did text her eventually. Out of boredom, mostly. We've been hooking up for a little over two months now. We both agreed it was nothing serious.

30

Especially because I only got off probation back in October. I still walk around with paranoia clinging to me like cellophane; one wrong move and I'm back in prison for another five years—or worse, for life.

I haven't gone out drinking much either.

But the thirst to just fuck it all to hell and drink until I black out is particularly strong tonight.

When I first spotted Connie strutting up to her table, I thought I had plucked her straight out of my overactive imagination. But then I realized even my imagination couldn't have conjured her up looking this good, with her tight black pants and a top that clung to her perfect tits.

I knew it was her birthday today. She wasn't very subtle about it online.

Twenty-nine ... and way out of my league.

The thought makes me bitter. Angry and pissed off with myself to even think I'd have a chance with her when she's done nothing but pretend I don't exist.

I was a big, fat *mistake.*

Story of my fucking life.

And who gives a shit anyway?

I barely know the girl. She can fuck right off for all I care.

Doesn't prevent me from spending the night tracking her movements from the corner of my eye, though. Selina is near the bar dancing with some friends. I'm sitting alone at our booth, stewing and drinking a watered-down rum and coke I made ages ago from the bottle at our table.

I should leave.

I should stop staring at Connie.

I do neither.

Looks like she came here with friends but has been flirting with anything that moves since we locked eyes a few hours ago. She hasn't glanced my way since. Now, she's dancing near the

DJ booth, a gaggle of losers around her as if she's the star of the fucking show or something.

I swipe my hand over the bottom half of my face, groaning under my breath. Finally having had enough, I leave the table and walk up to where Selina's dancing.

"I'm out of here," I say into her ear so she can hear me.

"What? Why?" she shouts back over the music, followed by a sexy pout. I can tell she's high and definitely not following me out of the club.

I make a face that sort of explains that I'm just not feeling it anymore.

She winds her arms around my waist and pushes her body against mine. Giving me a sultry look, she asks, "Can I still come over later?"

I consider saying no; the idea of having someone in my bed tonight feels suffocating, but I swear I can physically *feel* Connie on me. I need to get her out of my system.

"Sure," I say before giving her a quick kiss on the lips. "Call me when you're downstairs."

I turn around and head for the door. Unfortunately, I need to pass the DJ booth to reach the exit, and Connie is still acting like the club is named after her.

I weave through a throng of club-goers, resisting the urge to push everyone out of my way. I realize too late that Connie plans to intercept me. Her hand circles around my wrist, and I'm stopped in my tracks.

"Hey, kid," she says just loud enough for me to hear. She's visibly drunk, and her guard is down.

A storm of emotions flares inside of me. But the word *kid* rings in my ear, and I snap.

Anger wins.

I scoff and look at her up and down.

"Aren't you the star of the show tonight?"

I'm being sarcastic, but Connie is too far up her own ass to notice.

She giggles, eyes hooded with inebriation. "Well, it's my birthday, after all."

Her response does nothing to tame my irritation, and I go in for the kill.

"Considering your recent dating history, I should have known you were nothing but an attention whore."

I say it with venom and right next to her ear, as I rip my wrist out of her grasp. I linger just long enough to watch her face shutter in shock. I flash her a pleased but condescending smile and walk away.

It's all for show. Nothing about what I just did felt remotely good. By the time I grab my coat and the cold air of early December hits my face, I regret being such a dick. Outside, I pull my pack of smokes out of my pocket and light up before even thinking of hailing a cab. I need to calm down.

"What the fuck is your problem?"

I freeze, my hands still up near my face as I shelter the flame and take my first drag.

*Shit.*

She followed me out.

I keep the surprise off my face and slowly lift my gaze to meet hers.

She seems pissed but cold, having stormed out here without a coat. Her arms are clasped tightly around her chest while she waits for me to respond, nostrils flared and breathing hard.

"What the fuck is my problem?" I parrot back in disbelief while pointing to my chest. "What the fuck is *your* problem?" Two fingers now aimed at her.

She scoffs, a small puff of air leaving her glossy lips.

"What did I even do?"

Her question is meant to sound blameless, but she shifts on

her feet and looks away. I can tell she's feeling guilty. I don't bother answering. I just stare at her and smoke my cigarette.

Finally, she cracks and breaks the silence.

"It was a mistake, okay? I don't know what the hell I was thinking." She's being squirrelly, her eyes barely meeting mine. "You're Ozzy's little brother, for god's sake."

"I'm twenty-five," I reply flatly.

I don't know what it is about telling Connie my age, but it always feels like I'm trying to convince her of something. All it does is make me want to fling myself into traffic.

Her tongue smooths over her teeth behind her pursed lips as if deliberating what to say.

"It meant nothing." She says it much too softly, as if she's worried about hurting my feelings. I feel sick at the thought of her thinking I'm that fucking weak.

Her words hang between us while upbeat conversations from other smokers float in the air. We continue to stare at each other for a few rapid heartbeats.

I finally break the spell. Slowly shaking my head, I laugh dryly while flicking my cigarette to the snowy ground. I leave her standing there, not another word spoken between us.

**8**

## HUXLEY

"What's up *your* butt?"

I clench my teeth, exhaling deeply before sliding my gaze up from the book. I'm sitting near the window while Sophia is sprawled on the couch across from me, scrolling on her phone.

She's not even fucking looking at me.

"I haven't even said shit." My voice is flat and full of impatience.

"You don't have to. Your weird energy is stinking up the whole place."

She still hasn't looked up from her phone, the TV filling the silence between us with studio audience laughter.

"What the fuck are you even saying?" I answer with all the annoyance of dealing with a younger sister.

She huffs loudly as if I'm the one being difficult. Rolling her eyes up to the ceiling, she drops her phone on her chest, finally looking at me.

"You know, just because you were gone for five years, that doesn't magically erase that we grew up together. I just *know* these things, okay? You're not as misunderstood as you'd like to think."

She falls silent and quirks an arrogant brow.

I absentmindedly drag my barbell between my teeth as I try to choke down what she just said.

*Ouch.*

Sophia has a knack for calling it as it is without bothering to sugarcoat things.

My mind still spins with how my night ended yesterday. Calling Connie an attention whore wasn't my finest moment. I have trouble thinking about it without feeling ashamed. Then I remember her calling me *kid,* and I get angry all over again. But it was exactly what I needed to hear to snap me out of whatever infatuation I had for her.

She'll never take me seriously.

I was just an easy fuck.

An itch to scratch.

At least now, I know exactly where I stand with her. Although I should have known from the start. It's as if I lost all my social skills while I was rotting in prison. I hate how prison politics feel a lot more natural to me now. I got used to keeping my head down and my mouth shut. Simple. Straightforward. Even after more than a year, the outside still feels confusing. Stressful and overwhelming.

*Pathetic.*

I'm such an embarrassment.

I sigh, closing my book, and resign myself to admitting *some* of my anxiety to Sophia.

"It's just that ... I'm having — I don't know."

I stop talking, the words stuck somewhere between my heart and ribcage.

Sophia hums like a fucking therapist. "Great start."

My irritation flares. "Fuck off, Soph." I spit the words out, and she barks out a laugh.

"Come on, dude, give me something — What is it? Selina?" she asks innocently.

"No, it's not Selina, but —" I stop abruptly, rubbing my palm over the scruff on my cheeks.

I can't tell anyone about Connie. *Especially* Sophia. I know how close those two are.

*Shit.*

Maybe Connie was right.

We're just a disaster waiting to happen.

Sophia obviously picks up on whatever I didn't say out loud and springs up from her horizontal position. Her mouth drops open, blue eyes scintillating.

"Is there someone else?"

I shake my head, acting clueless. "No. Why would you say that?"

She extends her arm, pointing a finger at me, her mouth opening even wider. "There *is* someone else."

"It doesn't matter," I say quickly, now acting squirrelly.

"Why? Do I know them?"

I avoid eye contact and mumble, "It's nothing, drop it."

Sophia flashes me an unimpressed face. "Fine. You're no fun." She drops back onto her back. "You realize you haven't told me anything of substance, right?"

Guilt pricks at my conscience for being so closed off. I can't help it. I snap closed like a spooked clam in the ocean anytime there's even a whiff of vulnerability in the air.

I decide to move onto a less precarious subject.

"It's my first class tonight, I guess I'm just nervous."

"Woodworking?" Sophia asks with far too much hope in her tone.

As if the workshop Ozzy gifted me for my birthday back in October is somehow going to be the key to my rehabilitation. I hate how it felt like charity, especially from Ozzy.

But I still accepted the gift, unwilling to admit how much I wanted those classes. Ever since I learned a few basic skills in prison, it's something I've wanted to continue learning.

I guess Ozzy remembered.

I should be grateful. Instead, it makes me bitter, and I'm too messed up in the head to explore the reasons why.

"Yeah," I cross one ankle over the other. "Woodworking," I mutter.

"Oh, you're going to do great," she assures. "You've always had a knack for that stuff."

She's back on her phone. I think she knows if she pays me too much attention, I'll clam back up again. But she still lifts her gaze to meet mine and smiles before looking back down.

"Remember when you used Dad's old scrap wood and made a birdhouse out of it?"

I chuckle weakly. "Yeah, what a piece of shit."

"What?" she says, looking back at me. "The birdhouse? Or Dad?"

It's one of those jokes that are only funny to people like us —those who got the shit end of the stick and never caught a fucking break. Most people would find that kind of humor sad and morbid.

Instead, we fall into a fit of laughter.

I sit in the driver's seat of Sophia's parked car, watching the snow fall onto the windshield. It melts as soon as it hits the glass. I don't have a car of my own yet; my driver's license was only reinstated a few months ago. It was taken away when I was convicted. Another piece of my life to be ashamed of—stuck borrowing my younger sister's car like some fucking grade-A loser.

I arrived too early for the woodworking class. I've been wasting time in the car, landing on Connie's Instagram page like a moth with a death wish. She's posted a new video. It's one of those skits where she reenacts classic tropes from romcoms. It was only posted a few hours ago, and it already has thousands of likes and comments.

I watch the video a second, then a third time, smirking at her antics despite myself. She's funny and effortlessly charismatic, made to be an actress. I'm no better than any of her other lame-ass followers ... except *I* know what she sounds like when she moans. And how her tits fit perfectly into my palms.

I close the app with an irritated sigh, and my head falls backward onto the headrest. I watch the snow fall against the frosty glass for a little while longer before finally opening the car door.

I pretend my heart isn't beating against my chest as I make my way inside for my first real class since I was seventeen.

# 9

## CONNIE

S itting on the edge of my hotel bed, I stare at my phone. I'm gripping it so hard that the corners are starting to dig into my skin. I barely ever go into my Instagram requests; it's typically a minefield of men behaving badly. To put it lightly.

But it's Sunday night in Marsford Bay, and I'm crawling out of my skin, stuck with my spiraling thoughts and nothing to do. Jamie invited me for Sunday dinner, but I declined. One more flimsy excuse, and I know she'll soon be on to me.

I'll worry about the integrity of my friendship another day.

Right now, I'm staring at a mea culpa message from Oliver. It was sent a few days ago from a fake account. I feel *sick*, the shame and memory of being cheated on—and so publicly— threatening to pull me under. I've been running from the feeling for weeks now. I even flew back to Massachusetts to get away. But none of that matters when I can just open up my phone and find him there, waiting for me like a poisonous snake in the grass.

I'm biting my lip bloody, staring at his words.

*I'm so sorry ... Please unblock me ... It was a mistake ... You're the one I love ... I was fucked up ... Going to rehab ... Please forgive me.*

I can't believe him, blaming his affairs on his drug and alcohol addiction as if I'm just some inconsequential collateral damage. I fucking *hate* him.

Finally having enough, I throw my phone across the room, hoping it shatters into a million little pieces. It does not. I let out a pained shriek and fall backward onto the bed. I'm struggling to keep the tears at bay. Eventually, they do fall, silently traveling down my temples and disappearing into my hair.

I stare at the ceiling, the words from Oliver's message etched into my vision. I watch them flash one by one against the white paint, taunting me.

I can't stay in my hotel room for one second longer and jump up abruptly from the bed.

I settle for a late-night walk to clear my head.

MY MIND IS STILL RACING as I walk through the deserted streets of the North End. Although Marsford Bay is a large port city known for its many universities and bustling young demographic, the winters sometimes make it feel like a ghost town.

Especially when it's this cold outside.

I barely feel the bite of the wind, the hood of my red Burberry coat shielding me from most of it. The city is full of Christmas spirit, snow falling lazily from the sky and blanketing the streets in white. Seeing all the decorations as I walk makes my teeth ache with childhood nostalgia.

Christmas was always an extravagant affair when I was young, as if my parents were making up for lost time compared to their absence during the rest of the year. As a kid, I didn't care, as long as I was showered with gifts. The memory feels hollow now, but the nostalgia still lingers, especially when I'm feeling this lonely.

I had a good childhood, all things considered, if maybe a

little neglected. My parents weren't monsters, just not particularly present. At least they were supportive of my lofty goals, even when those aspirations were pipe dreams like moving to LA and becoming an actress.

*Maybe I should move back home for good.*

The thought knocks the wind out of me, and I stop in my tracks, sneakily looking around as if someone could have read my mind.

*No way.*

*I can't.*

I have a life in California. Not to mention that I'd feel like a giant failure if I moved back home right after my breakup with Oliver. As if I were a mistreated puppy running away with its tail between its legs.

*Nope—not a chance.*

I'm just having an existential crisis.

It'll pass.

Thankfully, I know exactly how to remedy it.

---

THERE'S a knock at my hotel door, and my heart skips a beat. I down the rest of my Chablis before giving myself a quick once-over in the full-length mirror. I opted for as little as possible—a braless tank top and silk shorts—considering the specific rendezvous. I don't want him to get any ideas, I messaged him for one thing and one thing only.

I slide the chain and unlock the door.

"Hi," I say breathily, adding just the perfect mix of flirty and sexy.

"Hey," Gael replies, quirking a smile.

He's the DJ from Eden. He started following me on Instagram after I spent most of the night dancing near his booth. I never followed him back, but he's been watching my stories for the past four days; I knew he'd be an easy catch.

I wave for him to come in, and he strolls in casually, making a show of pretending he's interested in the room decor, hands in his jeans pockets.

"Want any wine? I have a bottle open in the mini-fridge."

He looks over, his smile telling me he knows that we're both just dancing around the real reason he's here. His brown eyes darken, and I lick my lips.

"Sure."

I take my time pouring the wine, taking pleasure in the anticipation buzzing in the room. When I turn back to look at Gael, he's watching me, leaning against the desk near the window. His brown hair is cropped short, and my mind unexpectedly goes to Huxley and his shorn blue hair.

I bat the thought away as soon as it appears.

"Here." I hand him the glass with a smile.

His eyes are penetrating when he takes it from me, his fingers grazing against mine.

"Thanks."

I move to distance myself, but he hooks his arm around my waist, pulling me between his open legs. Enjoying that he's taking charge, I let out a husky laugh and wrap my arms around his neck.

"What about your wine?" I say playfully.

His free hand slips under my tank top, smooth fingers trailing up my spine. I shiver alongside the charged anticipation. He keeps our gaze locked, a flirty smile on his lips as he takes a slow sip, then carefully places it on the desk.

"I think you'll taste better."

He catches my lips with his, the tart wine still cold on his tongue. I moan into his mouth, and he pulls me closer to him. The kiss deepens, and the urgency of our desires skyrockets.

He pushes away from the desk while bringing his hands

under my ass, and I jump into his arms, my legs hooking around his waist.

As he blindly leads us to the bed, our kiss turns desperate before he drops me onto the mattress. He follows me down, bracketing me with his body as one of his hands finds my breast and squeezes. I arch my back, moaning in response.

And for a while, I forget everything.

I numb myself with pleasure and push away the harsh facts of reality in exchange for lackluster orgasms and one-night stands.

**10**

**HUXLEY**

Fresh out of the shower after staying the night, I walk into Selina's bedroom. I find her sitting on her bed, half-dressed in black panties and a t-shirt, grinning down at her phone. Holding the towel wrapped around my waist, I give her a curious glance, but she doesn't acknowledge me. She keeps giggling like a maniac as I try to find my clothes on the messy floor.

Selina might appear put together, but her bedroom begs to differ.

"What's so funny?" I finally ask, slightly irritated but unable to pinpoint why.

I step into my boxer briefs, standing near the end of the bed, waiting for her to answer me.

She's still grinning goofily when she glances up at me before her eyes dart back to her phone screen.

"Nothing, just gossip in the Eden group chat." It sounds like she's dismissing my question, but she then continues unprompted. "Just that, last week, Gael hooked up with that girl Oliver Campisi cheated on — she's in town apparently."

She says it so casually that I don't quite process the words until my mind finally catches up, and it suddenly feels like I'm going to puke up my own heart.

"Connie?" I croak.

My jeans are still unbuttoned as I stare at her dumbfoundedly for half a second too long.

Selina's eyes narrow as if reading my body language.

"Yeah, Connie Broadbent ... you know her?"

When I realize my slip-up, I quickly smooth away the shock from my face and look down as I finish buttoning up my jeans.

"Yeah — I mean not really. She's just a family friend."

*Who I fucked over a bathroom sink at my brother's engagement party last year.*

I look up just in time to see Selina's suspicion turn into excitement.

"Oh my god, really? Can you introduce me?"

"What? No," I mutter, feeling flustered. "Why?"

She shoots me a prissy look and shrugs, looking back down at her phone. "Why not? You know she's Instagram famous, right? She's got like over a million followers, plus she dated *the* Oliver Campisi — I'd die to get a picture with her."

We fall silent as she resumes typing on her phone, grinning and laughing under her breath. I itch to ask for more information on her latest work gossip.

*Was it only once?*

*Are they still hooking up?*

*Why him and not me?*

My thoughts make me sick, and anger soon surges through me like a deadly wave. Before I do or say something I regret, I find my t-shirt and hoodie and throw them on.

"I've got to go," I say dryly.

Selina looks up, slightly surprised, her phone now hanging loosely from her hand.

"I thought we were going for brunch?"

"I just remembered I need to help my brother with something."

It's a flimsy excuse, but I don't care.

Disappointment flashes across her face, but she conceals it quickly.

"Sure, okay," she says quietly. "Call me later?"

I nod, forcing a smile, and leave without kissing her goodbye.

---

"Are you stocking up for the apocalypse or something?" I hear Ozzy say from behind me.

I roll my eyes but don't say anything as I place a log on the chopping block, my back still to him. After positioning the axe so the blade lines up with the center, I take a large swing over my head, splitting the log in two.

"I just needed to think," I say, a little winded.

Ozzy approaches me from the left and surveys my work with an amused glint in his eyes.

"Well, according to the giant pile of wood, looks like you've been thinking for a while."

My first impulse is to bite his head off.

It always is when I'm dealing with my older brother.

If I were forced to psychoanalyze my resentment toward him, I'd probably blame it on him moving out when he was sixteen.

I was eight when he abandoned us. He left me and Sophia stuck in a house with an alcoholic father and a deadbeat mother; she was still around back then, pregnant with Charlie. Meanwhile, I did what I could to shield Sophia from most of the bullshit since she was only five years old.

Ozzy prides himself on having been there for us even when he moved out, claiming he was always around, making sure we were being taken care of. What a fucking lie. It's as if he selectively forgets those first few years when he just disappeared. He left us to struggle alone. And I always hated him for it. Admittedly, our relationship has gotten better since I got arrested, but I've never truly forgiven him for disappearing like that.

I take a deep swallow of cold winter air, wiping at my mouth with the back of my hand while still holding the axe. I look at Ozzy from the corner of my eye. He has this stupidly patient look on his face, and it's already grating at my nerves.

I *could* bite his head off, but I'm also currently standing in his backyard, unannounced, and chopping wood. Dropping the axe, I unzip my coat and take it off, throwing it atop the pile of wood. I pick up another log.

"So?" Ozzy says, still standing there, his hands stuffed in his jean coat pockets.

"So, what?"

I'm being intentionally dense, but I can't help it; he brings out the worst of me.

However, Ozzy's used to my attitude by now, and to my dismay, nothing about me really fazes him anymore.

"So what's on your mind, dummy?" he says in jest.

As the axe splits the log into smaller pieces, I let out a small grunt before shooting him a wary side look, but say nothing. I should have checked if he was home before I came over, he's always looking to fucking bond anytime we're alone together.

*Shoot me.*

"I didn't say I wanted to talk about it."

The words are a muttered hiss as I pick up the split pieces and place them with the—admittedly—ridiculously large pile of already cut wood.

I grab another log.

Ozzy watches me for a few minutes, the sound of the axe and my ragged breaths filling in the silence.

"If you don't want to talk to me, that's fine, but you have to talk to someone, Hux," Ozzy finally says.

I glance over at him, and the expression of concern on his face makes me want to hurl.

"Have you thought more about therapy?"

I pick up the split wood and scoff.

"Pass."

Ozzy sighs, raking a hand through his curls, but doesn't press the subject. I swallow the low throb of guilt at acting so difficult when all he's doing is trying to help.

*Too little, too late.*

We fall back into silence until finally, after a few more minutes of him watching me, he moves from his spot. "There's risotto in the fridge if you're hungry," he says before walking back inside.

**11**

## CONNIE

It's a sunny Tuesday afternoon, and the quaint coffee shop near my hotel is bustling with patrons. The tables are full of young professionals hunched over their laptops, some sporting expressions of deep concentration, while some are busy taking business calls while surrounded by total strangers.

I came here to do the same. Tucked in the corner near the windows, I've spent the past hour answering emails, and my stomach is now rumbling with hunger. I've been dodging my agent's calls for the past two weeks, and I know her patience is waning.

She's been trying to convince me that Oliver cheating was a blessing in disguise and a PR godsend. She's been trying to spin the story in my favor—without my help, as she keeps reminding me—since the news broke. I'm only now returning her *many* urgent emails, half-heartedly agreeing with her.

*Whatever helps my image, I guess.*

All of it suddenly sounds ridiculous to me. Was this really what I wanted? Was this really what I meant when I said I wanted to become an actress? I've always had such a romanticized image in my head of what it meant to be an actress. Move to LA, make it big and live happily ever after. Simple. Never did I imagine that it would mean cheating scandals and PR coverups.

I sigh, coming up for air from all the emails, and look at my phone for some distraction. There's a text from Jamie saying she'll be a few minutes late. Then there's a couple of messages from the few friends back in LA that I haven't ghosted yet since I've been dodging mostly everyone else. I feel too exposed. Too raw.

I open Instagram but ignore all my notifications. I never did reply to Oliver. I blocked his fake account and tried to push him out of my thoughts. By pushing Gael into my bed.

Ignoring Oliver doesn't seem to help with the angst, though, and it certainly doesn't seem to prevent my stomach from twisting every time I open the app, worried he'll just find another way to contact me.

Then again, even with all my efforts, I can't seem to get away from him. Every detail I've learned about him lately has been against my will, and I keep stumbling onto think-pieces about him online. Everyone seems to have an opinion about his mental health ever since he announced that he was checking into rehab last week.

I pause, my thumb hovering over the screen.

I deliberate.

Finally, I switch Instagram profiles and log into my secret account. The one I use when I want to go incognito. Only Jamie and a few others know I have one; even Oliver is oblivious.

I don't bother visiting Huxley's profile, the man has zero online presence. It's annoying. Instead, I type Selina's handle into the search bar.

It didn't take much sleuthing to find out who the girl was that Huxley was with at the club, especially after spotting her in Gael's Instagram stories and connecting the dots.

*Of course, she's a bottle service girl.*

Young, flirty, and always ready to party.

It's unclear what their situation is. The one thing I do know is that there isn't one picture of Huxley on Selina's feed, so it can't be *that* serious.

Not that I would care if it was.

I can't help but tap on her profile picture to access her Instagram stories. I tell myself that I'm not looking for anything in particular, just quenching my curiosity.

Her stories aren't revolutionary. Just the life of a typical young twenty-something: A few random reshares, a selfie, an aesthetic picture of a restaurant table.

Huxley appears on screen.

My heart sinks.

They seem to be at the same restaurant as in the previous picture. He's scowling at the camera, green eyes sardonic, black hoodie and arms folded over his chest. But there's the smallest of smirks on his lips, and I consider taking a screenshot of the picture just so I can zoom in closer on his mouth.

"Connie?"

I startle and slam my phone screen down on the table before looking up.

A brunette with wide brown eyes smiles down at me.

"Oh my god, Mary-Beth?" I stand up and give my friend a long hug. "I can't even remember the last time I saw you," I add when I let go of her, nostalgia creeping into my voice.

"I know, it's been way too long," she says with a similar intonation.

"Do you have time to sit?" I gesture to the free chair at my table.

She nods with a warm smile. "I only have a few minutes," she says while settling into the chair in front of me, "But I'd love to catch up longer if you're in town for a few days?"

"Of course! I'd love to. I'm here 'til January, actually," I say while I close my laptop and put it to the side so we have more space to talk. "So, how've you been?"

She laughs and looks at me mischievously. "How have *you* been?"

A small black cloud appears over my head, knowing exactly what she's alluding to, but I ignore it and laugh off her question. "*Please*, I'd much rather talk about you."

Thankfully, Mary-Beth takes the hint and smiles cheekily. "I've been good, got married last year. You remember Hugo from prep school?"

I pause and try to conjure up a face. One finally appears: Mousy and awkward. "Wait, are you talking about Hugo from *drama class*?"

She confirms with a nod, then says, "I married his sister."

She bursts out laughing, clearly tickled by her little misdirection, and I follow suit, barking out a laugh.

"Wow, congrats, I'm so happy for you," I say genuinely while I ignore the selfish sting of being single. "Are you still acting? God, I miss theatre."

My last comment is an afterthought, but one I realize is wholeheartedly true.

I *do* miss theatre. Those were simpler days. Nothing like the shit show that is Hollywood.

"I am!" she explains with stars in her eyes, but then her smile drops. "Well, I mean I was — it's such a shame that the Remi is closing down."

"The Remington is closing down?" I parrot back with shock. The regional theatre has been an institution in the artsy Marsford Bay world for as long as I can remember. I spent plenty of summers interning and helping out with production, daydreaming about my future as a serious actor. "Since when?"

"Pretty much now," Mary-Beth answers with a disappointed pout. "We closed out our last show back in November. They just haven't found any buyers."

My thoughts start racing. "So it's for sale?"

She shrugs and nods. "Last I heard." She looks down at her phone and then stands up. "Anyway, I've got to run." She flashes me another smile, hopeful this time. "Call me, okay?"

I agree with promises of a longer catch-up and plenty of margaritas, giving her one last hug before she walks out the door. I slowly settle back into my chair, my mind reeling.

The Remington is for sale?

# 12

# HUXLEY

"**H**uxley, can I talk to you before you go?"

I freeze midway through packing up my things. My first thought is that I'm in trouble. My second is to pretend I didn't hear him.

Begrudgingly, I look up and find my woodworking teacher standing near my work table. He's a gruff-looking dude who appears to be in his early forties and first introduced himself as Whitman, but everyone calls him Whit. I've been taking his classes for three weeks now, and after getting over my initial case of first-day nerves, I've been really enjoying it. Whit included.

Within a millisecond, I've analyzed his body language. It's a skill I perfected in prison. I conclude that his demeanor is friendly. He's sporting a backward cap and another one of his flannels, just standing there, smiling, waiting for me to answer.

I look back down and resume packing my things.

"Sure, what's up?"

"Well," he starts, and I feel him take a step closer to my bench. His tone is eager, as if excited about what he's gearing up to say. "Since this is the last class before the holidays, I just

55

wanted to tell you how great of a job you've been doing. You're definitely a natural."

I sneak him a glance from the corner of my eye. He's still smiling, and it's softening the look in his eyes, a proud expression on his face. Suddenly, I feel cornered—and incredibly awkward.

"Uh ... thanks, I guess," I croak, unable to look him in the eye.

"I hope to see you back in January," he adds.

Zipping up my backpack, I throw it over one shoulder.

"Yup. See you in January," I mutter and start for the door, barely giving him a final glance.

"Happy holidays!" he hollers from behind me

Without looking back, I send him a wave before bolting out of the woodshop.

---

Sophia had a shift tonight at Popol Vuh, Itzel's restaurant, so I had to take the subway back home. It's unusually warm for mid-December, and everything is wet.

The subway station is about an eight-minute walk to my place, and I just *know* that the dirty slush will soak through the small hole in my combat boot. Not to mention that my ratty earphones died while I was listening to them on the subway.

I sigh, shoving my hands in my bomber jacket, and accept my miserable fate for the rest of the walk home.

*What else is new?*

I'm cutting through an alley when I hear a faint sound coming from the dumpster. I don't pay it any mind until I hear it again. This time, I'm almost positive it sounds like a kitten's meow.

Stopping in my tracks, I slowly approach the dumpster, my ears perked.

I hear it again.

*Shit.*

It's definitely a cat—and it sounds like it's in distress.

I push up on my toes and stretch my neck to look into the dumpster, but can't see anything. The meows only get louder and more urgent as if it's somehow sensing me there. I look around the alley not really knowing what I'm looking for and curse under my breath when I realize I'm going to have to dumpster dive if I want to save this damn kitten.

I spot a milk crate near one of the back doors, most likely used to sit on during smoke breaks, and jog to go fetch it. Milk crate in hand, I return to the dumpster and set it on the ground, bottom facing up. If I base it on the sounds of the meows, the kitten is somewhere in the far right corner of the dumpster.

Pushing with my two hands, I heave myself up and swing a leg up so I can catch the ledge with my foot. I manage to perch myself on the side like some kind of fucking gargoyle, the stench of garbage hitting me square in the face.

I grumble another slew of profanities, trying to psyche myself up and finally maneuver my way down into the dumpster. My feet land on uneven ground, garbage bags full of god knows what squelching under my boots, and I start to uncontrollably gag.

The meows grow louder, but I can't see any sign of life in the pitch-black pit. I take my phone out and turn on the flashlight. Aiming it toward the sound, I still don't see anything. It's then that I realize the kitten is inside a bag. I fall to my knees and start ripping at the garbage until I find the plastic bag it's stuck in and rip it open.

*Goddamn sociopath.*

*I'd fucking kill whoever did this.*

Finally, a little black ball of fur appears, and all I see are watery eyes staring up at me, the meows not letting up.

"It's okay, little guy," I coo, softly picking it up, surprised at how gentle my voice sounds. "We're getting you out of here."

It's a lot harder to crawl out of this dumpster one-handed, but I manage to climb out without falling flat on my face. When back on steady ground, I plop the little thing on the asphalt and wipe my hands on my jeans.

The kitten stays put, looking up at me, all black fur save for one white spot around its left eye. It meows again, but this time it sounds more curious than distressed.

I flick my hand toward the mouth of the alley. "You're free now, little guy. Go." But it stays put, and we stare at each other for a long, quiet beat. "Okay, well ..." I say, clearing my throat. "I'm going now. Stay away from dumpsters, okay?"

I awkwardly wave to the kitten as if we're two old friends saying goodbye and turn my back to it, a small twinge of guilt plucking at my heart, but I ignore it. Walking out onto the main street, I turn to look over my shoulder just before turning the corner.

*Oh for fuck's sake.*

It's following me. I turn on my heels to face it, putting my hands up, signaling to stop.

"No, no. I'm not your mommy." I point in the opposite direction. "Go find other street cats or something."

It cocks its little head to the side and meows again. We face off once more but the damn cat is clearly not going anywhere, and I just want to get home.

"Fine," I mutter under my breath. "Suit yourself."

The kitten ends up trotting beside me all the way to the front door of my apartment building.

We have another one of our staring contests as I deliberate what to do. Nothing about this is my responsibility. I should just let it fend for itself, it's a feral cat for god's sake. I wouldn't feel so guilty if it were nice out, but it's wet and cold, and its fur is soaked.

I sigh and pick it up.

"Just for the night," I tell it.

---

I END up running a bath to clean its fur. From what I can see, it doesn't have any fleas, but the water turns brown instantly.

"Gross," I say out loud. "You're filthy, little guy."

The kitten lets out a little squeak, clinging to my hand and forearm, looking like a wet rat.

After the bath, I swaddle it in a towel and carry it with me into the kitchen while I riffle through the cupboards for something to feed it.

I find a lonely can of tuna behind a stale box of cereal.

I'm leaning on the kitchen counter, watching it devour the fishy pile of mush, when Sophia shows up from her shift. The front door is right next to the small kitchen, and I look up as she enters.

"Hey," she says absentmindedly when she sees me standing there.

Stopping in her tracks, bag and keys still in hand, her head snaps to my feet.

"Oh my god, is that a cat?!" Her voice is nearly a shriek, her eyes widening with glee.

"We're not keeping it," I answer flatly.

Sophia throws her shit on the floor, quickly pulling off her boots.

"The hell we aren't," she says as she drops to her knees next to the kitten, who's now pushing the plate across the floor with the force of its tongue against the porcelain.

"It's a stray, it belongs outside."

She lifts her gaze, eyebrows creased in suspicion.

"Okay, so why is it *inside* then?"

"It followed me home after I pulled it out of the dumpster." I scratch my head and shrug. "Figured I'd feed it."

Sophia laughs, her attention now back on the kitten. "You're a goner, dude."

I scrunch up my face. "No, I'm not. It's just a cat, it'll be out by morning."

She pets its little head, not even bothering to look up at me when she replies, "Sure it will."

# 13

# CONNIE

"Charlie, you're keeping Alec hostage with your shit, leave him alone," Ozzy says as he passes through the living room into the kitchen.

It's Christmas Eve at the McKennas, and the festivities have started to wind down. The few friends left are either in the living room or drinking coffee and playing cards around the dining room table.

I'm settled on the couch with Sophia and Jamie, while Charlie has Alec, Ozzy's best friend, cornered near the Christmas tree. He's telling him all about the Chernobyl disaster, his new hyperfixation.

Upon hearing his brother calling him out, Charlie whips his head around and looks at Ozzy disappearing around the corner, then back to Alec, his mouth open in outrage.

"I am not! Alec, tell him."

Alec barks a laugh, smoothing a palm over his mustache, and winks at Charlie. "All good, bud, finish your story."

Sophia, Jamie, and I are giggling at the spectacle when the front door opens, and Huxley reappears from smoking outside.

Our gazes slam together for a split second before Huxley walks back to his chair at the dining room table.

I chew my lip, feeling annoyed. It's the first time we're in the same room since we saw each other at Eden. We haven't spoken a word all evening.

Taking a sip of my wine, I stare at the Christmas lights reflecting off the living room windows. This is so childish. We're both adults, we can't keep on acting this way. I just don't know how to fix it. Especially now that ... I'll be around a lot more often.

"Jamie, I have something to tell you," I blurt out.

She stops halfway through her sentence and peers over curiously. Sophia does too. I let out a nervous chuckle, slightly embarrassed that I cut her off for seemingly no reason.

"It's no big deal, really." *Only the biggest of deals.* "I've just been waiting for the right moment to tell you."

"Connie," Sophia chides. "Spill."

I shoot Sophia a wary look before continuing my meandering confession, toying with the ring on my finger as I speak. "I'm moving back to Marsford Bay."

"No, you are not!" Sophia exclaims.

But my attention is solely on Jamie, whose hand is now covering her mouth, looking speechless.

"Are you being serious?" she mutters through her fingers.

I give her a small nod, pressing my lips together in a nonchalant confirmation.

Jamie falls silent again. Then bursts out crying.

"Oh god," I mutter, rolling my eyes in mock defeat, so incredibly used to my best friend's melodramatics.

As if summoned by Jamie's tears, Ozzy pokes his head out of the kitchen. "What happened? Why is Jimbo crying?"

"I'm just so happy," Jamie squeaks through tears.

"Connie is moving back home!" Sophia yells out over her

shoulder to her brother, officially announcing it to the whole house.

I cringe internally, infuriatingly sensitive to Huxley's reaction to the news while everyone explodes in yips of celebration at the announcement. I make sure not to look his way while I pull Jamie into a quick hug over Sophia's lap.

"Jamie, stop crying," I laugh. "This is *happy* news."

We pull away from the hug, getting out of Sophia's personal space, and Jamie chuckles tearily while dabbing the corners of her eyes. "I cry when I'm happy, you know that."

"And when you're sad, or angry,"—Sophia starts to enumerate with her fingers—"or when watching auditions on America's Got Talent."

We all burst out laughing, and Jamie playfully slaps Sophia on the arm. She then turns serious, eyes full of concern.

"But what about LA? What about your acting career?"

I turn a little awkward, thankful that everyone has returned to whatever they were doing and have stopped listening in, aside from Sophia.

My shrug is a little defeated, conveying a lot of what I refuse to say out loud.

All I end up saying is a quiet, "I just think it's time."

I follow it up with a meek but hopeful smile.

I didn't make the decision lightly; I stayed up most nights last week, weighing the pros and cons. But eventually, it became painfully clear that there was nothing of substance keeping me from moving back to the East Coast. I have a few friends that I'll miss in LA, of course, but it's not enough to keep me there.

Not when Marsford Bay has Jamie.

"There's something else," I say coyly.

Both Jamie and Sophia perk up, waiting for me to continue. I decide to blurt out the words like I did with the earlier news.

"I'm buying a theatre." Sophia gasps, and Jamie's mouth

falls open. I start to ramble, "I went to visit it last week — you remember the Remington? Anyway, it's definitely run down and will need *major* love and renovations, but the owners are dying to get it off their hands, and well, I've been wanting to invest in something since I got the inheritance from my grandparents, and so I made an offer, and they accepted."

I stop talking, taking a deep breath in while my eyes flit back and forth from Sophia to Jamie, who both look dumbstruck.

"Well?" I press. I don't miss the small tremble of nerves in my voice. "Do you guys think it's a good idea?"

I've addressed the two of them, but we all know I'm asking Jamie specifically.

Her smile turns watery, her eyes shining with a fresh batch of tears. "I love it."

---

"I can't believe you're moving back," Sophia whispers to me.

After all the guests had left for the night, Sophia tried to convince me, Charlie, and Huxley into a slumber party in the living room. We all agreed, except for the obvious curmudgeon, who barked his displeasure and disappeared upstairs into his old room.

I turn to face Sophia, both of us lying on a makeshift mattress on the floor while Charlie is muttering in his sleep on the couch.

"I know ..." I say thoughtfully, watching the shadows dance on the side of her face. "Are you happy about it?"

Her blues widen in delight, twinkling like the Christmas tree behind her as she smiles and nods. "We've never lived in the same city since we met."

Something about the innocence in her expression makes my heart ache, as if suddenly seeing the child she was when we met ... and all the hardships she's been through before and after.

I bring my hand to her face and tuck the blonde hair behind her ear as I return her smile. Melancholy smarts in my chest. "You know I love you, right?"

Sophia chuffs quietly as she watches me, the covers pulled up to her chin. "Feeling mushy?"

I snort and nod. "Something like that."

We fall into comfortable silence, simply looking back at each other for a beat. "Goodnight, cutie," I finally whisper.

"Okay, weirdo," she whispers back with a grin before turning around and settling into her pillow.

# 14

# HUXLEY

S tanding on Ozzy's small porch, I stare at the muddy grass peeking through the melting snow as I take a large drag of my cigarette. The temperature has stayed mild throughout the holidays.

It's the crack of dawn on Christmas Day, and I'm the only one up.

I couldn't sleep.

Thinking about life and all the things I've missed over the years.

It's my second holiday season since I've been out, and I still feel like an outsider. It's as if *ex-con* is written on my forehead wherever I go. Nothing but a loser who threw his life away and got arrested for stealing a car at seventeen.

I was wide awake in bed, staring at the ceiling for so long that the walls started closing in on me, my skin suddenly feeling too tight and suffocating. I needed to take in some fresh air before I spiraled deeper into my ruminating thoughts.

Ozzy says those *episodes* are probably panic attacks. I'll add it to the list of reasons he keeps harping on about therapy. Nothing a hit of nicotine through the bloodstream can't solve.

The front door opens, and my heart flips when Connie appears. She's halfway out when she realizes I'm standing there.

"Oh," she puffs out quietly.

Her red hair is sleep-mussed, and she's wearing one of James' long, puffy coats with too-big winter boots. The coat is unzipped, and she clutches at it against the cold, looking slightly uncomfortable.

"I didn't realize anybody was up," she adds.

I look away, having trouble keeping eye contact. "I was just about done, anyway," I grunt, stubbing the cigarette in the ashtray on the porch railing.

She closes the door behind her and steps closer to where I'm standing, keeping the coat tight around her by crossing her arms over her waist.

"Actually, can we talk?"

*Great.*

"Why?" I respond flatly, flicking my gaze her way, then back to the ground as I chip at a piece of icy snow with the tip of my boot.

I hear her sigh, and there's a shard of guilt stabbing my ribs for always acting so difficult.

I push it away.

"What happened to your knuckles?" she asks, her tone slightly shocked.

*Shit.*

As a reflex, I look down at my left hand, the knuckles bruised purple.

Last night, after hearing that Connie was moving back to Marsford Bay, I went out back to expel some of my frustrations and ended up punching the side of the shed. As irrational as it might be. The very thought of Connie moving back makes me grind my teeth together. I would rather she'd get out of my life altogether.

Shame forces me to hide my hands in the pockets of my bomber jacket. Even *I* know that bruising my knuckles because I can't deal with my emotions is fucking immature.

"Nothing," I mutter.

Connie blinks. Once, twice, three times; as if not knowing what else to say.

"Huxley," she says defeatedly, and my nape tingles with my name on her lips. "We can't keep on ignoring each other like this, especially now that I'm moving back."

I can feel anger wash over me like a protective shell. "Right." I chuckle dryly. "God forbid everything isn't perfect for Connie Broadbent now that she's decided to grace us with her presence."

Her mouth snaps closed, and she narrows her eyes. There's a tense beat of silence that passes between us before she speaks again.

"You know," she starts, and just by her tone, I know I'm not going to like what she's about to say. "If you want me to start treating you like a grown-ass adult and not like the teenager I once knew, maybe stop acting like such a fucking brat."

The word *brat* pulverizes my ego, and I'm left staring at her without any good comeback. She smirks, pouting her lips ever so slightly as if proud of her jab, and I hate that I feel so attracted to her, even now.

I maintain eye contact, chewing on my pride, but say nothing.

"Can we at least *pretend* to be civil for everybody's sake?" she asks hopefully.

Still, there's a touch of impatience in her voice as if *I'm* the one being difficult.

Because.

Well …

I guess I am.

Pushing off the railing, I give her a half-hearted shrug.

"Sure, as long as *you're* happy, right?" I step around her to reach for the door. But before walking in, I lean close to her side and hiss next to her ear. "*Your Highness.*"

I hear the small tsk leave her lips, but I don't look back. Smirking just like she did, I close the door and leave her standing alone outside in the cold.

---

"So, a theatre, huh?"

I look up just in time to watch Connie startle from Ozzy's seemingly innocent question.

After gifts were opened around the Christmas tree, we all gathered at the dining room table for breakfast. The table is full of large stacks of pancakes, plates of bacon, breakfast potatoes, and whatever else Ozzy felt like whipping up so that everyone could get their favorite.

My brother acts as if Christmas breakfast is a family tradition he needs to uphold or something. As if Christmas was anything but a big fat disappointment when we were growing up. Maybe that's why it appears to be so important to him now, especially with Charlie still being so young.

A confusing pang of jealousy throbs behind my chest at the thought that Charlie is forming happy memories that we older siblings never had the chance to experience. It's not his fault, and still, I find space to resent my younger brother for something he has no control over.

Connie nods wordlessly, bringing her hand to her mouth as she chews and carefully swallows. It almost looks like she's trying to bide her time now that she's been put on the spot.

Finally, she speaks. "Yup, kind of crazy, right?" She lets out a small laugh, waiting for Ozzy to respond.

"Not crazy at all." Ozzy smiles.

I roll my eyes.

*Always so fucking supportive.*

Connie's gaze shifts to James sitting in front of her, then back to Ozzy at the head of the table, and she smiles back.

"I know it's impulsive, but sometimes you just have to follow your gut, you know?" She takes a quick sip of her mimosa. She follows it with a nervous laugh. "And sometimes your gut tells you to buy a rundown theatre."

The table laughs, and I stab my fork into a breakfast potato.

"Oh my god," James suddenly says, her mouth falling open, as if something just dawned on her. With stars in her eyes, she looks over at Connie. "I'm assuming that you'll need to hire people to help you renovate, right?"

"Yes ..." Connie answers a little suspiciously, and my own suspicion spikes right along with hers.

*She wouldn't.*

My heart drops when James looks over to me, her smile widening. "You can hire Hux!"

My gaze slams into Connie's as we both look at each other with horror before returning our attention to James. We protest awkwardly in unison.

"No, no, no, that's fine," Connie blabbers politely.

"I don't think that's a good idea," I mutter at the same time, breaking into a cold sweat.

James watches us both in confusion, eyebrows dipping low, then finally settles on me, tilting her head.

"Aren't you in between construction jobs 'til spring?" she asks so fucking innocently that I just want to crawl under the table and pretend none of this is happening.

"Yeah, but —" I start to argue.

She doesn't bother letting me finish whatever excuse I was about to pull out of my ass before looking over to Connie.

"And you *will* need help, right?"

I watch Connie's throat work around a hard swallow.

"Yes."

James is now beaming as if having come up with the answers to all our problems.

"So that settles it then," she chirps.

Ozzy is sporting a similar expression to his fiancée when his gaze slides to meet mine.

*The insufferable duo.*

Connie looks over to me again. We've been pushed right into a corner. I give her a thin-lipped smile as a silent confirmation of our sealed fate.

Connie's smile is shaky, but no one at the table seems to notice but me.

"That settles it, then," she says.

# 15

# HUXLEY

I don't know what I'm doing here. There are too many choices, and I feel like an idiot browsing the aisles. I've managed to avoid eye contact with the sales clerk, but I need to pick something soon, or else they'll surely come find me and ask if I need help. And why the hell is cat food so damn expensive?

Finally, I choose two blue bowls with paw prints on them, a litter box that looks more like a spaceship than an actual box, and a large bag of cat food. At the last minute, I snatch some treats from a display stand while on my way to the cash register. I fumble with my card, anxiety spiking as if I'm wanted by the law or something, and pay.

Finally done with my bullshit errand, I head home.

---

Sophia's watching *Grey's Anatomy* when I get home. I've lost track of how many times she's watched the earlier seasons. She always tells me I remind her of Karev ... whatever the fuck that means.

"Hey," she mutters from her spot on the couch as she munches on chips from the bag next to her.

In reality, our apartment is nothing to write home about; most of the furniture is second-hand, including the sagging couch. The white walls have seen years of bad paint jobs, the wood floors creak no matter where you step, and the windows let in the cold air.

But it feels more like home than anywhere I've ever lived.

I might be a pessimist, but I can still find the joy in the small things from time to time.

"Where's DK?" I ask while disappearing into our narrow kitchen, dropping the bag of food and everything else on the counter.

"You've got to stop calling him that!" Sophia explains loudly from the living room. "Poor guy is starting to have a complex."

I swore I wasn't going to get attached to the cat.

Only for the night, and that's it.

But then a day turned into two and then three. By day four, I cracked and brought him to the vet just before Christmas. They told me the kitten was male, roughly four months old, and healthy.

I was surprised by how relieved I was by his clean bill of health. The visit solidified my decision to keep him, and I finally gave him a name.

Dumpster Kitty.

Sophia hates it, but I find it suits him.

"Oh yeah?" I ask sarcastically, coming out of the kitchen. "Did the cat confide that to you when I was gone or something?"

Sophia shoots me an amused but annoyed look. "Ha. Ha," she replies flatly. "Anyway, *the cat* is in your room, I think."

I walk down the dark hallway and flick the light on when I get to my room. My bedroom isn't much to look at either. Just the bare minimum with a double bed to the left of the window, a small desk with my father's old record player on top of it, and a few records leaning against it. I don't even own a dresser, all my clothes are stuffed into the small closet facing the bed.

The record player was the only thing I wanted from our childhood home. Ozzy kept it for me when Dad died while I was in prison. I missed that old record player more than I ever did my own father.

I find DK curled up next to my pillow. His head pops up when he senses my hand near his head, the white spot around his left eye stark against the rest of the black fur. He lets out a small squeaked meow and jumps to his feet, stretching his legs and paws.

It's hard not to find DK to be the most adorable thing I've ever seen. Something about the feeling makes me slightly uncomfortable, but I don't pay it much attention as I pick the kitten up and carry him into the kitchen.

Setting him down, I fill one of his new bowls with fresh water and the other with food. DK meows loudly at my feet, winding himself around my ankles and rubbing his little body against me.

"Here you go, little dude," I say under my breath as DK dive-bombs into his bowl of food.

Chuckling, I give his head a little scratch and lean against the counter, watching him eat. I smirk distractedly as I pull my phone out from my pocket. The smile fades quickly, the device nearly slipping out of my hand when I see the new Instagram notification on my cracked screen.

**@hiimconnieb started following you.**

I can't stop the irrational impulse to crouch as if she's watching me from the kitchen window.

*Idiot.*

Tapping on the notification, it leads me directly into the

app. There it is, clear as day, the small circular icon of her profile picture taunting me just as much as the blue *follow back* button.

My thumb hovers over it, wondering why the hell she'd choose to follow me now, then realize it must have something to do with the theatre gig. Christmas was two days ago, and we never did discuss our whole agreement after that awkward moment at the dining room table.

A part of me hoped she'd somehow forget.

I decide not to follow her back, *yet*. Instead, I go into my message requests and, as expected, find one from Connie. It was sent over an hour ago. I open it, peeved for reasons I can't express, and scan her message.

> Hey Huxley, thought I'd reach out since we can't really continue ignoring each other if you'll be working for me soon.

The message is so dry that I feel my eyes turn to dust just by reading it. I clench my jaw hard and consider ignoring her, but the word *brat* comes back to haunt me, and I drag a hand over my mouth before typing out an equally dry answer.

> Sure. Just tell me the time and place.

I turn off my screen but keep it clutched in my palm. Leaving DK eating in the kitchen, I walk into the living room and plop myself on the couch opposite Sophia. She doesn't acknowledge me, her eyes glued to the screen. I pop some chips in my mouth for something to do as I wait for Connie to reply.

It takes her two hours to answer me, and by then I've come up with ten different scenarios as to why it took her so long. None of them are good. Most of them involve that fucking DJ, Gael. I'm in bed reading when I see her name appear on my phone. I drop the book and tap on the notification.

So you still want to do this, then?

I roll my eyes.

I agreed, didn't I?

This time, she answers almost immediately.

Ok

I'm hiring a company. I guess you can work alongside them.

Her *I guess* makes me irrationally angry, but I take a deep breath and answer with a one-worded *Ok*.

Meet me at the Remington at 9 on the 5th.

That gives me about a week to mentally prepare, a feeling of dread at the thought of working for Connie already tightening around my throat. I type a quick *Sure* and log off the app.
I never follow her back.

# 16

# CONNIE

The smell of the theatre—*any* theatre—is a comfortable and familiar amalgamation of odors. The scent of wood and a subtle hint of dust. Then there's the tangy metallic scent of the stage lights when they're first turned on, or the faint perfumes and colognes clinging to the costumes.

It smells theatrical. Like the tears of tragedy and the hearty laughs of comedy. It smells like the otherworldly scent of the muses floating above the stage smiling over us.

And I couldn't be happier to be back on familiar grounds.

Today is the day.

I might not be the new owner *officially*, the paperwork is still ongoing, but it's mine in every other sense of the word. The previous owners handed me the keys a few days ago, and I've been crawling out of my skin with excitement ever since. I've been dying to get the ball rolling.

Now, here I am, making my way down the empty aisle of the auditorium, waiting for the renovation crew to show up at nine.

I arrived an hour early, wanting to introduce myself slowly to the Remington before I took on my new role.

Everything is happening so fast.

Just how I like it.

That way, there's no chance of backing out or getting cold feet. Full steam ahead. No thoughts, just gut feelings to help guide me through these life-altering changes.

Quietly stepping on stage, I turn to face the room and let out a pleased sigh, my palms flat on my hips.

The Remington might not be the biggest or most impressive theatre in Marsford Bay, but it's certainly the oldest, with a long history and heritage attached to it. It's revered fondly by all Marsfordian theatre nerds, including me.

The theatre opened at the turn of the century; the interior architecture influenced by the Italian Renaissance with accents of gold and red. Over the fan-shaped auditorium is a shallow balcony and a few box seats. My favorite detail of the spacious room is the domed vault ceiling paired with its opulent, but weathered, chandelier. It perfectly conveys the dramatic flair of theatre that we all know and love.

The regional theatre is beautiful and exudes a sense of wistful nostalgia that makes my insides feel all warm and tingly. But if I squint hard enough, I start to see the wear and tear of years past: Faded red seats, cracks in the wood, and even the paint peeling off the walls near the murals of lively theatre scenes. It's in dire need of some TLC, and lucky for the Remington, I have the money to do just that.

A whistle near the auditorium doors snaps me out of my daydream. Startled, my gaze lands on Huxley, casually strutting down the main aisle, arms crossed as he looks up and around the room. There's a grin on his lips that has me questioning if I'm seeing things.

"So this is the reason for your big return, huh?"

I can't tell by his tone if he's being sincere or if he's just trying to fuck with me, so I choose to ignore his comment altogether.

I glance at my phone.

"You're like, half an hour early."

Huxley drops his backpack and jacket on one of the seats in the front row and walks up to the stage, holding a thermos. His buzzed blue hair has faded into a turquoise kind of green. He's wearing the same boots as always, an old pair of blue jeans, and a black, faded Incubus t-shirt with white paint stains all over it. The short sleeves showcase the tattoos on his arms—if I'd have to make an informed guess, they were all acquired in prison— which just makes his whole ... *thing* that much hotter to ogle at.

*God, this was a bad idea.*

I step up to the edge of the stage, looking down at him. He's still sporting that unfamiliar grin, and I'm now convinced we have a serious case of a body-snatcher on our hands.

"Soph dropped me off on her way to class," he says. "I was waiting outside, but realized the front doors were unlocked."

I drop down and sit, letting my legs hang over the edge of the stage, my palms flat to the ground on either side of me.

"Yeah, I've been here since eight." I pause, still quite wary about how casual this moment between us feels. "No car?"

Huxley twists the cap off his thermos, and the soothing scent of coffee wafts between us, mingling with his own scent: A subtle mix of spicy black pepper and vanilla. My stomach immediately grumbles at the smell of coffee—I was too wired to eat this morning.

He takes a slow sip before answering my question, "I only got my license back a few months ago."

"Oh, because of ... yeah." I'm not sure why the mention of his prison sentence turns me into a fumbling fool, but I don't bother elaborating when Huxley just nods.

There's a part of me that hungers for more of his story and if it was anyone else I'd be unapologetically asking questions. But because it's *him*, I say nothing.

Silence settles between us just long enough for me to start

to squirm. Surprisingly, Huxley doesn't seem bothered by it, and I question his motives. Is this all an act? Did Ozzy tell him to be on his best behavior or else? It's not as if Huxley ever heeded Ozzy's warnings before.

Wordlessly and with a raise of his eyebrow, Huxley offers me his thermos. It takes me a second to move, but eventually, I take it out of his hand.

I take a tentative sip, not wanting to burn my tongue. I don't miss Huxley's eyes dipping to my mouth. The slow, deliberate slide back up to meet my gaze has my nape tingling.

"Black," I state, trying to break this already excruciating tension. "I should have guessed."

Huxley takes the thermos back and takes a sip, followed by another wry smile. "The coffee was such shit in prison. I used to put, like, three packs of sugar just to mask the taste." A pensive laugh rolls over his lips, and my body suddenly feels electric. "I've kind of become a coffee snob since getting out."

I can't help but stare at him for a beat too long. This is the first time I've ever heard him be so upfront about prison. Then again, we've never really had a legitimate conversation without being surrounded by his family.

What if this is just a version of him I've never seen before?

Maybe he's *actually* making an effort to squash the animosity between us, and this unassumingly flirty demeanor is a natural part of his personality.

"I'm a croissant snob," I blurt out.

"Oh?" Huxley says with another soft chuckle. He turns and leans his back against the stage looking onto the empty auditorium.

"Yeah." I chuckle a little awkwardly. "I spent a semester in Paris — been a croissant snob ever since."

"Paris, huh?" Hux pauses, letting out another short whistle. "Must be nice."

I expect his response to have more bite to it, but instead his words are laced with subtle melancholy. He hands me the thermos again, and I take it.

"It *was* nice ..." I trail off while studying his side profile, his gaze fixed straight ahead.

I notice small freckles peppered across his ear and it makes my stomach twist.

Given his past, I assume he's never been out of the country before so I venture with a question. "Would you like to travel?"

He nods pensively before looking over at me and flashing me a side grin. I take a sip of the black coffee just for something to do.

"I've always wanted to go to Brazil," he says, "I don't know why, it just speaks to me." His expression turns a little morose before adding, "Never left Marsford Bay, except for prison."

My heart sinks at the thought of how lucky my life has been compared to his, and I try my hardest to smooth the feeling away from my facial expression. I might not know Huxley as personally as I'd like to believe, but I *do* know he wouldn't take kindly to pity.

I'm about to respond when the doors of the auditorium open and a group of four file in.

I ignore the pinch of disappointment at having our conversation interrupted when Huxley was finally warming up to me and push myself off the stage so I can stand next to him.

Huxley's eyebrows furrow. "Whit?"

His attention is on the man leading the team; backward cap, flannel shirt, and a tool belt bouncing around his waist with every step he takes.

"Huxley? Well, I'll be damned," he says with a booming voice, brown eyes shimmering. "What a coincidence!"

Whit's attention turns to me, offering his hand. "You must be Connie," he says with a smile. "I'm Whit with Garafola and Sons. We spoke on the phone."

I shake his hand, adding a distracted, "Pleased to meet you."

But I'm far more interested in how Huxley knows the handyman. I decide to add more context myself. "Huxley is the extra set of hands I mentioned on our call." I take a breath. "How do you know each other?"

Whit's face lights up, looking at Huxley and then back to me. "That is *great* news," he exclaims with so much sincerity. "Huxley's in my woodworking class." He claps Huxley's shoulder with warmth. "He's my best student."

*Woodworking class?*

Huxley's cheeks pinken, clearly uncomfortable with the compliment. He stays silent, his gaze cast down to the floor before finally looking back up.

Whit turns to the three others. "This is Penelope, Maverick, and Bruno," he says, pointing at his team one by one.

They all wave, muttering a small *Hi* in response.

Silence settles between us while Whit smiles, watching Huxley and me just standing there.

He clears his throat. "Should we start with a tour of the theatre? See what we're dealing with?"

His request snaps me out of it, reminding me that all five sets of eyes are waiting for me to give clear instructions.

"Yes, of course," I say, straightening my shoulders. I plaster a smile over my nerves. "Sounds like a plan."

I lead them out of the auditorium to start with the building's facade, and we slowly make our way around the Remington, assessing what needs to be done.

---

It's late afternoon when I get a text that makes my heart fly into my throat.

"Shit," I say under my breath. "What the hell is he doing here?"

Scrambling out of my office, I rush through the backstage corridors, heading for the foyer.

I find Gael standing near the box office, holding a giant bouquet of roses.

*Oh jeez.*

Gael and I have been casually hooking up over the holidays, but nothing about our situation should have warranted him showing up like this on my first day at the Remington—with *flowers* no less.

I barely remember even telling him about it.

To my dismay, some of the renovation crew is also in the lobby fixing some lights and signage, Huxley included. I want to crawl into a hole and die.

"Gael," I squeak, walking up to him. "What are you doing here?" My tone is friendly, but inside, I'm peeved at his presence here.

"I thought I'd come by and congratulate you on your first day," he answers, beaming and clearly unaware of how weird it is for him to be here in the first place.

"Oh, well, uh — thank you," I say, awkwardly taking the roses from him while dodging his kiss.

Gael's back is to Huxley, who's up on a ladder near the front doors. Unfortunately, he has a front-row seat to our interaction, and I can feel Huxley staring at me without having to even look.

"I'm really busy today, though," I mutter with a thin-lipped smile, taking a step back while clutching the bouquet. "I need to go back to the office."

Gael smiles back, still not picking up on my body language.

Ignorance is bliss, I guess. Must be nice.

"No problem," he says with a wink as he slips his headphones on his head. "I was heading to the gym anyway." He bumps my chin with his fingers and winks. "Talk to you later, babe."

*Oh my god, kill me.*

I nod and smile, mentally pushing him outside the theatre myself. I watch the door close before I start back to life and bolt backstage, ignoring Huxley's prying eyes.

I've made it to the corridor outside my office when I realize I hear footsteps behind me. I let out a small yip, my heart flying into my throat when a strong hand grabs me by the arm and swivels me around. I come face to face with icy green eyes, narrowed and prying.

"Huxley! The hell are you doing?"

His hard stare is startling, his full lips pressed together in what I can only guess is disdain. He stays silent for a few seconds, the tension palpable, then cocks his head to the side.

"What is this?" he asks flatly, plucking a petal from the bouquet, keeping it trapped between two fingers.

I step backwards, keeping my chin high.

Something about his attitude is pissing me off.

"None of your fucking business," I reply, my tone dripping with annoyance.

I try to move away, but Huxley steps in front of me, not letting me pass.

I scoff. "Are you being serious right now? Are you trying to intimidate me or something?"

He chuckles wryly, his eyes so cold they burn. "Why so jumpy?"

He crowds me, and I take another step back, but I hit the wall behind me. The bouquet's plastic wrapping crinkles between our bodies, and my heart rate doubles. I can't tell what I'm feeling, all I know is that a confusing part of me is enjoying whatever is happening right now.

"Don't tell me you're dating that chump?" he says mockingly while plucking another petal from the bouquet, this time flicking it to the ground.

The need to rile him up gets the best of me. "If you call fucking, *dating*, then yes, I guess we are."

I watch his jaw clench, my heart slamming in my chest, my back still pressed against the wall. His expression shutters, and I feel the energy suddenly shift between us.

His voice is a lot softer when he speaks again. "So any loser will do, right?" His words sting, but his next sentence hurts even worse. "You fucked *me*, so I guess that checks out."

I'm stunned but manage to mutter out, "You're not a —"

But it's too late. Huxley is already storming down the corridor before I can even finish my sentence.

# 17

# HUXLEY

My breathing is shallow. I can barely take a full breath. I'm storming through the auditorium as my vision starts to blur. My mind racing, my throat tightening, and it feels like reality is slipping away from me.

I can't breathe.

I can't *breathe*.

I spiral into darkness.

*I'm going to die in here.*

The thought appears like a ghost, crawling out of the grave I buried it in. Flashes of memories. Torn pieces from my time in prison assault my senses, and I double over, resting my hand on the back of a seat.

*I'm going to die in here.*

The auditorium disappears, and I'm back there.

I try to take a deep breath, but I can't.

I can't.

I can't do anything.

*I'm stuck.*

*I'm stuck.*

*I'm stuck.*

*I sit on my cot. Frozen. Dead eyes staring back at me. My bunk-mate. He made a noose out of his bed sheets while I was sleeping. Now he's dead.*

I'm choking back air.

*I'm going to die in here.*

"Huxley, are you okay?" A hand lands on my shoulder, and I reel back. I shove the hand away and stumble backward. My eyes are wide as I snap back to reality.

Whit stands a few feet away from me, shock splashed on his face. I'm blinking fast, my breathing still shallow, trying as I might not to let myself slip into a flashback again.

"Hux," he repeats, "What just happened? You're white as a ghost."

"I'm ..." My tongue feels like cotton in my mouth. I look toward the exit. "I need some air."

I leave him standing in the middle of the aisle and bolt outside through the front doors. The winter air hits my clammy skin first, my bare arms breaking out into goosebumps, before I'm gulping down oxygen as if I'd been drowning until then.

I hear the door creak behind me, and I don't need to turn around to know it's Whit. I close my eyes and squat down near the wall, curling my arms over my head while shame spills over me like tar. I can't believe he's seeing me like this. At *work*.

I don't know what exactly about my run-in with Connie triggered this, but I blame her for all of it. I need to stay the fuck away from her.

She's nothing but toxic.

I take a few seconds, trying to ground myself with the icy feeling in my lungs, before standing back up and begrudgingly meeting Whit's concerned gaze.

He's the first to speak. "Want to talk about it?"

"Not really," I say a little too forcefully, as I swipe a hand over my buzzed head back and forth.

He shoots me a look that clearly conveys that he knows

I'm full of shit, but shrugs his shoulders and pulls out a pack of cigarettes from his shirt pocket. He wordlessly offers me one.

I stay still for half a second too long, then finally, step closer and pull one out of the pack. He lights mine first, then his. I grunt out a *Thanks* with the filter between my lips.

We smoke in silence, the white cloud of smoke and cold breaths mingling in the air between us. The weather eventually gets the best of me, and I start to shiver.

"Need the rest of the day off?" Whit asks offhandedly as he stubs his butt into the metal ashtray on the wall.

"Absolutely fucking not," I snap back, flicking my butt into the snowy street.

Whit chuckles, and I swallow hard.

"Alright then," he says, "Let's get back to it."

<hr>

NOTHING about this bottle of Jameson is going to help ease whatever happened to me today. But at least the burn of the alcohol down my throat helps to keep the thoughts at bay.

I'm sitting on the couch in the dark, drinking straight from the bottle. Memories of my deadbeat dad doing the same filter through my mind, and a bite of shame threatens to undo the numbing buzz I'm working on.

*Like father, like son.*

It's a cliché for a reason. It satisfies my need to wallow in peace. At least I've turned on the TV just to make the image of me a little less depressing, DK curled up and sleeping against my thigh.

I thought of texting Selina, but even meaningless sex wouldn't help quell my thoughts about Connie.

What the hell is it about her that has me in a chokehold? I feel as trapped under her spell as I did behind bars. She's strung me up like a puppet, pulling my strings, making me dance against my will.

I take another swig from the bottle.

On the living room table, my phone lights up with a phone call. I eye it numbly, but it's a number I don't recognize. I stare at the screen until it goes dark and deliberate if I should just turn my phone off for the night.

My phone vibrates with an incoming text.

Groaning loudly, I lean over and plop the bottle of whiskey on the table, picking up my phone. My stomach flips, despite my irritation.

Pick up, it's Connie.

Not a second later, my phone starts to ring again.

"*Shit*," I mutter out loud.

Being at least a *little* familiar with Connie's temperament, something tells me she won't be taking no for an answer, even if I ignore her call a second time.

I unconsciously smooth my shirt down as if this isn't just a voice call, and straighten up on the couch before answering.

"What?" I grunt.

She takes no time to jump right in.

"Are you ever going to apologize for what you said today?"

Guilt gnaws at my conscience like tiny razor-sharp teeth, but I don't let it be heard in my voice.

"How did you get my number?" I ask, my tone flat.

"Well, it wasn't fucking rocket science now was it?" she snips back. Sophia, probably. "You know, we're going to have to start acting civil, whether you like it or not."

The line goes silent, and I chew on my lip. Finally, I let out a long sigh and decide to act my age for once.

"I —" The words immediately die somewhere on my tongue. I clear my throat, smoothing my hand over my face in exasperation, and try again. "I'm sorry," I say a little more forcefully this time. "It's none of my business who you're seeing. It won't happen again."

Connie stays quiet for so long that it has me checking my phone to make sure the call hasn't been dropped.

Finally, she speaks. "Thank you. Apology accepted." She pauses. "I guess I'll see you tomorrow?"

I force a smile, even though she can't see it.

"Yeah, see you tomorrow, boss."

Connie snorts a laugh, and my heart skips a beat. I ignore the embarrassing flutters in my stomach and hang up. Dropping my phone beside me, I sit motionless while I stare at nothing, feeling everything.

Eventually, I snap out of it and swipe the bottle of Jameson from the table.

# 18

# CONNIE

I t's my second day as the owner of the Remington, and I'm trying my hardest not to let my nerves get the best of me in a room full of strangers.

With Mary-Beth's stamp of approval since she already knew the staff, I decided to keep the technical crew as is. I called a pre-production meeting for Tuesday morning so I could officially introduce myself to the director, stage manager, and designers.

I deliberated taking on the role of director for our first production but decided that the role of producer would allow me more freedom as I transitioned into my new life. Technically, the Remington is closed, but I wanted to keep the fast-paced schedule of a regional theatre as intact as possible and settled on a mid-April opening night.

That gives us three months to produce a play.

I know I'm at the top of the hierarchy, even though we're all sitting at the same table in the rehearsal space, but I feel a lot more like the new kid in school. They all share a past and camaraderie. I'm acutely jealous of that fact.

"So the play will be a modernized twist on The Taming of the Shrew," I declare, handing out copies of the play.

I give people time to look through it before speaking again, but Virginia, the director, beats me to the punch.

"Who wrote this?" Her tone is chilly as she flips through the pages, her eyes then flicking back to me. "You?"

Ignacio, the stage manager, coughs, shooting a wary look over to Virginia from the corner of his eye. I had the good sense to ask Mary-Beth to give me background on the major players before the meeting.

Especially Virginia; graduate of the Westmount School of Arts, exceptionally talented, late forties, known to be kind of a bitch.

Luckily, I've worked with my fair share of difficult people in my six years in the entertainment business, including Oliver.

I've always loved writing just as much as acting. I even wrote a screenplay titled *Love Lies Waiting* with some help from my ex last year. But this is my first chance to utilize my talent. I might have a lot more confidence in my acting skills, but I'm not about to show my insecurities to Virginia.

"Yes," I respond with a saccharine smile. "Problem?"

I hold her pointed stare until finally she relents and gives me a small shake of her head.

"Great," I say, my tone a lot more cheerful now. "Now that that's settled, I'll let Ignacio take the helm."

Ignacio quickly interrupts. "You can call me Nacho," he says, followed by a warm smile.

I return the warmth and grin in confirmation. "If you have any questions, just come find me or call. I'll give Nacho my number so he can update the contact sheet. Sounds good?"

Everyone nods in agreement, even Virginia, and with that, my very first meeting as a theatre owner comes to an end.

The swell of pride blooming in my chest is undeniable.

I'm exactly where I'm supposed to be.

---

BY MID-WEEK, both the technical crew and the renovation team have found their stride, and my sense of accomplishment only grows in size.

I might have never majored in business, but having a tech mogul as a father has certainly rubbed off on me; particularly the valuable lesson of knowing when to take a step back and delegate.

Pushing the lobby door with my backside while wrapping my scarf around my neck, I step into the January air. It's barely five p.m., but it's pitch black outside. I might not miss LA much, but I *do* miss the warmth and sunny blue skies on winter days like these.

I stop in my tracks when I find Huxley standing near the curb, cursing at his phone.

"You okay?" I ask casually.

Since I called him two days ago, it feels like we've finally turned a corner in our *platonic* relationship. I can tell he's been making an effort, and I am too.

Huxley whirls around when he hears my voice, his thick brows lifted as if surprised to see me standing there.

"Yeah," he answers. He stops as if that was enough information, but then, as if remembering himself, he adds, "Soph was supposed to pick me up, but something came up — she just canceled."

"I'll drive you," I say without much thought.

Huxley reacts as if I just told him that we're moving in together. He dismissively waves his hand in front of him as a way to decline my offer. "All good. I'll just take the bus or something."

"Huxley." My tone is slightly scolding as I look at him with a deadpan expression.

He returns my stare until finally, his shoulders sag slightly, and he relents.

"Okay. Sure, thanks."

"Great," I chirp. "I'm just across the street," I say as I unlock the car doors from a distance.

Huxley whistles as we cross the deserted street. It's a similar tone to the one he made the first time he saw the theatre, and something about it sends a shiver down my spine.

"A red Mercedes," he says slowly as he rounds the car. "I would have pegged you as a Porsche girl myself."

"Oh yeah?" I say with a laugh as we step into the car. "It's just a lease anyway — until I figure out what to do with my car back in LA."

Huxley settles in the passenger seat, his arms flung over his backpack on his lap. "And what's your car in LA?"

Pulling into the street, I shoot Huxley a wry grin, quickly looking over before my gaze lands back on the road. "I'm not telling you." My tone is playful, which is a stark relief from the tension plaguing our conversations as of late.

Huxley returns my smile, and his expression makes me unreasonably happy to witness.

"Don't tell me it's a Porsche," he quips.

I burst out laughing. "Maybe."

Huxley chuckles warmly, then falls silent, looking straight ahead until he says, "I can't believe you left California for this."

I'm not sure if he meant it so seriously, so I try to keep the conversation light. "LA isn't all that it's cracked up to be. Mostly smoke and mirrors. I'm *happy* to be back, I love it here."

It takes Huxley a few seconds to respond. "Can't relate."

"You don't like Marsford Bay?" I ask innocently but realize quickly that it might be a loaded question for him. "You don't have to answer that."

The silence returns, and I chew on my inner cheek, hoping the mood hasn't already been ruined.

"So, The Taming of the Shrew, huh?"

I smile as I glance over. His gaze is fixed on mine, and my heart skips a beat at the sight. I ignore my wayward reaction.

"You heard?"

"Yeah," he says casually. "I had lunch with Nacho yesterday, seems like a cool guy."

I hum in agreement as I turn on Fairview, entering Huxley's neighborhood.

"You ever read the play?"

I catch Huxley smirking from the corner of my eye.

He doesn't answer my question immediately, as if thinking about what to say next.

Finally, he speaks. "My tongue will tell the anger of my heart. Or else my heart, concealing it, will break."

My breath catches in my throat, and I almost veer off the road. Hearing Huxley quote Shakespeare has unexpectedly turned me on, heat pooling low in my stomach.

*Fucking. Hell. That was hot.*

I try to conceal my physical reaction with a surprised laugh, my knuckles turning white on the steering wheel.

"Well, well, well," I tease, desperately trying to shake it off. "Huxley McKenna, the secret thespian."

He scoffs with humor. "There wasn't much else to read in prison. Had to pass the time somehow."

Another one of his dismissive remarks.

I crave to continue our conversation and dig deeper into this softer side of him, but to my disappointment, I turn onto his street, his apartment just a couple of blocks away.

"I'll pick you up tomorrow."

The words rush out of me as I park in front of his building.

"No, you won't," Huxley says as he unbuckles his belt.

I sigh a little too loudly just to have him look at me. His green eyes flick up suspiciously.

"I *want* to. Just accept the offer, dumbass."

Huxley's lip quirks up when he hears me calling him a dumbass. He stares at me for a few seconds, then nods.

"Okay, fine." He pauses, his hand on the door handle. "Thanks for the ride." His smile is shy but genuine.

I smile back. "My pleasure."

# 19

# CONNIE

"He's cute," Jamie whispers beside me, pointing to the stage.

I look over at her, my mouth wide open in mock shock. "James Elizabeth Ferdinand," I whisper back. "You are a *taken* woman."

It's my second week at the Remington and the first full day of auditions. I called Jamie and asked if she wanted to come and judge the auditions with me.

She agreed immediately.

We've spent the past hour sitting in the far back of the audi-torium, eating M&Ms and critiquing the actors' performances.

Jamie quietly bursts into a laugh, hiding behind her hands. She clearly knows I'm just teasing, but says, "I still have *eyes*."

I smirk and glance back to the actor currently on stage. He is cute, I must admit. Lean but with broad shoulders, like a swimmer's body, his auburn hair falling in waves down to his shoulders. Talented too.

I make a note to tell Virginia that he'd make a good Petru-chio. As the director, she's in charge of the casting, but as the producer, I still have my fair share of influence.

"So, are you not going back at all? What about all your stuff?" Jamie asks, picking up our conversation from earlier.

I shrug nonchalantly.

"I'll just have movers pack it all up and ship it here when I finally find a place."

"Don't you —" Jamie pauses as if thinking. "Don't you want to have at least *some* kind of farewell to your life there?" Her tone is dejected, as if even thinking about it breaks her heart.

My smile is slightly morose when I look at her, but I break the moody tension with a joke. "I'm not the nostalgic sucker here."

She purses her lips as if insulted. "You're acting like a sociopath, Constance."

I chuckle behind my hand, and Jamie does the same.

"Wow," I say playfully, elongating the word for extra effect. "Did you just government name me? Must be serious."

"I *did*," she whispers harshly. "You can't lie and say that this isn't you running away from all your problems."

I turn thoughtful, my gaze sweeping over the Remington, a new actor now auditioning on stage.

"But look where it got me," I answer seriously. "You can't tell me this feels like a mistake."

Jamie's gaze turns watery, and she's seconds from crying, but miraculously manages to hold it in. She smiles weakly and shakes her head. "No, this isn't a mistake."

I didn't realize how much I needed to hear my best friend say those words until just now. Relief washes over me like a cool, rejuvenating wave.

"Have you heard from Oliver?"

My mood sours, but I answer her anyway, "Not since he checked into rehab before the holidays. And if there *is* a God," I say, being purposefully dramatic, "I'll never hear from him ever again."

"You never really had closure with that either —" Jamie starts, but I cut her off.

"Jamie." My tone is slightly irritated. "Drop it."

She holds up her hands in surrender and settles back into her chair, grabbing the half-eaten bag of M&Ms from my lap. We watch more of the auditions in silence.

I'm startled by Jamie's excited waving until I see Huxley walking up the aisle toward the exit doors. He looks like he's been working up a sweat, his white t-shirt and hands stained and dusty. Taking the bottom hem of his shirt, he lifts it up to wipe his face, giving me a full view of his toned stomach. I cough, trying to hide my audible reaction to his physique.

He's effortlessly sexy, and I want to crawl under my seat and pretend I never saw him like this. I swallow hard, trying to save face, especially in front of his sister-in-law.

Huxley waves back, barely a hand gesture at all, paired with a thin-lipped smile. He doesn't stop to say hi before disappearing out of sight.

"Huxley is allergic to small talk," Jamie mutters, then looks at me. "How is he? Staying out of trouble?"

I puff out a sardonic laugh. "He's not a teenager anymore, Jamie."

"I know," she whispers back, popping an M&M into her mouth. She chews, looking pensive. "We just worry about him, you know?"

"He's fine." I try to placate her feelings by adding, "Turns out the foreman is his woodworking teacher."

Jamie lights up as if I just told her the greatest of news.

"He is?"

Her smile is so sweet it makes my teeth ache.

"Yeah," I answer, chuckling at her reaction. "They seem to get on pretty well."

Jamie sighs wistfully. "I knew him working for you would be a good idea."

*Yeah ... Some great idea, Jamie.*

We both fall silent again, watching the actor on stage.

I chew on my next question.

*It's none of my business.*

I deliberate some more.

"Is uh — Is Huxley still dating that girl?"

I internally cringe, hoping my question is innocuous enough not to raise suspicion.

Jamie lets out a puff of air. "Hell if I know. *God forbid* Huxley tells Ozzy anything. We get all our information from Soph."

I laugh under my breath at her exasperation as I try to conceal my disappointment at the lack of information.

My next question slips out as if having a mind of its own. "I mean, you both wouldn't really care who he dates, right?"

*God, I'm so obvious.*

I'm uncertain why I'm even asking the question in the first place. It's not as if I have any intention of dating Huxley. Thankfully, Jamie doesn't pick up on my lack of finesse.

She's watching the next actor step on stage when she answers me. "As long as he's happy."

---

I watch Huxley half-jog up to the curb where I've parked outside his apartment. As promised, I've been driving him to and from work since last week. We haven't snapped at each other once since, and I'm starting to think that our shared secret history is *finally* behind us.

"Morning," I sing-song as he opens the door.

"Hey," he mumbles under his breath as he gets in. He drops his bag on his snowy boots and rubs his hands together. "It's cold as tits out there."

"Yeah," I answer distractedly as I pull into the street. "Says it's snowing all day. It'd be the perfect day to just stay in and watch movies."

"That's too bad," Huxley responds.

Something about his tone has my throat going dry, and I pretend I can't feel his eyes on me.

"Want to put something on?" I ask innocently, steering the conversation into a much safer territory—like who's in charge of the aux today.

"Sure."

He fiddles with his phone, and moments later, a song starts to play. Happily distracted, I tap my fingers on the steering wheel, and we listen to music in comfortable silence all the way to the theatre.

"I didn't know you were into Southern Gothic," I tell Huxley as I park the car, commenting on the playlist we were just listening to.

"Yeah," he says, a little surprised. "You like it?"

I shoot him a grin and a sideways glance. "I love."

Walking into the Remington, we're about to part ways when Huxley stops me.

"Hold up, I have something for you."

I swivel around to face him. "Me?"

"It's nothing," he says quickly as he unzips his bag slung on one of his shoulders.

He hands me a small paper bag. It looks like it's from some kind of bakery.

Shocked, I tentatively take it from him and try to catch his gaze, but he's avoiding eye contact.

"What is it?" I ask as I open the bag. I'm trying to keep my tone playful, but inside, my heart is beating like a drum

"It's nothing, really," he repeats again, making a dismissive gesture with his hand. "Probably stale by now."

Inside the bag are two croissants. They look buttery and flaky—just how I like them.

I'm suddenly warm all over.

My eyes flick up, unable to control the beaming smile on my face as Huxley's gaze finally meets mine. He looks nervous.

"There's a small bakery on Dulley," he says, obviously trying to sound casual. "I popped in before you picked me up this morning." He gives me one of his dry smiles. "Hope they're good enough for a croissant snob."

I laugh softly, smiling widely. "That's so sweet of you," I say. "Thank you."

He makes another dismissive gesture. "Just a thank you for all those rides," he says, avoiding eye contact again, his hand rubbing the back of his head. "Anyway, I should go find Whit. See you later."

And with that, he leaves with an informal salute, clearly uncomfortable with the entire exchange that *he* initiated. I stare at him walking away until he turns into a corridor, still clutching my bag of croissants, as a mystifying feeling blooms behind my chest.

# 20

# HUXLEY

My mind keeps bouncing back to Connie and the soft pink of her cheeks after I gave her the croissants this morning. I return to it again and again, the memory like the moon, and I am the tide.

Things are going smoothly between us lately, mainly because I haven't bitten her head off or acted like a complete fucking jerk. Anger and alienation are a heavy armor I've grown fond of carrying. It takes a lot more effort for me to act casual and at ease, but I won't let Connie know that. If pretending to be someone I'm not makes Connie finally warm up to me, then fine—I'll play the part.

I softly rap on Connie's office door to signal my presence. It's open, but I lean in the doorway just as her head pops up from staring at her laptop.

"Hux," she says with a smile. I mentally file away her smile with all the others I've kept in memory. "What's up?"

It's the first time she's shortened my name, and I get hit with an odd sense of glee at the sound.

I try to keep my face straight as I reply, "I know it's only two, but Whit told us to go home, the snow is only getting worse."

"Is it?" she says.

She uselessly looks around her windowless office, seemingly as a reflex, then down to her phone, most likely checking the weather app.

"Is everyone gone?"

I stuff a hand into my jeans pocket, still leaning against the doorframe.

"Not yet, but close. The tech crew is wrapping up, too." She hums distractedly, still looking at her phone. "Figured we should leave with them."

*We.*

The word hangs in front of me, taunting and mocking.

Connie doesn't seem to register the weight of the word, still stinking up the place when she looks up and smiles.

"I still have an hour or two here," she says, her brows creasing as she looks at her computer, then she adds quickly as if remembering herself. "You should go. No need to wait after me."

I scoff, pushing off the doorframe. "I'm not leaving you alone here."

She snorts a laugh. "The place isn't haunted or anything."

I stroll into her office. It's a pretty cramped room, but there's enough space for a small couch in front of her desk next to a row of filing cabinets.

I drop my backpack on the floor next to the couch and plop down into the cushions, legs wide and arms folded across my chest.

"Who said anything about ghosts, boss?"

Connie's laugh tickles my nape.

It feels good. Making her laugh.

Her lips are quirked, but her gaze is cast down, typing something on her computer.

"Don't call me that," she says lightly.

"What should I call you then?"

She's still smirking when her hazel eyes lift to meet mine. But when they do, her expression shutters as if suddenly trying to conceal her thoughts. Her gaze dips to my open legs, then quickly back up, her cheeks turning pink, just how I like them.

She laughs off her blunder as if I didn't witness any of what just happened. My throat turns dry, wondering what thoughts took over during her obvious moment of weakness.

I'd be lying if I said I wasn't waiting for another chance to make her squirm.

Although, was it even about me that night? Or was I just at the right place at the right time?

"You can keep calling me Connie," she says, looking back at her laptop.

"Everyone calls you Connie."

"Yeah?" She smirks. "And you're not everyone?"

"Aren't I?"

Connie's smile slowly fades as if turning apprehensive, her gaze slowly lifting back to study me from across the small space. I don't know what I'm playing at, but I don't care enough to figure it out.

The moment turns tense, and something about it makes my skin electric. I always feel the most comfortable when there's a whiff of unease in the air.

Feels familiar. Feels like home.

Connie licks her lips before she speaks, and my head starts to spin before I even hear the words come out of her mouth.

"I'm sure you'll think of something to call me."

She cocks her head, her eyes narrowing just a breath. She's challenging me. But I'm not a hundred percent sure *why*. It almost feels like she's playing chicken with me. To see if I have the balls to push our game even further.

*She takes my hand and squeezes it. She leads me down a dark-lit corridor, pushes me against the wall, and kisses me. Her lips are warm and hungry. She tastes like wine and sugar. And I'm fucking starving.*

I don't want to be careless this time. I suddenly feel like playing chess instead. I crave calculated moves pushed across the board. I hunger for a satisfying, well-deserved win.

"I'm sure I will," I say slowly.

*Her teeth sink into my bottom lip. I groan into her mouth, pulling her hips harder into me. Her laugh drips with lewd promises I ache to have come true. We stumble into the bathroom. The door locks behind her.*

Connie matches my stare for a few seconds longer before she clears her throat and returns to her computer.

Silence settles between us like a blanket of snow.

Eventually, I pull out a book from my bag and settle deeper into the couch, hyperaware of Connie's every move as the minutes tick slowly by.

---

"Oh ... My ... Fucking ... God."

Connie says the words slowly, spacing them and filling the silence between all four words with shocked horror. Her mouth is hanging wide open when she turns to look at me, but I'm still busy staring at the apocalypse happening outside through the glass doors.

The snowstorm is raging, I can barely see the building across the street. Whatever cars are still parked outside, including Connie's, have been completely buried. The street itself is nowhere to be seen.

"You should have told me it was this bad," she grumbles.

That has me turning my head to glare at her. "*I should have told you?*" Pointing to my chest. "*Me?*"

She turns sheepish, her gaze darting away, then back. "Well, yeah."

I chuckle sardonically. "You're not pinning this one on me, boss."

She smirks, and the urge to trace the curves of her lips overwhelms me. Luckily, just like life itself, the feeling is fleeting.

"Fine, it's nobody's fault," she says with pursed lips.

"It's yours," I deadpan.

She barks a laugh but still shoots me a worried look, dragging her hands down her face. "What the hell are we going to do? I can't drive in this weather."

I shrug my shoulders, backing away from the door. "I guess we're stuck here for now."

Connie's eyebrows dip as she crosses her arms. "You don't seem that alarmed by this."

I want to say, "*It's because I get to spend more time with you.*" Instead, I give her a dry smile and turn to the auditorium doors. "I've been to prison, being trapped inside is kind of my modus operandi."

I hear her puff out a laugh behind me, and I can't help but feel the sound somewhere deep inside my chest.

"Sorry, I shouldn't laugh about that."

There's still levity in her tone, but her comment falls much too close to pity for my liking.

"I want you to," I say as I keep the auditorium door open for her. "I wouldn't have said it otherwise."

Her eyes lift to meet mine as she passes through the doorway, a soft smile on her lips. Her body is inches from mine, the hem of her coat sweeping across my thighs, and it's as if she's pressed her palms flat against my chest.

My internal reaction is the same.

Flames licking through my veins.

Venom just as sweet as how her lips once tasted.

*Eager hands pull my sweater over my head. Our lips crash together again, and those damn eager hands now unbutton my jeans. She takes off her shirt, and I push her against the bathroom door. Fingers digging into her warm skin. A desperate palm wrapped firmly around her breast.*

I watch her skip down the main aisle.

"What are we going to do?" she asks innocently as she trots up the stairs and takes center stage. "I wish we had —"

Her mouth drops as she whirls to look at me. My gaze is questioning while I walk down the aisle to reach her. Connie's expression is one of mischievous delight.

"What?" I ask suspiciously.

My chin lifts the more she walks toward the end of the stage, her feet now at the height of my chest. I could very well be kneeling at her feet, the feeling is just as intense.

She looks down at me and smiles devilishly.

"Follow me."

<hr>

HER BIG REVELATION was a half-empty bottle of tequila in the staff lounge. She then dragged me up to the balcony to sit and share the bottle between us.

We've been taking swigs back and forth for the past half hour as we quietly stare down at the auditorium.

"I can't believe this is mine," Connie says with an awed sigh.

She has her feet pressed up against the guardrail, her arms over her thighs, the bottle of tequila hanging loosely between her legs. Her red hair is down, almost disappearing against the color of her black knit sweater.

I'm too wrapped up in drinking her in to say anything of substance, so I stay silent.

She looks at me with a sated smile, handing me the tequila bottle. I keep picking up on the warm florals of her perfume anytime she offers me the bottle, and I can't stop imagining myself burying my nose into the crook of her neck anytime I get a hit.

"You know ..." she starts, looking for her words. "Money has never been an issue for me, most of the things I've ever wanted I've gotten, but —" She looks back down at the stage and her smile widens. My heart swells with it. Her eyes meet mine again. "Buying the Remington feels different. It's not just another frivolous purchase simply because I *could*, it feels ..."

She falls silent again as if considering her next words. I decide to finish her thought for her.

"Meant to be?"

I take a swig of tequila as her face turns pensive, slowly nodding.

"Yeah, meant to be," she repeats softly.

I smile but don't say anything. We fall into a comfortable silence for a few minutes. Her fingers graze mine when she takes the bottle back. I pretend I don't feel it all the way up my arm.

*She's touching me. It's fucking bliss. A hand on my cock. My fingers finding her soaked. Breathy moans against parted lips. Heated exchange of words. Pleading. Begging. I shove her pants down. Bend her over the sink.*

Eventually, Connie breaks the silence with a question. "Do you believe that coincidences aren't just coincidences?"

I don't answer immediately. Instead, I mirror her posture and press my feet against the railing, settling deeper into my seat. Folding my hands over my stomach, I let out a long exhale before my head drops toward her. She hasn't stopped staring at me, waiting for me to answer her question.

"Elaborate," I finally say.

I know what she's implying, but something in me just wants to hear her muse out loud.

"You know," she says impatiently, elongating her last word. "Do you believe everything happens for a reason? That somehow every decision you make leads you right where you're supposed to be?"

*Foil wrapper ripped between clenched teeth. A hand trailing down her back, pressing her down. Groans. Moans. Breathing. Panting. The head of my cock pushing against her wet slit. A thrust of the hips. Bliss. Fucking bliss.*

I collect my thoughts before I give her an honest answer. I distance myself from the hard truth instead.

"You've been living in LA for too long."

Connie snorts a laugh before gulping down a healthy amount of tequila.

"I'm being serious, Hux."

The shortening of my name tickles my nape again. I chew on my words, my thoughts turning bitter. I don't want to ruin the moment, but how can I tell her that her woo-woo belief is one of privilege?

What a comforting thought to have, when everything has come so easily for her, while her *fate* gave me a shitty childhood and a one-way ticket to prison.

"Even the bad stuff, you know?" she says, breaking me out of my train of thought. She hands me the bottle. "If my ex hadn't cheated on me, I wouldn't be here now."

I study her for a little while longer before speaking again. "Ask me again when something good *actually* happens in my life. Maybe I'll have a better answer then."

Pain flits across Connie's face when she realizes the implication of what she was just inferring. This time, her reaction doesn't bother me. Maybe this girl needs a reality check. Life isn't a fucking magical journey full of wonder. Not for a lot of us, anyway.

"I'm sorry, I didn't mean it that way," she says helplessly.

I shoot her a crooked smile, trying to lessen the tension. "It's fine. I don't believe in that shit anyway."

She watches me take a large slug of tequila, the burn almost as soothing as her eyes on me. Her expression is serious when she speaks again.

"What about people?"

"What *about* people?"

"You don't believe that some people you're just,"—she looks up at the ceiling before her gaze lands back on me—"meant to meet? That no matter what happens, you were always destined to have them come into your life?"

"Like your ex?"

I regret the dig immediately, but Connie just rolls her eyes, letting out a large puff of air. She drops her feet to the floor and bends her knee flat on the seat so she can turn to the side and face me.

"Like Jamie?" she continues, her tone slightly annoyed while waving her hands animatedly. "Like, Like —"

*Her cunt squeezes. Flutters. Pulses. My thrusts are hard, my cock sliding in and out. Fucking her. Fucking Connie. My mind turns hazy. I'm burning up. My fingers dig into her thighs as her eyes stare back at me through the mirror. Her mouth is open. A moan slips out. I pull out. Flip her over and lift her up onto the sink. I catch her lips with mine one last time before it's over. One last time before this inevitably ends.*

"Like me."

It's not a question.

Her hands drop to the armrest between us, her eyes bouncing back and forth as she stares back at me. She chews on her lips as the silence turns into a perfume of unspoken desires.

If I can feel it, I know she can feel it, too.

"Like you," she whispers.

I don't second-guess myself before placing the bottle of tequila at our feet and leaning across my seat. I catch her bottom lip before she has time to protest.

The kiss isn't gentle.

It's lethal.

Pulverizing my universe into a million little pieces.

Connie wants this just as much, her lips parting for my tongue as easily as I remembered.

She lets out a small whimper as if she was waiting for this all along. As if she's been thinking about my lips just as much as I have hers. My head is spinning, and it's sure as hell not the tequila.

Her fist twists around my collar, pulling me closer. I feel crazed, my hands on both sides of her face as the kiss deepens and intensifies. It turns into a promise of her naked body against mine. I'm practically crawling out of my seat just to get to her.

Then, she pulls away.

"Huxley, we can't," she says.

Her eyes are wide as she pants, trying to catch her breath.

I don't give up so easily this time.

"What happened to everything happens for a reason?" I rasp as I try to kiss her again.

But she pushes at my chest, and I fall back into my seat with an irritated sigh, dragging a hand over my face.

"This is a mistake, and you know it," she says.

It almost sounds like a plea as if she's hoping I'll believe her bullshit just like she's trying so hard to do.

"A mistake," I repeat, laughing dejectedly. "So I guess all your woo-woo bullshit doesn't apply here."

She says my name again. This time, I hate how it sounds on her lips.

"Hux, please." She takes an anxious inhale. "Don't be mad at me. I don't want this to ruin what we were finally managing to build."

"What?" I reply in disgust. "A fucking friendship?"

She looks so innocent then as she blinks back at me with big owlish eyes. I forget for a second that she's almost four years older than me.

"Well ... yeah."

The bitterness only builds and builds inside of me. Before I start choking on it, I swallow hard and lick my lips. I break eye contact and pick the bottle back up from beside me. I take a swig of tequila and stare straight ahead.

"Fine."

I feel her stare burning a hole through me until finally, she sighs and straightens in her seat, facing forward.

"Fine," she repeats, ripping the bottle away from me.

This time, the silence that follows isn't comfortable. It's thick and insufferable. But neither of us seeks to fill it. We don't speak a single fucking word, passing the bottle back and forth until it's all finished and gone.

**21**

## CONNIE

"How long do we have?" Jamie asks. She blows a pink strand of hair out of her face as she fiddles with the table full of refreshments, her face scrunched up in concentration.

I check my phone. "Like, thirty minutes?"

"Perfect," she says under her breath. "I'm almost done with the table. What else needs to be done?"

"The booze is still in my trunk. Give me a hand when you're finished?"

Jamie nods and smiles, eyes sparkling with happiness as she returns to her task.

It's Saturday evening, just after audition week, and we're busy prepping for the cast party. Well, maybe housewarming is a more accurate word. A little something to mark this new era for the theatre.

Casting was pretty seamless; three days and we had the actors picked out. To my delight, Mary-Beth auditioned and got the part of Kate. It's a small comfort to have an old friend with me at the Remington.

I didn't waste any time planning the party. I invited everyone, from the cast to the technical crew and even the renovation team. The more, the merrier—and nothing to do with needing an excuse to invite Huxley.

Things have been ... *fine* ... since the big snowstorm four days ago. It didn't stop snowing until well after midnight. Eventually, I left Huxley to brood in the auditorium and took a nap in my office just to get away from the tense silence between us.

The torturous ride home wasn't any better, but by the next day, it was as if we both had decided to pretend the kiss never happened. We've been pretending ever since while I continue to pick him up and drop him off from work.

I don't even know why I stopped the kiss in the first place. What is it about Huxley that makes me so tentative?

Aside from that first time at Jamie's engagement party, that is.

I have a history of not thinking about the consequences. Our one-night stand is a classic example of my impulsivity.

But would hooking up with Huxley again really be such a giant mistake? I keep blaming my reticence on him being Ozzy's brother. But would that really be such a problem? Would Jamie even care?

It's not just that.

As much as I like to entertain the thought of him and me, Huxley could never just be a fling. It would be too messy, with the family ties and all. It already *is* too messy. And I'm nowhere near ready to consider anything serious after what Oliver did to me.

It doesn't mean I want Huxley out of the picture, either.

---

I'm standing near the stage with Jamie and Mary-Beth, sipping on a vodka soda. Most of the cast and crew have arrived, and I'm buzzing with excitement. With everyone here, there are about thirty of us, and the auditorium is alive with music and conversation. Even Virginia seems to be enjoying herself. After two weeks of killing her with kindness, she's finally warming up to me. No one can resist my infectious charm for long.

My gaze sweeps across the auditorium, but there's no sign of Huxley yet. I try not to make it obvious that I'm seeking him out in front of Jamie but thankfully she's too busy catching up with Mary-Beth to pay much attention to my nervous antics.

When I finally see him walk in, I swallow sideways, choking on my drink. He's cleaned up for the party. The burgundy sweater under his bomber jacket looks new, and even his blue hair appears freshly done. But I can't linger long on those details when all I can see is Selina hanging off him, all smiles and fake designer boots.

Letting my emotions get the best of me, I grab Jamie by the sleeve of her dress and tug her toward me.

"What the hell is she doing here?" I whisper harshly, pointing my chin toward the duo. "I specifically said no partners."

Jamie looks confused, then squints. "Wait, is that *the* Selina?" Then eyes me for half a second too long before she laughs, trying to defuse the tension. "But also, why were you expecting Huxley to follow the rules in the first place?"

I quell the urge to stomp right up to Selina and tell her to leave in front of Huxley and the whole cast. But I'm twenty-nine, for god's sake, I should maybe start acting my age.

I harrumph at Jamie's answer but don't reply. Taking another big gulp of my vodka soda, I let Jamie resume her conversation with Mary-Beth, and I make a show of pretending to listen. But try as I might, my gaze is fixed on the asshole who brought a date to *my* cast party.

He pauses near the doors and looks around, most likely looking for Whit, who's talking to one of the set designers. His green eyes land on me, and he pauses his sweep of the room just long enough to stare back and smile.

*God, his smile.*

It's calculated and inexplicably delicious. It's as if he thinks he's won something unsaid between us.

*Little fucker.*

Two can play this game. I turn away first before he has the chance to.

---

HALF AN HOUR LATER, I'm still fuming. He hasn't even come up to say hi to me or Jamie yet, and by my best friend's nonchalance, I'm the only one who seems to have a problem with his aloof behavior.

I'm *this* close to walking up and introducing myself to Selina just to spite him when he finally catches my eye. Leaning down to whisper something in Selina's ear, he keeps his gaze steady on mine, then turns and walks away.

Assuming he's going out for a cigarette, my curiosity—or more like suspicion—piques when he veers to the left and heads for the balcony stairs.

*Is he wanting me to follow him?*

I press my lips together, subtly rolling my eyes. He'll be waiting a long time for that.

I return to the conversation Jamie is now having with Nacho.

A minute passes. I'm not listening.

"I need some air," I blurt out. And before anyone has time to offer their company, I add. "I'll be right back."

I walk out of the auditorium and end up standing like an idiot in the middle of the lobby.

"This is so stupid," I mutter under my breath.

After barely thirty seconds, I loop back inside and bolt up

the stairs, praying that no one has noticed me. I find Huxley sitting exactly where we sat last time.

The night we kissed.

The memory of his lips on mine does nothing to quell the flames licking up my body.

Huxley is holding his beer with a loose grip, letting it hang between his legs as he stares down at the party downstairs. Even if he doesn't look at me as I approach, I can tell he knows I'm there.

With every step, I feel his presence like a magnet pulling me even closer. I stop just beside his seat. Placing my hands behind me on the railing, I lean against them.

"I said no partners."

He flicks his gaze up without moving an inch, staring at me from under his eyelashes. His smile is just as disarming as before.

His voice is low when he speaks. "She's not my partner."

I smooth my tongue over my teeth with irritation. "Whatever the fuck she is to you, she's not supposed to be here."

"James is here."

"Oh my god," I say dismissively as I look away, then back to him. "As if Jamie counts as a plus one."

He takes a slow swig of his beer before letting his arm fall back between his legs.

"I'll read the fine print next time."

I can tell he's goading me. He's trying to get a rise out of me, and to my dismay, it's working. I can't help but narrow my eyes at him and try to think of another lame comment to fling back at him.

"Nice dye job," I say with a snark. "Did you have your little girlfriend give you a hand with it?"

I realize I've walked right into it when Huxley shoots me an arrogant look, his chin lifting slowly so he can stare at me square in the eyes. He toys with his tongue ring, rolling it between his lips before speaking, and the sight has my cheeks flushing in heat.

"She gave me a hand, alright."

My stomach churns at the image he just painted, but I don't react, keeping my face as smooth as stone. I don't have any right to lay claim. Selina isn't doing anything wrong, even if I hate her fucking guts right now.

"Cute." My tone is dripping with condescension. "Is that supposed to make me jealous?"

I see his cocky expression falter, but he regains his composure just as fast.

It's enough for me to go in for the kill.

I drop my head backward and laugh before my taunting gaze lands back on Huxley. He looks rattled, and I feed off of it.

"Was that your master plan?" I push off the railing and surprise him by dropping sideways on his lap. Crossing my legs, I wrap an arm around his neck. While walking two teasing fingers up his chest, I pout mockingly. "You really thought parading a girl in front of me would make me fall at your feet?"

Too wrapped up in wanting the upper hand in this insipid game of chicken we're playing, I realize my fateful error when his green eyes darken.

His face is inches from mine, his hot breath tickling my parted lips. An entire lifetime passes between us before his hand slowly slips over my knit dress and settles on my upper thigh.

"It's working, isn't it?"

His voice is just as heated as the slow trace of his thumb across the dip of my hip. It's as if he's touched my core directly. My clit throbs in response as my breath catches in my throat.

I try not to react, caught up in how close his face is to mine.

I could kiss him. Part my legs and beg for him.

His tongue swipes slowly over his bottom lip before he flashes me another one of his infuriatingly smug smiles.

With it, his hold on me snaps.

And I suddenly remember the game.

I straighten in his lap and cock a grin, breaking the tension between us.

"Not even close, sweetie," I say while I pat him on the head and jump to my feet.

I don't look back and bound down the stairs, grinning with victory, knowing I must have left Huxley fuming in his seat. But it's done nothing to quell the fire still roaring inside of me.

Distracted, I realize much too late, when I get to the bottom of the stairs, that Selina is heading straight for me. My heart drops, thinking she might have seen something she shouldn't have. But her expression is one of forced friendliness.

"Hi!" she says excitedly, pressing both hands to her chest, eyes glimmering and mouth open wide in a smile. "I can't believe it's you, I've been following you for years! I've been trying to find a way to introduce myself all night," she gushes. She then points to her phone in her hand. "Can we take a selfie?"

My gaze lands on Huxley walking down the stairs on the opposite side of the auditorium. He's staring daggers at both of us, but Selina notices nothing.

I return my attention to my *fan* and flip my hair off my shoulder as I return her beaming smile.

"Of course we can!"

# 22

# HUXLEY

I t's the end of another woodworking class, and I'm packing up my bag when Whit walks up to me, his typical crooked smile fixed on his face.

"That's a really cool idea you got there," he says as he points to my workstation. "And your execution is flawless." His smile widens and with a proud laugh he adds, "You're a natural."

I've been attending his classes for two months now, and Whit has been *incessantly* encouraging me with every little thing. I haven't gotten used to it. I don't think I ever will. His words prickle against my skin anytime he opens his mouth.

At least, I've gotten used to simply nodding and smiling.

In a way, he reminds me of Ozzy.

They're both trying too hard.

I look over to the project I've been working on and feel embarrassed. I don't even know why I had the idea in the first place.

*Waste of fucking time.*

I look back to Whit.

"Thanks," I grunt as I swing my bag over my shoulder, getting ready to leave.

"Have time for a beer?" Whit asks.

I stop in my tracks and narrow my eyes. "With you?"

He barks a laugh. "Yeah, with me." He points behind him with his thumb. "There's a bar just around the corner from here. The place sucks but the beer is cold."

His invitation smells like pity. Like I'm a charity case that needs his attention. Why else would he invite me out for a beer? I almost say no, but something stops me.

Maybe it's loneliness that has me nodding my head and agreeing. Or maybe it's the fact that I lost all my friends when I went to prison. And that my only friend now is not even a friend at all but my sister Sophia.

*Pathetic.*

Whit's face brightens at the sight of my half-hearted nod.

"Great! I'll grab my coat."

WHIT WAS RIGHT, Stanley's is a dive bar. It's dark and dingy with a couple of pool tables in the back and a jukebox near the bathrooms. The bartender looks like he would rather die than be here serving us.

It's perfect and exactly what I like.

We sit at the sticky bar, and Whit orders us a round of beers. After a quick clink of our bottles, we fall silent as we take our first sip.

I don't know what to say so I blurt out the first thing that comes to mind. "My brother used to work around here."

"Yeah? Where?"

I feel stupid even to have brought it up but answer his question anyway. "Orso — it's a restaurant on Miller."

Whit gives me a toothy smile. "Oh yeah, I know that place." He takes a swig of his beer. "Fancy."

I wordlessly agree and suddenly feel awkward as if I've

completely lost the art of small talk. Come to think of it, I don't think I've ever known how.

"Older brother?"

I nod, swallowing a mouthful of beer. "Younger brother and sister too."

"Big family," he muses.

"Yeah." I chuckle dryly. "Always the ones who shouldn't have kids that end up having too many."

Whit laughs softly as if he's relating to what I said. "Don't I know it — I grew up in Pecket, shitty parents were the norm for most of us."

I fall silent, studying Whit as I pick at the label of my beer.

"What?" he asks casually.

"You grew up in Pecket?"

His laugh is slightly dejected this time. "Unfortunately. Born and raised."

"Me too."

Whit's eyebrows raise in surprise. We share a look that only people forced to grow up in the city's poorest and most dangerous neighborhood could ever understand. I'm suddenly put at ease, less guarded, as if we instantly share an unspoken history even though we just met a few months ago. Whit raises his beer and grins.

"To surviving that shithole."

---

I'M HOME from the bar, watching TV with Sophia. DK is purring on my lap as I pick at my lip, staring at my phone, lost in thought. It's the third time I've watched Connie's stories today and I'll probably have watched them a fourth time by the time I fall asleep tonight.

A picture of her coffee. Another of the cast rehearsing. Then a selfie. She took it during golden hour. The sun's rays look gold against her flaming hair, her hazel eyes almost green against the sunlight. I hold my finger on the screen, lingering on the picture.

"Is that *Connie*?"

I lock my phone and throw it across the couch as I hear Sophia's voice over my shoulder. Like a fucking idiot, I didn't realize she was behind me coming back from the kitchen.

"No," I say with a somewhat guilty scowl.

She snickers as she sits on the floor, resting against the couch. "That was totally Connie." She lifts her head to look at me, her eyes twinkling with mirth. "I didn't even know you followed her."

"Mind your fucking business," I mutter.

My threat falls on deaf ears as she continues to laugh. "You know people can see who watches their stories, right?"

My heart drops, still, I choose not to believe her.

I shove her head. "Sure they can, idiot."

"They do," she presses, still bleating like a fucking goat. "Look." She grabs her phone, and pulls up her stories on Instagram, then swipes up. "See?"

To my horror, a list of profiles appears. I want to dig my own grave and throw myself into it at the realization that Connie has known I watched her stories this *whole* time. Worst of all, I don't even follow her.

*Real fucking slick. That's what I get for being nosy—shit, am I sweating?*

Sophia chortles at the sight of my shocked face. "Don't worry she can't see how many times you watch them at least. You'd know this if you posted on your stories like a normal person."

I fall deeper into the couch, dragging my hand over my face and sigh. "'Cause you're a normal person?"

"More normal than you, weirdo," she answers through a mouthful of popcorn. She falls silent while she chews. Then abruptly changes the subject. "I haven't seen Selina around in a while, you guys still dating?"

I roll my eyes at her prying. She's not being subtle but I answer her anyway.

"We were never dating in the first place."

"So that's a *no,* then."

I give DK a little scratch on the head before answering. The last time I spoke to Selina was the night of the cast party last week. I don't owe anything to Connie, but after our little face-off on the balcony, I felt weird continuing to sleep with Selina. I broke it off with her that same night and went home alone. Her ego was bruised, but I'm not worried about her. I was just something to pass the time with, she'll soon forget all about me. They all do.

"No," I finally answer.

---

A FEW HOURS LATER, I check my phone while walking into my bedroom for the first time since Sophia caught me gawking at Connie.

*Speak of the devil ...*

She texted me about half an hour ago.

We've been circling each other since the cast party, as if we're both trying to see who's going to fold first. Connie loves to play innocent, and it's been four days of car rides where the tension is so thick I can barely think. Everything out of her mouth sounds like an innuendo, and I just know she's doing it on purpose.

I swear she's getting off on the theatrics of it all.

I'd be a fucking liar if I said I wasn't also.

I click on the notification, and my phone opens on our conversation thread. I nearly choke on my tongue when my eyes land on the picture she sent.

It's a fucking nude.

A mirror selfie. She's naked sitting on her knees, back straight, her ass resting on top of her pointed feet. Her back is facing the camera but she's twisted her torso just enough to take the picture so I can see the tantalizing curve of the side of her tit. I don't know what to do so I throw my phone for the second time tonight, on my bed this time. My mind is reeling, and my cock is instantly hard, but I try to ignore it, pacing in short circles.

*There's no way.*

*Ain't no fucking way.*

I dive for my phone and look at the picture again. It takes me another thirty seconds to peel my eyes away from Connie's nude to realize she sent a text right after.

> Omg! That was not meant for you!! I'm so embarrassed.

It's followed by a string of emojis that I can barely decipher except for the monkey covering its face. My stomach sinks reading her text.

She sent this by mistake? It was meant for someone else?

Jealousy curls tight around my throat. For that fucking *DJ*?

My grip tightens around the screen and I'm about to throw my phone again—this time against the wall—when it suddenly dawns on me.

*She's fucking with me.*

I let my head drop and groan out loud. But I can't help but grin maniacally. She must be getting desperate to do something like this. My mind races thinking of ways to retaliate.

Send a dick pic? Or a video of me jacking off?

I settle on the bed, sitting up against the wall as I deliberate. I palm my hardened cock through my sweats, mindlessly groping myself as I stare at Connie's naked body.

"Fucking tease," I groan under my breath, memorizing the curve of her ass as I pull my cock out.

I realize then what to do in retaliation. My laugh is dark and twisted. It's followed by a low hiss when my hand wraps around my hard shaft.

The best revenge is to ignore her. Connie thrives on attention.

The thought has me dropping my head against the wall, a quiet moan leaving my lips. I can stare at her picture all I want. I know she wants me to. Fuck myself dry staring at her perfect heart-shaped ass. I can do all of those things and more—she just doesn't need to know.

She can't win this round.

Not when I know I've already lost the game.

**23**

**CONNIE**

**I** 've just gotten to a massive plot twist in my audiobook when a call interrupts my concentration. I'm in the hotel's gym, running on the treadmill, but don't slow my stride as I glance down to see who's calling.

*Shit.*

It's my agent. I groan out loud and let out a long sigh. Slowing down to a fast-paced walk, I tap on my headphones to pick up the call.

"Hi Janet," I say as sweetly as possible while out of breath, bracing myself for what's to come.

Too busy to beat around the bush, she promptly goes in for the kill. "You can't ignore me forever, Connie. You need to get your shit together. Brands are getting impatient — they're breathing down my neck, and I'm starting to run out of excuses."

I roll my eyes, wiping a palm across my forehead and into my hair.

"I moved across the country, is that not excuse enough?"

"Not *nearly* excuse enough. Listen, sweetie, you might have turned your back on your acting career — *fine* — but you're still an influencer with prior engagements."

The way she hissed the word *fine* tells me it's *not* fine, but I ignore her tone. I suck on my teeth, my hands on my hips while I think.

*I could quit it all.*

*Start over fresh.*

It's not like I need the money. But for once, I chew on my words and don't say anything rash.

Yet.

"I just need some time," I finally say.

Something in my tone must convince Janet.

Her voice is softer when she speaks next. "All I'm asking is for you to fulfill the contracts you already have, and then we can talk. Deal?"

I sigh. "Fine."

"I also need you to attend an event in Marsford Bay next month."

I groan so loud that the man jogging a few treadmills away from me looks over. Smiling awkwardly, I give him a small apologetic wave.

"*What* event?"

"Just this influencer thing — sponsored by Hendricks Gin, something to do with Valentine's Day."

"Oh great," I mutter under my breath.

She ignores my petulance. "I just sent you an email with all the details. Anyway, I've got to go. I have a meeting in five. Talk soon."

I mumble my goodbyes and hang up.

My audiobook begins to play automatically when the call ends and I start up my run again, now desperately needing to expel some of my frustration.

I despise those influencer events. The downside to all this internet fame bullshit.

For now, I try to push it out of my thoughts and run for another half hour, my lungs burning but my mind clear when I finally step off the treadmill.

"WHAT ABOUT THIS?"

I bring a silk blouse up to Sophia's chest so she can see it against herself.

She wrinkles her nose and shakes her head. "Pass." Then smiles. "But it would look great on you."

Sophia turns back to the rack of clothes, slowly rifling through it as I inspect the blouse further, now for myself.

It's her twenty-first birthday on Monday, and I promised her a shopping spree to celebrate. She's being surprisingly picky for a no-holds-barred shopping spree. I return the blouse to the rack and continue my perusal.

"So," I say, "What's going on with you? Any good restaurant gossip?"

She smirks but doesn't look up when she answers, "One of the dishwashers got caught snorting Adderall in the dish pit."

I snicker as I pick out a pair of jeans to inspect. I show them to Sophia, and she takes them to have a closer look.

"I meant more like —" I waggle my eyebrows to convey my meaning instead of finishing my sentence.

With all the stories I've heard from Jamie, the restaurant industry is just as messy as the world of acting: Toxic flings, cheating, and *so* much drama.

Sophia puffs out a laugh. "I mean ... Yeah, I guess." She turns a little shifty, avoiding eye contact. "I'm kind of hooking up with the day bartender."

"You bitch," I hiss playfully, slapping her with the shirt I'm holding. "And you led with the dishwasher story? Classic Aquarius, keeping the best secrets for themselves."

She giggles, placing the jeans back where I found them. "It's part of my allure." She strolls to another rack of clothes, her hand idly dragging against the fabrics. "It's no big deal, really. He's so full of himself." She makes a face, and I can tell I won't like what she's about to say. "And thirty-three."

My jaw drops. "*Sophia.*"

"It's *fine*," she says, elongating her last word as if it's going to help ease my shock.

I stare her down, but her attention is on a blue baby tee. Finally, she looks up and cocks her head to the side, shooting me an unimpressed look.

"Please," she says, "As if you weren't *also* making dumb decisions at my age."

I puff out an irritated sigh. "Yeah, and look where it got me. Twenty-nine and single."

Sophia flings the baby tee over her arm, the pile of clothes she's chosen to try on finally getting bigger.

"You're being dramatic," she deadpans. "*Anyway*, enough about me."

She narrows her eyes, and my stomach drops. I know that look: She knows something.

*Oh god.*

She knows something.

Never the one to skirt around a subject, she goes straight for the kill, her smirk never wavering. "So what's going on with you and my brother?"

I hate how she used the word *brother* instead of his name. It feels deliberate, and I hesitate for a few seconds too long, which only cements the suspicious look on her face.

I shrug my shoulders and look away. "Nothing, we just work together."

She stares at me, and I pretend to be focused on a lace top that would never go with my complexion. She lets out a sarcastic hum, and I start to sweat, hoping she'll drop the subject. Why would she? I wouldn't.

"You know he watches your stories, like, *all* the time. I think he's kind of obsessed with you, actually."

She says it much too casually, but her words feel like a bomb detonating inside my chest. It's a confusing reaction, especially since I've been aware that Huxley has been watching my stories. I only noticed it when I came back for the holidays and wonder if it's been happening for much longer than that.

But obsessed with *me*?

That's a stretch.

Not to mention that the little shit hasn't followed me back on Instagram yet. I know it's a tactical move. And a great one at that because I check every day to see if he has. I was so sure I had him hook, line, and sinker when I sent him that nude two days ago.

But he stayed infuriatingly silent about it. Then, I thought I'd see *some* kind of tell when I picked him up the morning after, but his poker face was rock solid. He just handed me a coffee and put on a playlist he'd been working on.

I've been stewing since yesterday, morbidly curious to know where our precarious game will take us next. It's like watching a car wreck in slow motion, there's nothing I can do but watch. Or cause the wreck in the first place. It's an intoxicating, albeit unhealthy, feeling.

Knowing Sophia is waiting for some kind of reaction from me, I scoff, trying to look as disinterested as possible in her little theory.

"Huxley? Obsessed with me?" I say as if the mere thought is ridiculous. "Isn't he dating that Selina girl?"

I wasn't *specifically* looking to pry, but the opportunity is right there; it would be a shame not to take it.

Sophia slowly walks around a rack of sweaters but gives me

a quick look before returning to the rack. It's obvious she knows I'm full of shit. I play dumb nonetheless.

"Apparently not."

"Oh?" I squeak out, smiling to myself.

From the corner of my eye, I watch her grin, and I realize she won't be giving me anything but that small morsel just to spite me. And if I want to keep my cards close to my chest, I can't do anything about it.

"So you're coming tomorrow then?" she asks.

I scrunch my eyebrows together. "Tomorrow?"

"Tomorrow," she repeats with a bit of an attitude. "Sunday dinner? My birthday?"

"Oh! Right ... Um ..."

I've known about this dinner ever since Jamie invited me a few weeks ago, but I've been trying to find a way out of it since. The thought of having to dodge the minefield that is Huxley and me, in front of Jamie and Ozzy, has me breaking out in a sweat anytime I think about it.

It was one thing when Huxley was pointedly ignoring me, but now? I'd rather do anything to avoid it.

"Well," I say much too tentatively. "I thought since we were hanging out today that I could ..."

Sophia's green eyes are hard and penetrating.

*Oh god, she won't let this go, will she?*

"Why? Something better to do?"

My mouth hangs open, my half-hearted protest evaporating into thin air.

"I mean, not really, but ..." I stammer out.

"Great!" she chirps, smiling sweetly when there's nothing *sweet* about her. She tucks her short blonde hair behind her ear, the very picture of innocence. "Settled then. You're coming."

She turns on her heels and heads toward the fitting rooms,

giving me no other choice but to agree to her coerced invitation.

**24**

## CONNIE

I t's Sunday evening at the McKennas. I arrived an hour ago and I've already had two—maybe three—large glasses of Burgundy. I'm hoping it chills me out and stops my gaze from constantly seeking Huxley's presence even when I'm busy speaking with *anybody* else.

I'm so desperate for some distraction that I even let Charlie recount, beat by beat, the latest K-drama he's been watching. At least with him, I just need to be half-listening and nod once or twice for him to be happy.

Thankfully, Huxley has spent most of his time in the kitchen helping Ozzy with dinner. Jamie and I have migrated to the dining room table, Jamie sitting across from me, catching up while we wait.

"Have you thought more about your bachelorette?" I ask her, taking a sip of my wine.

Jamie presses her lips together as if thinking, her finger circling the lip of her wine glass, nails painted chrome pink. The only ring on her fingers is her engagement ring. A silver ring with a simple row of three pearls.

I wouldn't believe the story behind the pearls if it didn't come directly from the source.

When Ozzy was still working at Orso, he found three pearls, one after the other, while shucking oysters. It's extremely rare to find a pearl in an oyster, let alone three.

That's the thing. Nothing is impossible when it comes to Ozzy and Jamie. Their love is so fated that Ozzy finding pearls in oysters feels *normal*—like just another sign from the universe proving that they are meant to be.

It's sickening. And achingly beautiful.

"I don't know ..." she says, "Ozzy and I were maybe thinking of a joint party? Like maybe renting a cottage or something."

"Oh, so you're old and boring."

Jamie bursts into a laugh, and I grin at my little jab.

"Why don't we go somewhere?" I press, "My treat."

Jamie waves her hands in front of her, shaking her head. "No, no, no, I don't want you to pay, absolutely not."

"Why not?" I say, a small whine in my tone. Resting my arm against the table, I press my chest against the edge as if trying to get closer to Jamie across from me. "Let me do this for you? As a wedding gift."

Jamie continues to protest. "No way." She tilts her head in that meaningful way of hers. "I don't need anything big, I just want you there."

Leaning back into my seat, I slowly shake my head, pretending to be disappointed in her, taking a sip of wine. "You've changed."

Jamie snorts in her wine glass. "Bitch."

We're busy giggling like teenagers when Huxley appears holding a large bowl of paella.

His gaze finds mine, and his crooked grin makes my stomach flip.

While placing the steaming bowl in the middle of the table,

Huxley calls for Charlie and Sophia to come sit. Ozzy follows from behind with two more dishes.

Everything smells incredible, as usual.

Expecting Sophia to sit beside me, my spine snaps straight when Huxley beats her to it and pulls out the chair beside me. Sophia gives me a knowing look that makes me want to shrivel up and die, and settles across from me beside Jamie.

"What are you doing?" I harshly whisper from the corner of my mouth.

Huxley's smile widens as he looks at me. "Celebrating my sister's birthday."

He scoots his chair even closer, and I try to hide my full-body cringe. Just his good mood alone should be enough for his family to start getting suspicious.

"You never sit beside me."

Thankfully, everyone is talking over each other, too busy passing around plates of food to overhear our exchange.

"Yeah, well," Huxley says with a small pause, shoveling spoonfuls of paella onto his plate. "View's better over here."

I look away and sigh under my breath, hoping I can survive this without Jamie—or worse, Ozzy—picking up on our new dynamic.

---

"So the Remington is going good, I hear?" Ozzy asks.

He rakes a hand through his curls as he leans back into his chair, waiting for me to answer.

Dinner is winding down, plates cleared, dessert being eaten, and I can finally see the light at the end of the tunnel. I even stopped drinking an hour ago, so I can promptly leave when the opportunity arises.

I smile and nod proudly. "Yeah, really good, we did our first read-through last week, so that was exciting."

"That's great." His smile widens. "And Hux isn't giving you any trouble?"

Ozzy's eyes crinkle, clearly just teasing.

As soon as Huxley's name is out of his brother's mouth, his hand lands on my thigh.

My shoulders straighten, and my heart rate triples.

*What the fuck is he playing at?*

My knee-jerk reaction is to shove his hand away, but the sudden movement would be much more obvious than whatever the hell Huxley is currently doing. His palm is scalding against my thigh, only my tights separating me from him. He squeezes once, then lets his hand relax, his index finger making lazy circles near my knee.

I stutter out a nervous laugh, answering some kind of pleasantry while all my attention is now on Huxley's hand slowly moving up my thigh.

A deranged part of me is curious to see how far he'd try to push this, but thankfully, that part of me is small enough that I manage to squash any desire to be reckless.

Instead, I do the only thing that comes to mind and abruptly stand up.

Jamie looks up at me. "You're leaving?"

*Perfect, an out.*

I give her a small pout. "Yeah, it's getting late — big day tomorrow." I look over to Ozzy and smile. "Thank you so much for dinner, it was amazing."

"Can I bum a ride?" I hear Huxley say from his seat.

Slowly, I look down, widening my eyes at him, trying to convey my exasperation.

I try to protest as innocently as possible. "What about Soph? She drove you here."

I glance over to Sophia, hoping for some backup. But the knowing smile on her lips tells me she's not planning to do any such thing.

"I had one glass too many," she says, "Apparently I'm a lightweight, so I'm just going to crash here."

"Great," Huxley says as he stands up. "I'll grab our coats."

---

I WAIT until we're alone and Huxley has slammed the passenger door closed to snap.

"What the hell was that?"

I don't wait for him to answer to start driving, pulling out of the driveway, indignation bubbling through my veins. Even with my eyes on the road, I still catch his smirk as he fastens his seatbelt.

"What was what?" he asks slowly.

"That little stunt you just pulled," I hiss.

"Ah, that." His tone is flat as if I'm boring him. "Sorry, I thought you were someone else."

My reaction is instantaneous. I start to laugh. It's dry and cold, my knuckles turning white around the steering wheel.

"You know what?" I say, suddenly feeling a *lot* calmer than I've felt all night. "I'm too old for this shit."

I make a hard right and park on the side of the deserted street, ignoring Huxley's confused protest. I turn to face him, one arm over the steering wheel.

"Get out."

I don't know if I even mean it or if this is just a desperate attempt to take back control.

Huxley's face is impassive as if he doesn't believe the threat. His posture is relaxed, his head lolled to the side against the headrest while he watches me. His eyes rove over my face, seemingly busy thinking while staring at me. His gaze on my face feels like he's actually touching me, like a slow caress of his hand on my skin. I burn up right along with the sudden shift in the air between us.

His voice is low when he speaks. "You know what I did after you sent me that picture?"

It's dark, smooth, and delicious. I want to bathe in the sound. I swallow hard, my heart in my throat, as my lips part like they have a mind of their own.

I match his smoldering gaze, my expression just as serious as his. I shake my head only once, barely noticeable. But I know he sees it.

A smug grin sweeps over his face just as quickly as a deadly riptide, a small dimple appearing on his left cheek.

"Why don't you use your imagination?" His tone hints at his condescension as he squints. "And try to guess?" He tongues his cheek as if trying not to laugh and I feel his tease directly on my clit. I've lost my voice, too wrapped up in witnessing Huxley like this. "Maybe next time you show me more of yourself, I'll send you a thank you back."

*I pull his sweater over his head, and our lips crash together as I feverishly unbutton his jeans. I take my shirt off, and he pushes me against the bathroom door. His fingers dig into my heated skin. A desperate palm wraps firmly around my breast.*

"Are you thinking about it?"

I snap back to reality.

"About what?" I croak.

His eyes are the darkest of greens. Neither of us has moved an inch since I parked the car; the only sound between us is the idling rumble of the engine.

Huxley stays silent for a long, tense beat.

When he speaks next, his tone has changed into something a little more desperate. "Why are you resisting this?"

There's just enough angst hanging off his words to make me close my eyes and inhale deeply, the notes of vanilla and black pepper of his cologne making my head swim before my gaze lands back on Huxley.

"You shouldn't want this," I whisper, my voice cracking on the mouthful of desire I'm choking on.

"I've already *had* it," he growls between his teeth.

Silence crackles between us as we stare at one another.

Finally, I sigh and settle back into my seat.

"We can't."

I pull back onto the street.

## 25

# HUXLEY

**I** don't know how much more of this I can take.

Connie is a walking contradiction. Every time I think I have her figured out, she goes and does something that has me questioning her intentions *and* mine.

She's so fucking frustrating.

Sometimes, I just can't stand the sight of her. But I can't stay away for long either. She's catnip, and I'm a feral cat. For once in my life, I feel alive. And maybe this tug-of-war between us is actually leading me toward something good. As frustrating as she is, I haven't lost my patience *yet*.

"Shit," Connie says under her breath.

It's Monday morning and, as usual, Connie is driving us to work. The car still reeks from our tense conversation last night, like a sentient perfume digging its claws directly into my brain. I ignore it as best I can.

Letting my head fall to the side, I look at Connie driving.

"What is it?"

"Nothing," she says. Her eyes are on the road, but she's clearly distracted. "It's just that I realized I left my laptop back in my hotel room."

"So, let's go get it."

She glances over. "You sure? I don't want to make you late."

I shrug. "Whit won't mind." I pull my phone out. "I'll just text him."

"Okay, great," she says, sounding relieved. "It won't be a big detour." She bangs a uey. "We're not far from my hotel."

A few minutes later, she parks in front of the hotel entrance, and I let out a long whistle.

"So you're rich, rich."

She laughs as she takes her seatbelt off. "The suites are pretty affordable, actually."

When she hears my seatbelt click open, she looks up.

"What are you doing?"

Her question sounds more like a warning, but I ignore her tone.

"Coming up with you."

"No, you're not."

I shoot her a searing look and hope my intimidation will work on her this time. It's always a hit or miss with her.

"I'm not waiting in the car like your lap dog. Plus, I want to see how the other half lives."

She scoffs, then shoots me a quick smirk. "If you stay in the car, I'll call you a good boy afterward."

Rationally, I know that her comment was meant as a joke, but my body immediately tingles all over, the words *good boy* ringing in my ears. Suddenly, there's a lot more I want to hear coming out of Connie's mouth. I try to hide my reaction, but by how her smile slowly fades, I'm not doing a very good job of it.

The familiar electric charge between us returns full force, but Connie is quick to move on.

"Fine, you can come up. Just don't touch any of my shit."

I conceal my grin by turning to open the door, my expression back to casual disinterest by the time I round the car and meet up with her. Connie tells the valet she'll be right back, but gives them her keys just in case before we walk in.

The interior of the hotel is even fancier than the outside. I lack the words to describe the decor; all I know is that everything is imposing and shiny. It's also impossibly quiet as we head for the elevators, as if rich people live on a different sound frequency than the rest of us.

I feel the divide between my world and Connie's widen as the elevator doors slide closed. She swipes her card before pressing the PH button. My skin starts to itch. We don't speak, our eyes glued to the flashing floor numbers rising.

Our tense silence is at an all-time high by the time she opens her hotel room door. I had no intention to come on to Connie when I invited myself up. I just wanted to press a few of her buttons and ruffle some feathers. But now, watching her step into her suite, glancing back at me as I follow her in, it's unclear where either of our intentions lie.

"This is it," she mutters. Bending down, she unzips her boots. "Take those off if you plan to sniff around. I don't want that winter muck on the carpets."

I snort under my breath but do as she says, unlacing my boots as she steps further into the living room area.

"I think it's in the bedroom," she says, obviously talking about her laptop.

She disappears through a doorway, leaving me standing in my socks near the door.

My eyes sweep around the room.

Connie's personal belongings are everywhere I look. A pair of jeans over the back of the couch. A hairbrush on the coffee table. A phone charger hanging from the wall. Something about seeing her life out in the open like this feels too intimate. I look away and turn around, spotting the door leading to the bathroom.

*It probably looks like a fucking spaceship in there.*

Curious, I stroll in, hands in my pockets. The bathroom is huge for a hotel room. Then again, how the hell would I know? I've never seen anything but the interiors of rundown motel rooms in Pecket. I'm almost done with my quick perusal when something in the shower catches my eye.

"What is *that*?"

My voice is loud enough to drift out into the living room, and I hear Connie screech.

"Oh my god!" she says, her footsteps fast approaching until she runs into the bathroom with wild eyes. "Close your eyes! Get out of there!"

She dives in front of the shower glass, trying to block my view, but it's too late; I'll never unsee the dildo suctioned onto the shower wall.

I bark out a laugh while Connie blushes profusely.

"Kinky," I casually tease as I lean on the side of the sink.

She huffs and rolls her eyes. Her body language shifts as if trying to save face, and she straightens her shoulders, crossing her arms.

"It's really not," she says with an annoyed tone.

"Oh? So every girl you know has a dildo in their shower?"

She shoots daggers at me with her eyes, and my grin widens. Before she has time to come up with a smart-ass response, I step closer to her.

"Is that where you do all your thinking?" Connie doesn't move. Doesn't react. I take another step forward. "What do you think about, huh?" I grab one of her belt loops and drag her closer. Her eyes grow wide, but she stays silent. My voice is lower when I speak next, my head cocked to the side, inches from her face. "You think about me, don't you, baby?"

Her shocked reaction has me wishing my finger was on her pulse just to feel the effect those words had on her.

This time, when she speaks, her tone is not as self-assured.

Her voice is a lot quieter and hesitant, almost a mumble. "You wish."

I rarely feel like I have control over Connie, but right now, I do. It's going to my head *fast*. I slowly drag my gaze down her body and then back up, my finger still hooked on her jeans.

"I wish for a lot of things." I smile tauntingly. "More money. A luckier life. But right now, the only thing I'm wishing for is for you to show me how you use that thing."

I'm eighty percent sure she'll tell me to fuck off, but there's still a twenty percent chance I witness a miracle today. She stares at me as if *actually* considering this, and my heart rate quickens while she fidgets with the gold ring on her finger.

"We'll be late for work."

Her voice is so low, I barely hear her even though I'm standing right next to her. I don't miss a beat, refusing for this moment to pass like all the ones that came before it.

"We're already late."

The silence returns, coiling around our limbs, threatening to snap a bone.

I can tell the very second Connie changes from apprehensive to determined. She cocks a brow, her face deadly serious when she finally speaks. "Put some music on."

*Holy.*

*Shit.*

I swallow hard and lick my lips, trying to sound as casual as possible. "Sure."

Walking backwards until I hit the counter behind me, I fish my phone out of my jeans pocket. I pick the playlist I made for our car rides together and slam my phone down, in a hurry to see what Connie does next. We lock eyes, and a faint grin appears on her face.

I'm already forgetting how to breathe.

She lets the first song play for a few seconds before beginning to take her long winter coat off. It slips down her shoulders, then holds it away from her body with one arm. With a flick of her fingers, she drops it to the ground, her eyes fixed on me.

I'm not sure how I'll survive her undressing in front of me like this.

Next, she turns and leans into the shower, turning on the water before stepping back out. Facing me again, she pulls her knit sweater over her head, her red hair tumbling down over her shoulder when it's all the way off.

The song's tempo picks up, it's now just as fast as my beating heart.

This isn't a slow, sultry striptease. It's a declaration of war.

I forget what to do with my hands.

I cross my arms, uncross them, and then lean back on the counter.

Her t-shirt comes off next. The effect is as violent as a punch to the gut. Freckles pepper her shoulders and arms, and her black bra is see-through, the shadow of her hard nipples peeking through the fabric.

This is fucking torture.

But I don't move from my spot as I watch her unbutton her jeans and slowly push them down her legs, revealing striped blue panties underneath.

I grow harder by the second, my cock pressing against my jeans. She's so fucking beautiful, it's almost painful to look at her. But I'd rather die a painful death than look away.

Memories of our one-night stand flash in my mind as she reaches for the back of her bra and unhooks it. Her hungry gaze studies me when she drops it next to her feet.

I realize this is the first time I'll see her fully naked.

And I'm having a hard time keeping calm.

She doesn't waste any more time after that. Hooking her thumbs under the sides of her panties, she pulls them down so they fall to her feet. The steam of the hot water rises behind her as she steps out of them.

Connie is now naked, standing in front of me.

She's naked because of me.

I *am* witnessing a miracle today.

There's a blush crawling up her chest and neck, and I wish I could press my palm against her skin so I can feel the heat seep into my veins. It'd keep me warm for lifetimes.

Breaking eye contact, she turns and steps into the shower. It's open-concept, with tiles on the floor and walls with a glass panel dividing us.

I shift a few steps to the right to get a better view.

The music changes to something a little angstier. I consider skipping the song, but the ache it conjures up inside of me is just as addictive as the sight of her right now.

Facing away from the shower head, she closes her eyes and tilts her head. The water sluices down her hair and body as she drags both hands over her hair and down the back of her head.

She then lets one hand drift down her stomach, her eyes still closed. When her hand reaches the center of her legs, her mouth falls open, and I think I might lose my mind. My balls squeeze painfully, and my fingers grip the counter as I try to choke in an inhale.

Her lids flutter, finding my gaze through the glass.

I'm a fucking deer in headlights.

She steps toward the toy, her body now just a few breaths away from the jet of water. Her expression is serious but wanton when she faces me. Reaching around, her hand wraps around the silicone dildo. Although I don't technically see her do it, I can picture it vividly. She bends over, and her gaze stays fixed, watching me through her eyelashes. Her breasts pull taut with the weight of gravity, water dripping down from her nipples.

Not being able to watch her from behind is a special kind of torture. I can only imagine her pussy stretching around the thick head of the toy. I do just that when I watch her lips part, the moan lost somewhere between the sound of the shower and music.

The edge I'm teetering over is excruciating, and I might be a masochist because the pleasure it gives me is just as intense.

She starts rocking back and forth, fucking herself on the dildo, and I consider crawling on my knees to have a better look. Her gaze is pure fire. Visual adrenaline, the flames burning me raw.

While one of her hands claws at the wall beside her, the other finds its way back to her clit.

"*Fuck,*" she moans just loud enough for me to hear, closing her eyes with the pleasure she's giving herself.

With the sound of her voice, I can't bear being this far away any longer. Not when her eyes fly back open and something in her devouring gaze tells me she's close to coming. I push off the counter and stalk toward the shower just as her rhythm picks up. Her moans rise higher and higher in volume as her tits bounce with the fast-paced movement. An unexpected wave of pleasure barrels through my body, and I shakily exhale before my hand wraps around the edge of the glass pane, my eyes locked on hers.

I watch the orgasm possess her, her eyes squeeze shut in ecstasy, and I wonder if I'm about to come too just by watching her.

Her eyes snap back open. She surprises me by quickly straightening up and gripping my coat, pulling me into the shower.

Her lips are warm when they find mine.

She craves me.

*Me.*

My mind empties, and I become this giant mass of *need.* I wrap my arms around her, my hands smoothing up and down her wet back, then down to her ass, squeezing it with hungry palms. We stumble into the jet of water, my clothes quickly getting soaked, but I don't care. Not when my dream girl is finally kissing me. Not when I just watched her fall apart for me.

Turning us around, I push her into the glass pane, my hands now holding the sides of her face, deepening our kiss. Connie's giggle bubbles out of her lips as she grips the back of my wet shirt with her hand.

"You're soaked," she says against my lips, giggling again.

I smile, kissing her again and again, feeling weightless and free.

"Like I give a shit."

## 26

# HUXLEY

The elevator doors ding open, and a blonde middle-aged woman with a chihuahua tucked into her large purse walks in. She gives me a double take but says nothing, slowly turning to face the doors while Connie is barely keeping it together beside me. She's holding in her laugh, a small snort coming out from her nose. I can barely manage to save face, either.

I'm soaking wet.

My jeans are now dark blue and sticking to my legs, seeping water into my boots drop by drop. Given my current predicament, we agreed to stop at my place before the Remington so I don't freeze to death.

I didn't stay in the shower for long, but I wish I could have stayed in forever, if only to exist in that happy feeling until I died. But I couldn't excuse my absence from Whit for much longer, although the thought of playing hooky sounded much better than working.

Connie continues to snicker beside me, trying to keep silent, and my smile is so wide it's hurting my cheeks. I'm vibrating with a feeling I can't quite place; all I know is that it's making me feel good, like *really* good.

I might not know what this all means for Connie, but right now, I don't care. Sharing a private laugh with her in the elevator of a fancy hotel is good enough for me.

Following her through the lobby, I stop us before we reach the exit. I grab her hand and pull her into my arms. Something tells me that as soon as we walk through those doors, the spell will be broken. Whatever happened between us in her hotel room was a fluke, a bizarre shift into an alternative universe, and as soon as the icy cold air hits our skin, we'll revert back to our old timeline. I just know it.

Her lashes flutter as she looks up at me, a smirk still on her flushed lips. I kiss her effortlessly and with no resistance. To the strangers passing us in the lobby, we're a couple in love sharing a tender kiss.

I like the idea.

I like that idea *very* much.

---

THE BELL above the door clangs as I walk into my brother's restaurant, Enter Sandwich. It's a quarter to six, and the place is full of young professionals grabbing a bite to eat on their way home from work. I scan behind the counter for Ozzy but don't see him yet, so I sit at a free table and text him that I'm here.

I'm not in the habit of visiting his restaurant out of the blue. But he called when I was still at the Remington today. Told me I hadn't come by since they had changed the menu and that I should come try it out.

Ozzy's always so eager for us to hang out. Might as well get some free food out of it. It might also have to do with the need to keep my mind occupied after the morning I had with Connie. As predicted, things reverted back to casual friendliness almost instantly, and I'm trying not to let it sour the memory.

After a few minutes of waiting, Ozzy appears from the back, his usual smirk at the corner of his lip. He might get on my nerves most of the time, but I can't deny the brotherly resemblance. Even down to the clothes we wear. Dickies and band tees. Shitty stick and poke tattoos that make it look like we've never seen the inside of a professional tattoo shop before. His keys jangle from his carabiner on his hip, and I unconsciously toy with mine.

"You made it," he says, his smile widening. "Sorry, it took me a second. I was making you a sandwich."

He slides a plate in front of me and the smell makes my mouth instantly water.

"What is it?" I ask as I force a disinterested look on my face.

Rotating the plate a full three-sixty, I pretend to inspect the sandwich, but it's all a facade. I know exactly what this is: Sourdough bun, mortadella, melted provolone, Dijon, and mayonnaise.

"It's your favorite," Ozzy says casually, his elbow resting on the table as he sips a small cup of espresso. "Remember? From that small Italian deli near our old place."

My heart unwillingly squeezes painfully at the childhood memory. It's an ache that feels too vaporous to locate and soothe. It just haunts and haunts until it eventually dissipates if I ignore it for long enough. I'm not sure I would have remembered that Italian deli myself if Ozzy hadn't mentioned it. Or placed the sandwich directly under my nose.

I don't remember much from our childhood. It's like a black void, consuming anything that comes close to its orbit. Good or bad, it doesn't discriminate. But if I strain and concentrate hard enough, I can conjure up the memory. It's frustratingly vague but somehow also *feels* extra bright. Like a single ray of light poking through a cloudy day. Like one impossibly small positive amongst the total mess we had to live through.

I toy with my tongue ring absently, staring at the sandwich. He even served it with a side of plain potato chips, just how I like it.

"Is this off-menu?" I ask, not knowing how to show my gratitude.

The feeling is uncomfortable, like a pair of boots two sizes too small. I distract myself by lifting the bun and shoving a few chips into the sandwich.

He shakes his head and grins. "It's from the new menu. I called it the Huxley."

I'm hit with another disarming emotion. Love dipped in glass shards. It hurts. But I also desperately crave it.

I snort, grinning from the corner of my lip, trying to cover my actual reaction. "You're so fucking cheesy."

I take a bite of the sandwich, and I'm suddenly transported back to the Italian deli.

Barely seven years old. Back when one single afternoon felt like a lifetime. Ozzy felt so old to me back then. Like an adult, when he was just a teenager.

Ozzy's eyes shimmer as he takes another sip of espresso. And maybe it's the happiness that I constantly see in his gaze that makes me hate him. Jealousy so profound for how his life turned out that I can hardly put it into words.

"You like it?"

I take another bite and nod. *Fuck, it's good.*

"You know," I muse after swallowing my bite and placing the sandwich back on the plate. "That Italian deli is pretty hazy, but I *do* remember you never getting anything anytime we went. You'd always just take a few bites of my sandwich."

Ozzy laughs, but it's a sardonic kind of sound. He slowly smoothes his hand over the bottom half of his face, his gaze distant as if recalling something. His eyes then flick to mine. His expression is friendly but I can see behind the bullshit.

I don't think I'll like what he's about to say.

"I never had enough for two sandwiches. That was your treat, not mine."

The jagged, broken feeling returns. This time, it slices straight through my heart, and vague anger wafts in like a hot breeze on an equally hot day. This time, the anger isn't directed at my brother like it usually is, just at … life.

At the injustice of it all.

My voice cracks when I speak. "You never told me that."

Ozzy studies me for a few seconds, then presses his lips together and shrugs.

"I didn't tell you a lot of things. You were just a kid, Hux." His gaze turns mournful while his index finger taps idly on the linoleum table. "I was trying my best to keep it that way."

I stare at my older brother. Nine years separating us. I stare at him long enough for all of our miserable childhood to pass us by. Somehow, I feel like a failure, and I don't even know *why*.

I want to run out the door. I want to spit on Ozzy's stupid fucking sandwich and flip the table over. Instead, I sigh and take another bite of the sandwich, our silence speaking volumes.

Then I surprise us both. It's as if our exchange stirred something deep in me, and the words pour out of my mouth before I can convince myself how stupid the question is.

"Do you still have the contact for that therapist?"

Ozzy jolts as if I just confessed to murder, but he recovers quickly. He smooths his shocked expression into one of nonchalance and smiles.

"Yeah, of course I do."

I can tell he wants to press the issue. Probably ask me why now? But I'm relieved he's still treating me like an easily spooked dog because I wouldn't have an answer.

Only maybe ...

This constant suffocating anger is getting old.

Maybe aiming for a better version of myself isn't a bad idea after all.

"Send it to me?"

Ozzy smiles warmly and nods.

I return to my sandwich.

**27**

# CONNIE

From the corner of my eye, I see Huxley stroll into my office, but I keep my head down, busy finishing up an email to my publicist. He doesn't say a word, just plops himself onto the couch facing my desk. He must be done with his workday.

It's been a couple of days since I took our game a little further than I wanted. I still don't know what came over me. Oh, who am I kidding? I know exactly what came over me. The reason is sitting right in front of me casually scrolling on his phone like he didn't watch me fuck a dildo in my shower two days ago.

The thought should embarrass me.

But looking at him now. The subtle landscape of muscles down his forearms, honed by hours of working with his body. The casual wear and tear of his clothes, with paint smeared here and there. I linger on some rogue droplets of paint on his neck, imagining trailing my finger down his skin and finding his quickening pulse.

*God.*

There's no embarrassment in sight.

Somehow, whatever transpired between us that day has alleviated the tension between us. Just like that, our little game of chicken is no more. It's now replaced by a confounding sense of ease and casualness. And I can't help but wonder if it's because we're both far too adept at navigating meaningless flings.

Because that's what this is, isn't it?

Deep down, I'm running out of excuses for why he and I are a bad idea. I list them in my head like a hymn, protecting me from my impure thoughts.

He's younger than me.

He's Ozzy's brother.

I just had my heart broken.

He's ...

I don't know—

An ex-con?

Please. Like I give a shit. As if I'd ever want to hold that mistake against him. Plus, his bad boy aura, hard exterior, and permanent scowl are probably what led me to sleep with him in the first place. Come to think of it, I don't think he'd be all too pleased to know that.

I give my head a small shake when I realize where my thoughts have gone. Sighing, I rub my eyes with my index finger and thumb. I hear the tell-tale sound of an incoming email ding, and I glance back at my computer screen.

My heart skips a beat.

"Oh my god," I giddily say out loud, as I hurriedly open the email.

Huxley stops what he's doing and looks up, but I'm too busy skimming through the email to give him any attention.

"Oh. My. God," I repeat, my smile widening.

"What is it?" Huxley asks as he sits up straighter on the couch.

Meeting his gaze, I let out a small chuckle.

"I think I finally found a place!" I look back down, finishing the last few lines of the email.

"An apartment?" Huxley asks, and I nod enthusiastically, my gaze back on my computer.

"Oh shit," I add. "She wants me to come visit it now." I glance back up, hesitating for half a second. "Do you mind coming with me before I drop you off? It's kind of time-sensitive."

Some cryptic emotion passes across Huxley's face, but he quickly erases it and smiles. It's one of his genuine smiles. The one that makes his green eyes sparkle and shows off his dimple.

His effortless charm has me feeling like I'm slipping under his spell just by staring at him.

I can't imagine the effect he'd have on me if he actually *tried*.

"I don't mind." He claps his hands once while he stands up as if geared up to go.

"Great!" I grin and close my laptop. "Then we should leave right now."

---

THE POTENTIAL CONDO is a twenty-minute drive from the Remington in one of those skyrises lining the Marsford Bay boardwalk. I considered buying a house instead of another luxury condo, but even though I'm twenty-nine and just *bought* a theatre, something about owning a house felt too permanent. Too grown-up.

I settled for a penthouse with amazing amenities instead.

It took driving all the way here and meeting with Dusia, my real estate agent, to realize that maybe bringing Huxley along was a mistake.

This is a *couple's* activity.

Dusia certainly thought so.

Huxley turned bright red at the assumption, and I would have laughed at his spluttering reaction if I wasn't so busy trying to hide my own flaming cheeks.

But Dusia is a professional and navigated through the blunder with charismatic ease. She jumped right into the showing and slowly led us through the penthouse, pointing out feature after feature.

"I'll leave you to it," Dusia says with an assured smile.

Dressed head to toe in Prada, she's the picture of class with her minimal makeup and straight black hair tucked behind her ears.

"Look around. Take all the time you need." She points to the door while clutching her phone. "I have a few calls to make, so I'll be right outside when you're ready."

I nod and thank her, waiting for her to step out before looking over to Huxley, standing near the kitchen island. I watch him idly drag a finger over the countertop, his gaze upward as he looks around the spacious living area.

It's late afternoon, but the sun is already setting, the rays glowing orange against his face, the shadows slowly extending over the hardwood floor.

I have an inexplicable urge to capture this moment.

Without much thought, I pull out my phone and take a few pictures of Huxley in the afternoon light.

"Did you just take my picture?"

I take another while he's looking straight at me just for kicks.

"Maybe." I pocket my phone. "So? What do you think?"

He appears to be considering what to say.

"I can't imagine being this rich," he finally mutters, his gaze back on the professionally staged decor.

A strange guilt flutters across my conscience, and I suddenly feel gauche to be flaunting my generational wealth to

Huxley like this. Then again, I shouldn't be made to feel guilty for a reality I was simply born into.

Not wanting to dwell on the feeling, I let out a small puff as I strut closer to him.

"Not the question, do you *like* it? Could you imagine yourself living here?" Realizing I misspoke, I stumble to fix it. "I mean me — *me* living here."

Huxley watches me with what I *think* is curiosity. His expression has softened since Dusia stepped out, and I've never wanted to know what another person was thinking more than I do now.

Huxley is a mystery. Especially right now, while he's studying me with an intense gaze. My heartbeat quickens under his attention. Finally breaking eye contact, he heads toward the large sectional facing the living room windows.

"You'd be a fool to pass this place up," he says over his shoulder before sitting on the couch. He gives the cushion an experimental bounce as if testing out the furniture. "Did you see the *size* of the bedroom?"

I laugh under my breath, but the sound dies halfway out of my mouth when his eyes slowly slide up to meet mine. The sight of his cocky grin has my mind cycling through all the other things we could be doing in that bedroom.

I pretend not to notice his loaded gaze as I sit close to him ... but far enough that we're not touching. I turn my body so I can face him, an elbow resting on the back of the couch as I rest my head on my closed fist.

From the side, I gaze out the windows and let out a pleased sigh. "Can you imagine those sunsets?"

A crooked smile pulls at the corner of Huxley's lip, but he says nothing as he watches me with a casual ease I rarely see on him.

"What?" I can't help but ask, craving to know what's happening behind those broody eyes.

He smiles. "Nothing." His voice is soft, almost a whisper, and a pleasurable shiver skitters down my spine at the unassuming sound.

We fall into a comfortable silence as we look out over the harbor.

"I've never seen Marsford Bay from this high up before," he mutters. "Almost feels like I'm in another city."

"Yeah ..." I say pensively. "I guess I take these things for granted."

We share another beat of silence before Huxley speaks.

"What *don't* you take for granted?"

I furrow my brows and look straight at him, feeling slightly insulted by his question, but his innocent expression stops me in my tracks.

He appears curious, as if waiting for me to answer; his body language is open. He's leaning back into the couch with his fingers loosely laced over his stomach while his head is turned slightly to the side, watching me.

"That's a genuine question?"

He nods, his expectant gaze roving over my face.

I suddenly feel vulnerable. As if he's asking for more of me. As if he's asking me to strip naked, but this time he wants to see the inside of me.

I chew on my lip and look away.

What don't I take for granted?

Love, friendship ... *life.*

But all those answers sound so flat when I rehearse them in my head.

Generic. With no real meaning.

After a few seconds, I glance back at him.

"The moon."

Huxley bursts out laughing, the corners of his eyes crinkling. He shoots me a look full of amused shock, clearly not expecting my answer. In all honesty, I wasn't expecting to land on *the moon* as my answer either.

"The *moon*," he repeats, his whole body shaking with laughter.

I realize then how nice it feels to make Huxley laugh. The feeling blooms behind my chest.

I could get used to this.

"Okay, hear me out." I straighten on the couch, now ready to defend my answer at all costs. "I know it's cliché, but you know how they say, no matter where you are in the world, if you look up, we're all gazing up at the same moon?"

Huxley chuckles while shaking his head. "You've watched one too many romcoms."

"*Listen*," I say. Leaning over, I grab his forearm with both hands as I scooch closer. I notice his eyes dip down to where I'm touching his sleeve, but I'm too busy needing to prove my point to really care. "Don't you agree that's a beautiful senti-ment? That,"—I look up to the ceiling for half a second while thinking, then back down—"that something so much *bigger* than any of us can make us feel a little less alone? That the moon, in a weird mystical way, can connect us to the people we love?"

"*You're* weird and mystical."

I playfully slap his arm. "I'm being *serious*."

Huxley's laugh rumbles in his chest, and he smooths his tongue over his teeth, flashing his black barbell, as if getting ready to mock me again. But then his expression softens for the second time today, and I'm suddenly acutely aware of how close my body is to his.

He slowly falls serious, his eyes roving over my face just like they did earlier. As if seeking something I'm not privy to. I wait for him to speak, my cheeks growing warm under his pointed attention.

"I guess I've never craved that kind of connection with someone before."

One by one, his words slowly drift down between us like delicate petals falling from a cherry tree. His penetrating gaze is locked on mine.

Our chests rise in unison.

One deep breath until finally—

The kiss is burning hot the second his lips touch mine, and I scramble up to my knees. Huxley catches me as if he was expecting me all along, his hand holding on to my waist as I quickly straddle him. Pressing my hands against the sides of his face, I deepen our kiss, relishing the unexpected feel of his tongue piercing, mindlessly grinding my hips against his. He groans into my mouth, pulling me harder onto him.

My lust spikes to a feverish degree, and I stop thinking clearly.

My mind narrows into one singular thought.

Never breaking the kiss, I slip my hands between us and fumble with Huxley's studded belt, but his hands quickly find mine. Wrapping his fingers around mine, he stops me.

"You're not getting me that easily," he says in between kisses.

His tone is playful, but his hands tighten, holding me captive.

I straighten on his lap so I can look at him.

I smile coyly. "I thought you wanted this?"

Teasing him, I grind my hips against what I'm *pretty* convinced is his hardened cock.

His smile is dark and steamy, but he doesn't let go of my hands.

"Not like this," he says, his voice nonetheless dripping with want.

"Why?" The word is close to a whine. I nibble at his bottom lip. "Because Dusia is right outside?" I lean down and pepper his jawline with kisses. "We can sneak quickly into the bathroom, for old times' sake?"

Huxley's body stiffens under me, and I realize too late that I've said the wrong thing. My head pops up, and I study his facial expression.

But Huxley has retreated, and his expression is giving me nothing.

"I'm not something you can use and throw away whenever you feel like it." His voice is soft like a whisper, a small thread of pining woven throughout his sentence.

"Who said anything about —"

He gently pushes me off him, and I don't resist, too stunned by the shift in mood to protest.

"I thought I could do this with you, but I can't," he says as he stands up. He paces up to the windows, swiping his hand over his buzzed head, the other against his hip.

"Do *what* exactly? What just happened?" I'm annoyed, but try to keep my voice calm.

He lets his hands fall to his sides; he's still facing away from me, but I catch his defeated shrug before he turns around. I'm not ready for the vulnerability I find in his gaze when he faces me. The pain that he's trying to hide under such nonchalance.

It makes me hate myself.

And the way we've both been toying with one another.

"I can't do meaningless with you, Connie. You — you're —"

The door opens behind me, and reality snaps back in place like a well-tuned string.

I jump up from the couch and swivel to face Dusia as she walks back into the penthouse. Her eyes survey us both, quickly picking up on *something,* but she simply shuts the door behind her and smiles.

"So what do we think?"

# 28

# CONNIE

"Your brother is ignoring me."

It's late Saturday morning, and I'm having brunch with Sophia at a trendy restaurant in the Central Business District. I've been trying to find an opening for the past half hour, but I lost patience and blurted it out.

Sophia's eyes dart up while taking a bite of her chicken and waffles. She slowly straightens in her seat and grins. A large part of me didn't want to get her involved in the shitshow that is Huxley and me, but ever since whatever that was last week, it's the only thing I can focus on.

Dusia wanted me to go over some contracts, so Huxley left without me, and he's been avoiding me since. The only communication we've had is him texting me, saying he didn't want me to pick him up anymore. When I asked why, I was met with no response. His behavior pissed me off, but I didn't press the subject. We haven't talked in over a week, and it pains me to admit it, but I now need some backup in understanding what's actually going on with him.

"Who? Ozzy?" Sophia's grin is far too mischievous to pass as innocent.

"Ha. Ha," I deadpan as I pick up my mimosa and take a sip. Then, because I'm already desperate, I add, "Has he mentioned anything to you?"

Sophia drops her fork and rests her elbow on the table. Sighing, she lifts her eyes to the ceiling and rubs her forehead in an amplified show of exasperation.

I don't know if it's because she basically had to fend for herself most of her life, but I often forget how young Sophia is. She's always acted far older than her actual age.

"I'm not answering that until you finally tell me what the hell has been going on between you two."

I feel like I'm about to burst into flames. Or suddenly develop a life-threatening rash. I pick at my fruit cup with my fork and avoid eye contact.

Eventually, I begrudgingly match her gaze and say, "It's complicated?"

"Great." She lifts her hands and widens her arms as if challenging me. "Because I have all day." She drops her arms and checks her phone. "Actually, that's not true, I work at three, so you'll need to hurry this up."

I roll my eyes, and she snickers, digging into her second waffle.

Chewing on my inner lip, I wonder how much I should tell her.

"I just don't want anybody to know about this ... for now — even Jamie."

Sophia pretends to zip up her lips and throw away the key. I stare at her for a few seconds, not knowing how to start. Finally, I let my shoulders drop and sigh with defeat.

"We hooked up at Jamie's engagement party."

By the sheer shock on Sophia's face and her gaping mouth, I know she didn't expect me to say that.

"You hooked up at ..." Her words trail off as if suddenly recalling something, then mumbles under her breath, "That's where he disappeared to." Her eyes dart back to me, eyebrows furrowing. "Weren't you dating Oliver back then?"

I wave her off and shake my head. "We were barely in the talking stage." I pause. "But to your point — after that night, I sort of just went back to my life in LA and pretended it never happened."

"This explains why he's been stalking you for so long," she puffs out then shakes her head, laughing dryly. "Oh, Connie, he was barely out of prison, what the hell were you thinking?"

I lean forward, my wrists pressing against the edge of the table. "*I wasn't*," I hiss. "And well —" I lean back into the booth. "You can't deny your brother is hot, he just looked very appetizing that night."

"Gross," Sophia sniffs. She takes a large sip of her coffee, staring at me while she swallows, then asks, "So that's it?"

I slump my hands onto my lap, picking at my nails.

"Not exactly. That was just how it started." Sophia raises her eyebrows as if urging me to go on, and I exhale slowly. "When I came back for the holidays, I thought we could at least be civil, which was harder than expected." I mutter those last words under my breath, staring down at my plate. "Plus, I had just broken up with Oliver, Huxley was dating someone, and I was kind of seeing that DJ, but things still kind of ... happened."

Sophia chuckles, leaning back into her chair. "You guys are so messy."

"We haven't hooked up since I've been back," I say quickly, hoping that will help my cause. "*Anyway*, things were getting kind of hot and heavy last week —"

Sophia grimaces. "Spare me."

I sigh loudly. "Then out of nowhere, he said he couldn't do it anymore and then told me, 'I can't do meaningless with you'." I pause and watch Sophia's expression gradually fall somewhere close to concern. Her reaction has my heartbeat quickening, but I add one final thing before letting her speak, "He's been ignoring me ever since."

I break into a sweat under her careful appraisal.

"What do you mean by *it*?" she says slowly.

"It? Like what are we?" Sophia nods. "I don't know," I whine. "I thought we were just having fun — I literally *just* broke up with Oliver."

"Are you still hooking up with that DJ?"

I'm not sure where she's going with this but I answer nonetheless. "I ghosted him after he showed up with flowers on my first day at the Remi."

She smirks. "Classic." She pops a piece of fried chicken in her mouth and licks her lips while dusting off her fingers. "And was that the *only* reason you ghosted him?"

I blink.

*Oh.*

"No," I answer sheepishly. "I guess, Huxley was another reason. I didn't want to flaunt someone else in front of him."

"Because you ..." She elongates her last word as if waiting for me to finish her sentence, one eyebrow lifting expectantly.

Miffed, I reply, "Because I *what*?"

She crosses her arms. "Because you care about his feelings, dummy."

I squirm in my chair, feeling pretty toxic when thinking back on how I've acted with Huxley since returning to Marsford Bay. The guilt makes me want to act out and reply as brattily as possible.

"Why does this have to be so serious? Obviously, Huxley has had casual flings before. How is this any different — he was literally fucking another girl just a month ago for god's sake."

A little harsh. But not too bad.

Sophia stays silent for a beat. "Connie." The tone of her voice makes me look up, my heart dropping into my stomach. Her eyebrows furrow with worry. "Huxley went to prison when he was eighteen years old ... how many flings do you think he's had?"

I suddenly don't want to have this conversation anymore. The reminder that Huxley spent his early twenties in prison has my nose starting to tingle as if threatening a deluge of tears.

I swallow hard.

*God. I must be PMS'ing.*

Sophia notices my inner turmoil, and her expression softens. She pushes her plate toward the middle and folds her arms on the table, leaning forward.

"You know, Huxley has always been the most sensitive out of all of us. He hates it. He fights it constantly, but it doesn't change who he is deep down. And one thing we *do* have in common is that we avoid talking about our feelings. So if he's gone far enough to tell you that this isn't meaningless to him, I suggest you listen."

I don't know what to say, so I say nothing, mulling over what she just divulged.

Then Sophia blinks, and her face switches from serious to something a lot more unhinged.

"*Basically.*" She grins and tilts her head as she stares me down. "Don't fuck with my brother or I'll kill you." Then, as if she didn't just threaten my life, she swivels her head around to look behind her. "Where's our server? I need a refill."

# 29

# HUXLEY

D K is meowing at my feet as I boil water for my instant ramen. I made an effort tonight and boiled two eggs to go with it. DK lets out another long whine as if he's never been fed in his entire life before. He's gotten so much bigger in the past month.

"Dude, I *just* fed you," I tell him. "I can still see food in your bowl."

He looks up at me with big watery eyes and meows again, throwing himself on his back to show me his stomach. We stare each other down for a few seconds, but I finally crack. I slowly shake my head and open the pantry, pulling out his treats.

"You're so spoiled," I say as I drop a few kibbles on the floor.

DK lunges for them and barely chews before swallowing them whole.

Leaving him to it, I pad to the living room, carefully holding my steaming bowl of ramen with the tips of my fingers. DK follows me from the kitchen but beelines right in front of me, almost making me trip. I sidestep, the noodles dangerously sloshing around.

"Jesus fucking Christ, you're an absolute menace," I curse under my breath but make it to the couch all in one piece.

Unpausing the show I'm watching on TV, I absentmindedly check my phone for any notifications.

My stomach sinks.

**Missed call: Connie**

The timestamp says I just missed her phone call. The feeling of seeing her name flash on my screen is confusing; I'm not sure if it's aversion or excitement. Maybe both.

I don't have time to dwell more on how this makes me feel before my phone lights up with three back-to-back notifications.

It's Connie again—texting me this time.

Placing my bowl of ramen on the coffee table, my knee starts to bounce nervously as I bite at the skin on my thumb. What would she even have to say after almost two weeks of silence? To be fair, I'm the one who called it off, but she didn't even protest. It's as if my sudden absence in her daily life was a non-issue. I'm such a fucking loser to lose sleep over this girl when I'm obviously nothing to her.

Feeling myself get riled up all over again, I drag my hand over my face as I deliberate if I should even read her texts. The safest option is to ignore her. It's been working pretty well for me until now. I stare at my phone some more, my ramen getting cold as I continue to chew on my thumb, my knee bouncing, bouncing, and bouncing.

Finally, I sigh, pick up my phone and tap on her name.

Can we talk?

I hate that you're ignoring me.

Can you pick up please?

Her messages irk me; she's assuming I'm not busy, and I'm just sitting here screening her calls. She's not wrong but it pisses me off nonetheless. My phone vibrates with another incoming call.

It's her.

I groan out loud and hesitate. Finally, I cave.

"Yeah?"

"Hux, uh ... hi." She sounds surprised.

As if she didn't expect me to pick up.

"What is it?" My voice is curt, and she falls silent for a few seconds.

"Look, I — I'm sorry, okay?"

My heart unexpectedly squeezes at her rushed apology.

It pisses me off more than anything. It's as if she's just trying to get it over with.

"Sorry for what?" I say slowly, my jaw tight with withheld irritation.

"For ..." It takes a few seconds for her to continue. "For being a jerk, I guess."

"You guess," I repeat with a mocking laugh.

"You weren't necessarily a perfect little angel either," she volleys back with a hard bite to her words, and a grin inexplicably forms on my face.

I lean into the couch, my head falling backward against the edge.

"At least I know what I want."

I hear her sigh through the phone, clearly annoyed by my pushback.

But the thought of me irritating her only makes my grin widen.

*Spoiled brat.*

Probably so used to always getting her way.

"Can I make it up to you?" The nervous hope in her tone takes me aback, and my smile fades. But her next sentence surprises me even more. "Can you come over? Like, now? I want to show you something."

My throat bobs on a hard swallow, and I lick my lips before replying, "To your hotel?"

"No, uh, to the penthouse actually. I'm not moved in yet, but ... Can you just meet me there?"

What would she want to show me at the penthouse? Memories of the last time I was there dig their claws into my brain, robbing me of any rationality. I consider refusing her invite just to get back at her, but the ache to see her stirs alive inside of me.

Reckless curiosity wins.

"Okay."

When Connie opens the door to her new place, I'm racked with nerves. I've gone over multiple scenarios in my head, and I still have no idea what to expect.

"Hey," she says softly with a timid smile.

She's dressed casually in white jeans and a knit sweater. When she opens the door wider to let me in, I'm left even more perplexed about the visit.

"There's no furniture in here."

I take one step inside. Just enough for her to close the front door. She laughs nervously, tucking a lock of red hair behind her ear.

"Yeah, like I said, I'm not actually moved in yet."

She doesn't add more to her statement, as if it's perfectly normal to invite me to an empty condo. She leaves me to take off my boots, casually strolling into the kitchen.

"Are you going to tell me why I'm here?" I ask while I peel off my coat and sling it over the kitchen island.

She rounds the island and faces me. "In a minute."

Her smile is tentative, and I realize then that I might not be the only one handling their nerves badly. Picking up an open wine bottle from the counter, she pours us two glasses and slides one of them toward me.

"Here — I thought we could have a drink first." She holds onto her glass in front of her with two hands as if it's some kind of shield. She quirks another timid smile. "Talk a little."

I nod, feeling equally timid. "Sure."

The silence turns awkward as we both stand there not knowing how to start this goddamn conversation. I take a sip of the wine just for something to do, the dry bite of it hitting the back of my tongue.

Connie lets out a long exhale through her nose and leans onto the island, perching on her forearms in front of her. She's practically bent over, but I don't think she realizes how suggestive her position is, the curve of her ass on full display. I try to keep my mind out of the gutter, but I'm not doing such a great job at it.

Connie toys with her glass as she watches me and smiles. "So, how you been?"

"Good." I pause, looking down at my wine, then back up. "I started therapy last week."

I blink, suddenly mortified.

*What the fuck? Why would I say that?*

Connie pushes herself up, straightening a little.

"You did?" she asks, surprised.

"Never mind, I don't know why I said that."

Her eyebrows dip. "So you didn't?"

"No — I mean yes." I chuckle nervously. "I don't know why I brought it up."

She smiles warmly, and I feel it trickle through my ribcage.

"Well, that's great." She looks away, staring out at the twinkling lights of the city. "I think therapy should be mandatory." She says it almost like an afterthought.

"Do you, now?" I place my glass down, resting my hip against the side of the counter and cross my arms. "So you've been to therapy, then?"

Her gaze swivels back to mine, and I catch the guilty expression fluttering across her face before it's gone.

"No."

We both fall silent for a long beat until she snorts, and we both start laughing.

Our laughter slowly wanes as the seconds tick by, but thankfully, the awkward tension seems to have dissipated, and I suddenly feel a lot more comfortable in my own skin.

"So are you going to tell me why you invited me here, specifically?" I tap my index finger on the counter to punctuate the word *specifically*. "A little weird, don't you think?"

She smirks while pushing herself off the island.

"It's a surprise. Just something to show my ..." she trails off, fidgeting with her fingers, clearly getting nervous again. It's as if she doesn't know how to end her sentence. So she doesn't. "Anyway." She waves it off, the nerves back in her short laugh. "It's in the office."

Connie signals for me to follow by giving a quick jerk of her head. I scamper behind like a puppy that's just been promised a treat as she leads us through the hallway.

The first thing I notice when we walk into her office is an air mattress near one of the walls with a throw blanket covering most of it. If that wasn't odd enough, there's a table in the middle of the empty room with an open laptop and what looks like three projectors pointed at three different walls.

I shoot her a quizzical look. "What's going on?"

Connie simply grins and ushers me to the mattress.

"Sit," she says expectantly. "I just need to set up a few things."

Slowly, and with a lot of suspicion, I sink to the floor. I settle myself onto the very edge of the mattress, not knowing what the hell to expect. My heart rate picks up as I watch her fiddle with the equipment on the table. Deep in concentration, there's an adorable crease in between her eyebrows.

Turning on her heels, she walks to the light switch and flicks it off. The office falls into darkness save for the glow of the computer screen. Promptly, she returns to the table.

Then suddenly—

The white walls are no more. Transformed into a landscape of blue skies and miles and miles of white sand, the three walls projecting the same video image. The scenery is so beautiful and nothing like I've ever seen before that it catches me off guard. I'm overwhelmed with the beauty of it all. From my vantage point, I'm immersed. Transported.

My gaze flicks to Connie as she walks toward me, her eyes sparkling with anticipation. I lift my chin to keep eye contact as she approaches.

My question is unspoken, but she still reads it clearly through my inquiring gaze.

"That first day at the Remi," she says softly, "You told me you'd always wanted to visit Brazil. It's silly —" She shrugs her shoulders as if trying to dismiss the grandness of her gesture. "But I thought, the closest thing to *actually* visiting Brazil was to maybe ... bring Brazil to *you*."

My eyes are still fixed on hers, a thousand thoughts tumbling over one another in my head.

No one has ever done something like this for me.

No one has ever thought about me long enough to surprise me like this.

Or ... cared enough.

I lack the words to express how I feel.

It's too big—larger than life.

She shifts in place as if getting antsy, waiting for me to react.

"Here." She hands me a remote control. "The footage is from a drone live stream, you can control where it goes." Then, she starts to babble. "I wasn't sure what exactly you'd like to see, like are you a beach guy? Or more of an Amazon and waterfalls kind of guy? Then I remembered about these really cool sand dunes in the Maranhão state and —"

Slowly, I raise my hand and curl my fingers around her extended wrist. As soon as our skin touches, she stops talking, her eyes wide and penetrating.

"Thank you," I rasp.

She bites her bottom lip, never letting her gaze stray and swallows hard. Her mouth falls open as if wanting to say something, but it takes several seconds for her to speak. And when she does, my chest cracks wide open.

"You're not meaningless, Huxley."

# 30

# CONNIE

Huxley hasn't said a word since I last spoke, and my heart is beating so fast I think I might pass out. He hasn't broken contact, his gaze steady, and the tension builds between us with every silent breath we take.

I don't know why I'm this nervous—why Huxley's hand around my wrist is affecting me this much.

But it is.

Like a red hot brand, his fingers burn through my skin, forever leaving a mark on me.

Finally, he breaks the silence and speaks, slicing through every unspoken thought and desire lingering between us.

"Come here." His voice is low and needy, and my head starts to spin.

He pulls me down to him, my knees hitting the mattress first, but Huxley pushes my shoulder and flips us so that I fall on my back, Huxley's torso on top of me.

My hands slip around his neck as a feeling of giddiness envelops me. I giggle, and he chuckles too, smiling against my lips before kissing me softly. The kiss is tender and slow, his tongue exploratory as if we have all the time in the world.

His hand is just as patient, caressing up my thigh and hip, slipping under my sweater then dipping back out. There's something quite possessive about the casual slowness of his touch. It's as if he knows that I'm not going anywhere, that he has all the time to make me his.

He isn't wrong.

I'd seek eternal life if it meant staying in this moment with him forever. It's a pure feeling, untainted by any of the other bullshit trying to ruin it for us.

Huxley pulls away, his eyes now a shade darker. They're intense and focused. His gaze makes me feel like I'm the only thing that matters in the world right now.

He pushes himself up and sits, taking off his hoodie as he does so. Then he reaches for the back of his t-shirt but pauses, his arm still raised as if needing to see some kind of confirmation in my gaze before baring himself to me.

I answer his question by sitting up and helping him pull off his shirt. Still, we keep our same slow pace, our actions unrushed. It only makes everything more intense, more intentional.

Seeing Huxley's naked torso, peppered with prison tattoos just like his arms, makes me realize I've never seen him naked before. The thought has my mouth watering, and liquid heat coils low in my stomach.

I waste no time climbing onto his lap, my hands cradling his face as I kiss him with a little more urgency this time. He chuckles darkly in between kisses, the sound traveling directly to my clit as he palms my ass with both hands.

"Take this off," he says against my lips, tugging on my sweater.

I lean back on his lap, Huxley watching me intensely from underneath me.

"Take it off for me," I say playfully as I raise my arms over my head.

He cracks a smile. It's crooked and reveals just enough of his teeth to have my head spinning again. It's the most disarming thing I've ever seen. He could tell me to do anything right now, and I'd do it, no questions asked.

He doesn't waste any time, pulling my sweater off along with the shirt underneath. He flings it somewhere behind me, his arms curling around my back. While his hands slide up to unhook my bra, he presses a kiss to the middle of my chest, then trails his lips over the curve of my breast.

My bra loosens, the straps falling over my shoulders, but Huxley doesn't look up. His hands slowly caress down my arms, pulling off my bra at the same time while his mouth takes no time to find one of my peaked nipples.

I arch my back as a moan catches in my throat, my hand smoothing up his nape. His tongue flicks around my nipple, and the heat in my core turns into a blazing fire. Closing my eyes, I lose myself in the pleasure of his hot tongue against such a sensitive area.

I grind my hips into his lap trying to find some relief, but feeling the hard curve of his cock through his jeans is a tease I can't bear.

"Hux," I say breathlessly.

He groans at the sound of his name, his mouth still against my breast, his hands moving up my back, pushing me even closer to him.

Before pulling away, he softly bites the curve of my breast, and I gasp at the feeling, my skin tingling.

He leans back and looks up at me, a dark grin pulling at the corner of his mouth. Slipping a hand between us, he presses it against the seam of my jeans.

"You want me, baby?" he says slowly as his thumb slides up and down the seam.

My mouth falls open, my eyes fixed on him as my clit throbs with need, my fingers digging into his shoulders. My thoughts scatter, and I lose the ability to speak. I bite my lip and nod, rolling my hips against his hand, chasing the pleasure, wanting more—so much more.

He starts to toy with the button of my jeans, never quite loosening it through the hole.

"I want to hear you say it, Connie." He pauses, then adds, "*Please*." His voice is hard but drenched in so much desire that I feel myself grow wet at the authority in his tone.

"*Fuck*," I say with raptured defeat, catching his lips with mine for another passionate kiss before we do anything further.

He continues his slow tease, unzipping my jeans and caressing the soft skin just above my thong, never venturing further down.

"Say it," Huxley rasps, and this time, I abide by his hungry demand.

"I want you, Huxley — I *need* you."

His groan is somehow celebratory, his cocky smile devastatingly sexy as he pulls me up by the waist with strong hands and lays me on my back.

This time, he doesn't tease, pulling my thong and jeans down with a hard tug. But before taking them off, he grabs my foot and lifts my leg, taking my socks off one by one. The act shouldn't be sexy, just another one of those rushed awkward moments toward getting naked.

But the way Huxley is looking at me. His eyes devouring, his hands steady and confident, it makes me flush with heat. I'm practically vibrating with the anticipation of what he'll do next.

When my jeans are finally off, I'm left naked under Huxley's brazen appraisal, and I've never felt more wanted than right now.

His hand slowly pushes my legs open, and he crawls between them. His mouth is now inches away from my pussy, and my core squeezes greedily as I grow even wetter.

He hums hungrily as his eyes dip down.

"Pretty thing," he says under his breath as if talking to himself. "God, you're gorgeous."

He swipes a knuckle up my slit as if casually assessing my arousal, and I gasp at the feeling, immediately craving more. Taking two fingers he spreads me open and tongues my clit, and the drag of his tongue ring heightens the sensation deliciously. Quickly, he does it again, and my back arches off the mattress, pleasure exploding throughout my body as if I've been waiting for him to do this my whole life. Moving down, he dips his tongue into my entrance and fucks me with it while his thumb circles my swollen clit.

"Oh god," I mewl, my fingers trying to find purchase on his shoulders, nails digging into his heated skin.

He replaces his tongue with a thick finger, slowly pushing it into my throbbing core while his mouth latches onto my clit with mind-numbing skill.

After only a few torturous pumps, he adds a second finger, and I bite my bottom lip at the pleasurable stretch. He curls both fingers against the sensitive spot inside of me, and I feel myself drench his fingers. My orgasm tingles up my body, a powerful wave of need and desire.

"Kiss me," I beg Huxley urgently before the feeling crests and carries me over the edge. "*Kiss me.*"

Huxley must hear the ache in my voice because he's kissing me with devout passion mere seconds later, his fingers still pumping steadily inside of me.

I climax just as he slides a third finger alongside the other two, the fullness finally pushing me over. My mouth falls open on a long moan as he tugs my bottom lip with his teeth, his hips thrusting against my thigh.

His fingers turn, still deep inside of me, as I come and I'm blinded with pleasure until finally I slowly float back to reality just as Huxley slips them out of my pussy.

He flashes me another one of his dark grins, and I can't believe how beautiful he is like this, when he seems to have not a care in the world.

"You're so wet," he says with a sexy drawl, bringing his fingers up to my lips. "Taste."

He pushes his fingers against my tongue, and I fight to keep my eyes from rolling into the back of my head at his lewd action. My core throbs with need all over again.

He kisses my upper lip just over his fingers as if wanting another taste. As if wanting to taste me at the same time as I am.

I grow desperate and claw at his jeans, needing them off immediately. Needing to wrap my hand around his cock. Needing to know and *feel* how aroused I've made him.

He lets out another teasingly dark laugh, and I feel undone. Splintered open.

He doesn't break our kiss as he helps me with his jeans, pushing and tugging them down his legs. When they're finally off, he pulls away. His thumb digs into the meat of my thigh before he fully straightens up, kneeling in between my opened legs.

I push myself up onto my elbows, needing to see Huxley naked, and *god* ... it's better than I could have ever imagined.

The flex of his thighs as he leans onto his heels. The lean but carved muscles that can only be acquired by repetitive tasks of manual labor. The light trail of brown hair under his belly button leading down to his hard cock. Long and thick, and so *fucking* erotic.

I swallow hard, craving the slow stretch it promises. I try to invoke how he felt the first time we had sex, but I'm having trouble recalling it now that I have him in front of me again.

He leans over and grabs his wallet, the chain connected to

the loop of his jeans. I quirk a smile when he pulls out a condom, refraining from teasing him that he's come prepared because *thank fucking god* he did.

I watch with rapt attention as he rips the foil with his teeth and rolls the condom over his shaft. My heart kickstarts its drumming beat again, wishing I could speed up time and feel his cock inside me right this second.

My hand snaps forward, and I grab his arm, pulling him on top of me.

"Fuck me already," I moan impatiently.

Huxley gifts me with another one of his teasing chuckles. The sound invades me as he kisses me. It's a sloppy, hungry kiss as if we're both trying to devour the other.

"I'll fuck you anytime you want, baby. Just say the word, and I'm there."

I hum with pleasure, feeling Huxley notch himself against my entrance as I wrap a leg around his waist.

"Is that a promise?" I tease.

"It's a fucking vow," he answers, voice thick with lust.

He says the last word at the same time as he punches his hips forward. His cock sinks halfway into my pussy, and we moan in unison.

"*Fuck*," he hisses, his forehead falling against mine, then back up to look me in the eyes. He slides even deeper, my heel pushing into his ass, coaxing him on. "I thought I remembered how good you felt, but this is ..." He trails off and shakes his head as if lacking the words to continue.

Instead, he slides his cock out up to the head and punches his hips so that this time he sinks to the hilt. The sound that escapes my lips is closer to a keen than a moan, my pussy fluttering around his cock, still so sensitive from my first orgasm.

I won't last long. Not when Huxley's body cradles me so perfectly, his skin so warm I feel lit up from the inside out. His hand slides up to my chest and gropes my breast with hungry possession as he pistons in and out. His mouth is just as hungry, his lips trailing down my neck and then back up my jaw.

Tasting. Devouring. Consuming.

"I need to see all of you," he says into my ear before wrapping his arms around my back and flipping us over so I'm now on top.

I slip back onto his cock with a satisfied moan, Huxley's mouth falling open with pleasure, eyes steadfast as he drinks me in from underneath. He grips my hips with both hands as I start to rock back and forth. I love the way he's watching me. Like I've turned into the stars and moon right in front of him. It's pure and staggering.

Spurred on by his attention, I decide to give him a bit of a show just to tease him further. I lean backward, placing a hand on his thigh and arch my back as I play with my clit with the other hand, fucking him with slow but steady curls of my hips.

I know I have him right where I want him when he squeezes his eyes shut and groans, his head pushing into the mattress underneath him.

"You're being so good for me," I hum, and Huxley's eyes snap open in surprise. He curses under his breath, his hands tightening around my hips, his neck straining with the continuous exertion. I flash him a sexy pout. "Do you feel how soaked you're making me, baby?"

Huxley's eyes widen, and I smirk, knowing all too well that he wants me to talk to him like this some more.

"Here." I take one of his hands, my hips still rolling back and forth, and bring it to where his cock disappears into my pussy. "You feel that?" I taunt as I glide his fingers through my arousal. "You feel how wet your cock is making me?"

"*Fuck*, Connie," Huxley croaks.

I know he must be close by the hard dip of his eyebrows, as if he's trying to concentrate. I decide to tease him some more.

My moan sounds more like a low, satisfied hum as I close my eyes for a few seconds, relishing the sensation—*every* sensation his body is giving me.

My eyes lock back on his, and I tilt my head before saying, "Good boys let me come first."

With the sound of my voice, Huxley shoots forward and sits up, catching me in his arms as he cradles me with his body.

"I've been a *good* fucking boy," he says with gritted teeth, his face inches from mine. "Now give me my reward, Connie."

The way he slowly elongates the word *good* has an instant effect on me, my walls squeezing around his cock. That paired with the change in position, my clit rubbing against his pelvis, has me seeing stars. I fall victim to Huxley's intense gaze as his hands slip down my ass and grip my cheeks with such intoxicating force that I finally snap.

He bites my bottom lip as I climax, and he follows me over the edge seconds later. The tug of his teeth turns into an impassioned kiss as his cock throbs inside of me, buried so deep I know I'll feel him for days after.

Our kiss lasts much longer than both of our orgasms, as if neither of us is ready for it to be over. Huxley's arms are strong around me as I stay seated on his lap, his cock still sheathed inside of me as his hands rove all over my body, the passion potent between us.

It never wanes, only simmers under our skins, promising to ignite all over again the next time we touch.

## 31

# CONNIE

**H**uxley peeks his head in my office as if checking if I'm busy before strolling in and dropping a bag of takeout on my desk.

"Lunch?" he says casually before tipping my chin up and kissing me on the very corner of my lips. "I grabbed some Thai and thought you might be hungry."

Butterflies explode in my stomach as I look up and smile. Somatic memories of our time together last night resurface, and I suddenly feel warm all over.

After we had sex, we spent the next couple of hours finishing the bottle of wine and exploring the sand dunes of Brazil via the remote drone. His easy smile throughout the night left me so giddy that I could barely sleep after we left the condo, and I returned to my hotel alone.

We didn't necessarily talk about what this meant for us, but things definitely feel a lot more serious between us, even if nothing has been made official yet.

*God, I should really tell Jamie what's going on.*

"Is that for me?" I say giddily as I take an exploratory peek inside the brown paper bag.

Huxley takes his usual spot on the couch.

"Of course. I didn't know what you'd like," he says, opening his own takeout bag. "So I got you a Tom Yum soup and some Pad Thai."

"You're too much," I sing-song, taking the container of soup out of the bag, my mouth watering. "How much do I owe you?"

Huxley snorts. "Don't insult me."

I look at him from across my small office and grin. "Thank you, that's really sweet of you — I was starving."

He shrugs and looks down as if uncomfortable with receiving gratitude for any of his positive actions.

We fall into comfortable silence for a few minutes as we eat until Huxley speaks again. "So when can I see you next?"

The way he smirks and watches me from under his eyelashes with those deep green eyes tells me his question is loaded with shameless intentions.

A small thrill zips through my body, and I grin, poking at my Pad Thai distractedly.

"How about tomorrow night?" he presses.

I'm about to enthusiastically agree until I realize my dreaded influencer party is tomorrow, the day before Valentine's Day.

I drop my shoulders along with my smile. "Ugh, I can't. I have this stupid fucking event I need to go to for work and —" I stop in my tracks and lift an eyebrow as my grin returns. This time, far more conspiratorial. "You could always come with me."

Huxley sits up a little straighter, brows lifting in surprise.

"As your ... date?"

"Yeah, silly, as my date, what else?" I say, trying to sound as natural as possible while swallowing around a large lump in my throat.

Huxley's eye turns suspicious. "What *kind* of event?"

"Just this influencer thing. We can leave early, I just need to make an appearance."

Huxley quirks a smile. "Why? 'Cause you're so famous?"

"*As a matter of fact*, I am," I say, pretending to be insulted, my grin widening the more I speak.

He coughs a laugh, but I can tell he's trying to conceal his nervousness.

Suddenly feeling insecure, I quickly add, "No pressure, obviously, we can always do something today instead. I just figured, why not? No biggie."

*Jeez, way to act casual, Connie.*

"I can't today." He pauses as if considering what to add next. "I have therapy after work, then my woodworking class with Whit at seven." He studies me for a second. "You actually want me to come with you?"

"Yeah," I say expectantly.

Huxley's smirk turns slightly mocking. "In public. Where people will see us together."

I laugh dryly. "God," I say with an amused smirk, poking at the noodles just for something to do. "You're making me sound like a total jerk."

Huxley smiles into his Pad Thai. "If the shoe fits," he mumbles before taking a bite.

"Little shit!" I say, pretending to be gravely insulted while Huxley falls into a fit of laughter. "Do you want to come with me or not?"

His gaze lifts to meet mine. "I do." His tone is a lot more serious than his earlier teasing, and my stomach flips with excited nerves. "But I don't think I have anything appropriate to wear."

I scoff, dismissing his worries. "It's an influencer party, you'll fit right in with your blue hair and prison tattoos."

I cringe immediately.

Why did I have to say it like that? Huxley doesn't seem insulted, but I still feel the need to appease him.

"Sorry, I didn't mean for it to sound so rude. I just meant, like, influencers would pay a lot of money to have your look."

He chuckles, playing with his food. "No offense taken." He gives me another loaded look before speaking again. "So it's a date then."

He words it as a statement, but I can still hear the question in his tone.

I smile warmly, feeling my cheeks getting warmer before I answer him. "It's a date."

The comfortable silence returns as we take a few bites of our respective food. But I have another burning question sizzling on my tongue, and I don't know if I'll last much longer without blurting it out.

"So," I tentatively start, trying to sound as casual as possible. "How are you liking therapy?"

He harrumphs, and the sound makes me think he's immediately dismissing my question. When he answers, I hide my surprise by stuffing a bunch of noodles into my mouth.

"It's okay," he sighs. "I've only been to a few sessions. But she's a little woo-woo." Huxley lifts his gaze and smirks. "Kind of like you."

I snort. "Okay, what does that even mean?"

Placing his takeout container on the small table next to him, he leans back onto the couch. He folds his arms upward so that the back of his head is resting against his palms. The movement makes his shirt lift, and a sliver of skin appears just above his jeans. My gaze darts down and then back up before he notices my distraction.

"She says that I have a bad case of negative self-talk." He rolls his eyes as if that statement is ridiculous. "And that I should practice gratitude and recite positive affirmations in the mirror or some shit."

I conceal my laugh in my hand. "I'm sure that was just a suggestion. Positive affirmations don't have to be so corny."

"Oh, because you're an expert on gratitude and positive affirmations?" he says from his sprawled-out pose on the couch.

I chuckle. "Well yeah, I *did* live in LA for years, where do you think I picked up all that woo-woo shit." I lift an arrogant brow. "As you like to call it."

He snickers under his breath but doesn't add anything to the conversation, and I realize he's waiting for me to continue. I think about what I should say for a few seconds, and an idea pops into my head when I spot his pack of cigarettes.

"Pass me those, please," I say, pointing at them.

"Why?" he says suspiciously. "You only smoke when you drink."

"Can you just — *Please*."

My stare is steadfast as I hold out my palm, hoping he'll stop being so stubborn. Eventually, he lets out a long exhale before grabbing the pack and throwing it at me from the couch. I catch it and grin, opening the pack and dumping all the cigarettes on my desk.

"I bought that pack today," he grumbles. "Besides, I'm not sure what this has to do with what we were just talking about in the first place."

"You'll see," I say with some exasperation. "I'll give them back to you. Promise."

After placing the cigarettes into a neat line, I look up at an inquisitive Huxley who's now perched on the edge of the couch, his forearms against his thighs.

"So the trick is to make it as painless as possible, especially for someone who thinks everything is cringe." He flashes me an unimpressed look, and I laugh, tonguing my cheek. I grab a cigarette and a pen. "You're a smoker, so why not incorporate it into something you already do daily? So tell me one thing you're grateful for?"

Huxley's face turns comically blank as if I asked him to tell me the meaning of life. "I don't know," he mutters with an indecisive shrug.

"Well, that's your problem, isn't it?" I say teasingly. "You have to stop taking it so seriously, it's pretty simple, really. For example,"—I point to the takeout— "I'm grateful for this Pad Thai, I'm grateful for Jamie, I'm grateful for my health. You see where I'm going with this? Whatever brings you joy, however small." He slowly nods as if too busy thinking to be fully present. "Now your turn."

"I'm grateful for DK," he finally says.

"DK? What's that?" I ask, but still write it down on one of his cigarettes.

The Surgeon General probably frowns at people inhaling ink, but he's already a smoker—I'm sure a few words on his cigarettes won't kill him. He chuckles softly and rubs a hand over his buzzed head as if slightly embarrassed.

"It's short for Dumpster Kitty. He's my cat. I rescued him from a dumpster over the holidays."

I blink, a nauseating warmth blooming inside of me at the visual he just painted. Luckily, my head is still down, and I can conceal my reaction before looking up.

"And you called him Dumpster Kitty?" I scoff with a smirk.

He smiles wryly. "It suits him."

We grin dumbly at each other for a beat before I break the spell.

"Alright, next?"

Huxley stays silent for a few seconds, then says, "Freedom."

I diligently write the word onto another cigarette, trying not to dwell on the heavy feeling that one word must mean to him.

One by one, we go through all his cigarettes, sliding them back into their rightful place as we work through the pack.

Huxley lists his gratitude, and I continue to write it down until we're left with only two cigarettes.

"Okay, two more things and we're done," I titter, somewhat giddy about how fun this little exercise turned out to be.

Huxley lifts his gaze to the ceiling, most likely running out of things to list off at this point.

"My vinyl collection and —" He pauses, his eyes finding mine. His Adam's apple bobs on a swallow. "You. I'm grateful for you."

My pen hovers in the air as we share a quiet but *very* loaded stare, my stomach exploding with butterflies. I don't have time to comment before I hear a rap on my open door.

It's Nacho, looking slightly disheveled and clutching his huge binder.

"Do you have a minute?"

I glance at Huxley, then back at Nacho, and smile.

"Of course, we were just finishing lunch. Come in."

Quickly, I write *vinyl collection* on the second to last cigarette, and then hurriedly jot down my name with a small sun on the final one, sliding them both into Huxley's pack, hoping Nacho isn't paying that close attention to what I'm doing.

Huxley jumps to his feet, giving Nacho a quick clap on the shoulder, then grabs his takeout, strolling up to my desk.

"I'll take those off your hands," he says casually, sliding his pack of cigarettes into his back pocket before grabbing my bag of takeout. He smiles shyly. "See you later, Connie."

# 32

# HUXLEY

I'm not sure how I let Connie talk me into this. But if I'm being perfectly honest, it didn't take much arm-twisting either. She had the idea this morning and had me agreeing to it in under a minute. Besides, how can I ever deny her?

Now, it's a few hours before the influencer party, and I'm sitting on the edge of her hotel bathtub with a towel around my neck while Connie paints black hearts over my blue hair with hair dye.

She giggles above me. "This is going to look so good. I'm a genius."

I grin but keep my head down. The dye is cold on my head, but the wet strokes of the brush feel nice on my scalp, especially knowing who's holding the brush. A vague but thrilling feeling tingles down my spine; the sensation is hard to describe with words.

I've been trying to keep my hands to myself while she works on my hair, but it's getting harder and harder by the second. Her tits are directly at eye level, all snug in that little tank top of hers, and I'm starting to feel like a feral stray desperate for a hot meal.

"Can't wait to show you off," she says under her breath. It's said so casually that it takes me a second to register what she just said.

When I do, my stomach flips with the implications.

"Yeah?" I reply, trying to sound just as casual as she did. "Are you going to show me off online, too?"

*Idiot. You sound so desperate.*

Connie falls silent, and I wish I could take it all back. Her fingers smooth over my buzzed head, followed by the stroke of the brush, and the tingles continue their descent down my body.

"I told Jamie about us last night."

"Oh?" I wasn't expecting that answer, and my voice cracks around my reaction. I cringe, but I power through, needing to know what *us* really means to Connie. "What did you say exactly?"

"That we were ..." She pauses. "You know, seeing each other."

Vague. But I'll take it. It also explains why my brother called me this morning. There's no plausible universe where James would keep such a thing from Ozzy.

But that's only speculation since I didn't actually pick up his call.

"How did she react?"

"A lot better than I expected, actually. I think she's just happy that I'm moving on from —" She stops in her tracks as if not wanting to name her ex out loud. "Everything that happened back in LA." She laughs, but it's a little dejected. "I guess I was the only one who thought you and I getting together was such a bad idea. I'm not sure why I thought it'd be a much bigger deal than it is."

"I should tell Sophia," I mutter.

"Oh, she already knows."

"What?" I say, slightly alarmed. "When?"

Connie takes a step back as if assessing her work, then her eyes flick to mine, and she smirks. Her smile slowly widens, seemingly finding my reaction amusing. She rubs her forehead with the back of her gloved hand, still holding the brush.

"I don't know, like, a few days before I called you?"

I can't believe my sister didn't mention it.

She's a fucking vault that one.

"Why would you tell Soph before James?"

"Because you were ignoring me, and I needed advice, so I went straight to the source."

"And what did *she* say?" I ask with a bite of impatience.

I suddenly feel way too perceived, my shirt collar tightens around my neck at the thought of being discussed and dissected like a lab rat.

She winks. "That's between her and I." She doesn't give me a chance to react. Throwing the dye brush in the sink, she takes her gloves off before swiveling back to face me, her hazel eyes sparkling. "I'm done. Want to see?"

She holds out both hands for me to take and pulls me up to my feet. I know she wants me to see myself in the mirror, but I take the opportunity to circle my arms around her waist instead and pull her into me.

I kiss her softly and with no urgency. She hums in response, her hands slipping up my pecs to rest close to my shoulders, and my body tingles from my nape to the very tips of my fingers.

After finally having a good, long taste of her lips, I pull away but keep my arms circled around her. Connie's only a few inches shorter than me, so her chin lifts slightly, gazing longingly into my eyes.

"What was that for?" she says dreamily, rubbing my shoulders.

I smile warmly and give her another lingering kiss before answering, "Because I can."

Her gaze turns hooded, and she giggles, kissing me back. Quickly breaking away, she takes my hand and pulls me to the mirror.

"Look," she says proudly. "Do you like it?"

I take a step closer, leaning the upper half of my body toward the mirror while I stare at my reflection. A dozen or so black hearts adorn my head, contrasted against the fading blue of my hair. I turn my head from one side to the other and grin, finding her gaze through the mirror.

"I love it."

She beams and lifts her heels up and down while clapping her hands as if she won a prize.

My grin widens as I turn around to face her and lean my palms against the bathroom counter.

"So we need to wait, what? Like thirty minutes before rinsing it off?" I ask.

She grabs her phone from her back pocket and checks the time. "Yeah, more or less."

"Do you need to start getting ready?"

When her eyes slide back to me, her excitement has turned into something a lot more sensual. She shakes her head and quirks a smile. Sauntering up to me, she delicately places her phone on the counter beside me.

I haven't moved, my palms still pressed up against the cool marble. There's a look in Connie's eye that has me turning into stone, not wanting to miss a single one of her movements. As she leans close to my ear, I feel her fingers working on my belt.

"Actually," she whispers before catching my earlobe with her teeth. I shiver. "We have some time to waste."

I don't have the chance to react before she sinks to her knees, my belt now unbuckled. I curse under my breath and let my head fall backward for just a few seconds, my lust going from quietly smoldering to burning hot.

Quickly, I return my attention to Connie kneeling at my

feet. I can barely believe my eyes. How many times did I imagine her like this?

Needy. Willing.

And wanting me.

*Me.*

"Connie," I rasp.

I say her name breathlessly. Like a wish. Like a prayer.

When she hears me call her name, her lashes flutter, her hooded eyes slowly moving up my body to meet mine. Something in her gaze tells me she knows I didn't say it because I had something to say, but simply because I needed to say her name out loud.

I still haven't moved when she undoes my button and zipper. My forearms strain and flex with the heady anticipation of her mouth wrapped around my cock.

With a hard tug, she pulls my boxers and jeans down to the middle of my thighs. My already hard cock springs out, and I'm weak in the fucking knees by the time her hand wraps around the shaft.

She hums under her breath as her palm slides up and down in a slow and exploratory pump, her tongue dipping out for a quick, teasing lick around the head. The euphoric sensation of her hot tongue on my cock explodes in ripples of pleasure inside of me.

"Fuck," I hiss as my palms turn into fists on the bathroom counter.

She looks up with a devilish smirk. It's in that very moment that I realize how much power she holds over me. I'm the one on my knees, not her.

"If you stay nice and still for me," she says, her voice like the softest of velvets. Her smirk curls upward, her stare darkening. "And keep your hands to yourself. I'll let you come on me wherever you want."

My mind catches fire at the tone of her voice. Sexual and

with tantalizing authority threaded through every word, vowel, and consonant. She lets go of my cock, and I whimper at the loss of pleasure. But I stay perfectly still as I watch her lean back on her heels.

Keeping her eyes on mine, she opens her mouth and flattens her tongue, placing the tip of her index atop it.

"Here," she says. Her finger slides to her cheek. "Or here."

Her movements are slow and so utterly fucking erotic. I almost forget not to move, my cock aching to be touched. I watch with rapt attention as the pad of her finger moves down to her neck and then down the middle of her chest.

"Here, maybe?" she teases as she circles her breast.

My nails dig into my palms at the sight of her.

So confident and so fucking beautiful. She's going to kill me if she continues like this.

*She's going to fucking kill me.*

She pursues her slow descent into madness, *my* madness, her finger meandering down her stomach. When she reaches the top of her jeans, she slides her knees open, deliberately slow, and places a dainty finger at the very middle of her legs.

She lifts a brow, her tongue swiping over her bottom lip before saying, "Or here?"

My head falls backward again, and I groan so loud, I feel it vibrate in my chest. I snap my gaze back to Connie on her knees.

"Then hurry the fuck up, baby, and wrap those pretty lips around my cock."

It's almost a bark. Impatient and demanding. But Connie is unfazed, her tongue pushing against her cheek in delight as her eyes turn from hazel to black.

"Now, now," she says with a soft drawl as she lifts from her heels and smooths her palms up my legs and thighs. Her gaze is intense and smoldering. "Good boys do *not* give orders." Her words are a lit match to my skin, exploding into goosebumps.

"They *take* what they are *given*." Her hands make their way over my bunched-up jeans, teasing the sensitive skin just above. I'm vibrating with need when Connie's hands finally wrap around my twitching cock. "Understood?"

I swallow hard, already feeling so close to the edge just by Connie's teasing words. I nod ardently, desperate and eager.

She smirks, and after what feels like an eternal, liminal moment between us, she breaks eye contact and looks down. She flattens her tongue against my cock and licks my shaft from base to tip before her mouth swallows the head.

My relieved whimper turns into a long moan, and I'm suddenly lightheaded from the wave of pleasure washing over me.

My arms shake as I struggle to keep my hands to myself when all I want is to touch her. To stroke and caress her hair as I watch her head bob up and down.

My knees buckle when Connie's cheeks hollow around my shaft, and she swallows me even deeper. Her gagged, throaty moan zips through my cock and up my spine as she keeps her hands fisted around the base of my length, stroking upward and then down with the same rhythm as her hot wet mouth.

I start to babble. Telling her how amazing she feels, how perfect she is, how utterly and painfully fucked I am for her. My fingers grip the edge of the counter, and with every swipe of her tongue, every slurp of her mouth, and pump of her hands, I move closer to delirium. My palm slips sideways, and my hand bumps against Connie's phone. As soon as I look down, the urge to take her picture takes over.

I stare at her phone. Deliberate.

Finally, I pick it up and open the camera with one hand.

*Technically*, I'm still keeping my hands to myself.

Connie doesn't notice as I take a few pics, the vantage point is nothing but delectable. A fucking masterpiece and I beg the heavens that she'll agree to send them to me.

My cock hits the back of her throat, and another wave of pleasure surges over me. No longer able to multitask, I drop the phone beside me and grip the counter again. I won't last long at this pace. I'm already trying to hold it off, desperate to feel her mouth on my cock for as long as I humanly can.

"*Fuck*," I croak, my chin falling to my chest in a vain attempt to see more of Connie on her knees and my cock disappearing into her tight throat.

Her eyes lift up, watching me, studying me, never stopping her maddening rhythm.

"Lift your shirt up, baby," I say with a clenched jaw and a tremble in my voice. "Let me see those perfect tits."

She slides me out of her mouth, a string of saliva still connecting her lips to the tip of my cock. Falling back on her heels, she carefully slides her fingers over her open mouth wiping her face, so lewd that it makes my cock twitch.

Pulling on her tank top, she tugs it over her head, revealing her lacey black bra underneath, red hair tumbling down her freckled shoulders. Her attention falls back on me, pinning me with her stare, and I shiver. She tilts her head to the side and grins.

"You listen so well, baby," she rasps, and I think I might come right then and there. She licks her lips, hooded eyes glazed dark and penetrating. "You can touch me now."

The relief is immediate. I take a step forward, tilting her chin up before threading my fingers into her hair. I tug hard on my cock, fucking my fist, knowing I'm only a few pumps away from absolute bliss.

"Look at you," Connie whispers. There's genuine awe in her voice, and my cock swells, my muscles cording with pleasure. "You're so beautiful like this."

"*Fuck, Connie*," I say breathlessly, my eyes slamming into hers while I come all over her neck and chest. My release lands in milky spurts on her skin, and I've barely finished before I fall to my knees in front of her.

My actions are primal, my mind blank, as I place a wide palm on her heaving chest. I slide my hand up her neck, coating my release all over her heated skin before curling my fingers around her jaw. I dip my fingers into her mouth before taking them out to kiss her with all the energy left in me. Her body responds immediately, pushing herself against me, her hands around my face, deepening the kiss.

We kiss like we mean everything to each other.

Like nothing will ever come between us.

**33**

# HUXLEY

I'm not sure what I was expecting at this influencer party, but it certainly wasn't this. The event is sponsored by Hendrick's, the location kept secret. From the meeting point, we're all chauffeured in cars reminiscent of the 1920s.

The second location is a converted Catholic church. The pews are missing, and the interior is decorated with hundreds of artificial candles. There are a few bartenders stationed near the altar, dressed just as old-timey as the chauffeurs. Even actors have been hired for various roles, like an indentured mermaid in a bathtub full of treasure placed in the middle of the church floor.

I feel just like the mermaid—a fish out of water.

There must be hundreds of us inside the church. And it seems like everyone here is extensively documenting the event with their phones, except for me. I've never seen such outlandish fashion choices in one room. It's as if they're all trying to outdress one another.

Then there's Connie.

*God*, then there's Connie.

I was stunned when I first saw her outfit back at the hotel.

Her white dress appears wet at first glance, the fabric hugging her curves as if she just climbed out of the sea alongside the mermaid. Even her hair and makeup appear wet, and it's hard not to feel like a chump beside her with my ripped jeans and leather jacket I stole from Ozzy.

But I don't let it ruin my night. Not when all eyes are on Connie, but her eyes are on me and only *me*.

We've been here for over an hour, and Connie keeps telling me she doesn't know anyone here, but people continue to come up to her to chat and take selfies. She must be way more famous than I thought. It's a weird concept to wrap my head around when I've always only ever known her as just James' best friend from LA.

"Drink?" Connie asks, rattling the half-melted ice in her empty rocks glass.

I nod. "Sure."

Not wanting to ruin her lip gloss, I press a quick kiss on her forehead before I weave us through the crowd. While we wait for our drinks, she pulls out her phone from the small pearl purse hanging from her wrist. It's not the first picture she's taken of us tonight, but my stomach still flips as if it is. I feel silly reacting to something so small, but for once, I ignore my negative thoughts and just enjoy the moment.

"We look really hot together," Connie says matter-of-factly, as she zooms in on our faces, studying the picture.

As more time passes between us, the more things feel solid. Like we're slowly becoming an official couple. Although I know we're not there yet, it sure as hell feels like we are when she says shit like that. I chuckle under my breath, resting an elbow on the bar.

"It's your sex appeal, it's rubbing off on me."

Connie giggles. "Oh, is it now?" she says.

Her hands smooth up my torso and end up resting on my shoulders. I take the opportunity to wrap an arm around her waist and pull her against me. We share a loaded look, our faces close together. It only lasts a few seconds, but it makes the crowd around us melt away.

I tug her even closer.

"You're so pretty, it hurts," I whisper.

Her smile is gradual, almost like she's slowly processing what I've just said. But the way she smiles back … It's warm and thoughtful, as if she's heard my silent confession between the words I've spoken out loud.

The moment fades when the bartender returns with our cocktails. I let go of Connie and grab our drinks, stuffing a twenty in the tip jar since it's open bar. I still have my back turned when I hear a commotion behind me. It sounds like it's happening close to the entrance, and I can practically feel the air shift as excited shouts and murmurs ripple through the crowd.

Curious, I turn to see what's happening.

Shock ripples through me like a threat when I spot Connie's ex walking into the party.

He's strutting like a peacock, his black hair perfectly coiffed and slicked back. There's a smug look on his face as if he knows all the attention is on him. The surprise I initially feel seeing him wears off, and I scoff, not wanting to waste any more of my time on that loser.

"What the fuck is he doing here?" I say as I turn my attention to Connie.

It's when I see the look on her face that my stomach truly sinks. She doesn't appear to have heard me; her eyes are still tracking her ex across the room. I was expecting some kind of disgust or anger, but her expression is far more complex than simple repulsion. It's hard to pinpoint what she might be feeling, but all I know is that it's not clear-cut, and it's confusing as all hell to witness.

There's history there that I'm not privy to, and I suddenly feel like the stranger in this stupid fucking equation.

"I need a smoke," I mutter, abandoning our drinks at the bar.

Connie's attention finally snaps back to me, and her eyes widen as if experiencing a whirlwind of emotions all at once.

"Wait," she says, her hand reaching out for me, but she drops it before ever making contact. "I'm not — I just —"

She gives up trying to make sense and just stares at me, dewy lips slightly parted.

"It's okay," I say calmly, even though there's nothing *okay* about how I'm feeling. "I just need some air."

I leave her standing near the bar and head for the exit, suddenly feeling sick, dread crawling up my throat like bile. I don't know what's about to happen next, but years of shitty luck prepares me for the worst.

Because nothing good ever lasts.

---

I WATCH Connie's scrawled handwriting fade and burn with the cigarette until it's nothing but ashes. I'm not exactly *grateful* right now, even if it's something as simple as my vinyl records. I'm stewing, picking my thumb raw with nerves, knowing that I eventually need to go back inside.

I'd rather just walk away now. Pretend these past couple of weeks never happened and fade back into the void.

Instead, I flick my cigarette butt into the street and jog up the church stairs.

Inside, I'm met with the worst-case scenario.

Her ex has replaced me at the bar beside Connie. Both their heads are down as if deep in discussion. Everyone is giving them a wide berth, and something about it pisses me the fuck off. I feel like a fool stepping up to them like *I'm* the one inter-rupting and not the other way around.

"Huxley!" Connie squeaks, her expression just as alarmed as before, her eyes bouncing from me to him.

She seems incapable of properly handling whatever is happening right now.

So I make it easier for her.

"I'm going to head out."

"Wait, no," she hurries to say, taking a step forward.

I don't miss her ex's hand landing on her arm as if he has every right to touch her. My fist curls instinctively at the sight.

His pompous gaze flicks to me, but he barely gives me the time of day. He assesses me quickly, then simply says, "Let him go, babe."

His term of endearment hangs between the three of us like a ghost risen back from the dead. If I weren't just fresh off of probation, I'd be punching this idiot square in the jaw.

Like I give a flying fuck who this guy is or how much he's worth.

My laugh is chilling when I look over to Connie.

"Yeah, *babe*," I repeat slowly. "Just let me go."

I don't leave Connie the chance to reply before I head straight back for the exit. But this time, I hear Connie's protest rise up from the crowd.

"Huxley, stop!" She's following me out.

I'm halfway down the church steps when I finally turn around.

I'm struck by the vision of Connie in her white dress, the church looming behind her with the moon hanging low in the starry night sky.

But at that very moment, I hate everything about how breathtaking she looks. A cruel taunt of the unattainable dream of being with her.

"Go back inside, Connie," I spit. "It's where you belong."

"What am I supposed to do?" she says, a small plea in her voice. "Ignore him?"

I stare back at her, slightly dumbfounded.

"After what he did to you? Yeah, actually, that'd be a great start."

She wraps her arms around her body against the cold, and I'm reminded of our spat outside the bar on her birthday. The memory stings. Although it didn't feel like it back then, everything was a lot less tangled between us.

"It's not that simple, okay?" Her voice rises as if she's getting riled up. "It's complicated — we were together for a year. I *loved* him. You just wouldn't understand."

Her frustrated expression falls as she realizes what she just said. I don't even let her words sink far enough to do any real damage. I lock myself out and feel nothing.

"I didn't mean —"

"You're right," I say, my voice cold and emotionless. "I wouldn't understand."

This time, she doesn't protest when I turn around and leave.

# 34

# CONNIE

The chill crawling through my veins as I watch Huxley walk away has nothing to do with the cold wind blowing through the flimsy fabric of my dress.

My eyes sting with the threat of tears, and I bite down on my quivering lip to make it stop. I never meant for this to happen. I would have never brought Huxley here if I knew there was any chance Oliver would show up.

In *Marsford Bay,* of all places?

I've never been good with words—scripted words, yes—but those that come from the heart? It feels like any time I try to explain myself to Huxley, I just end up making it worse.

The more I linger on the feeling of failing Huxley once again, the more it turns into an acute sense of loneliness. A soul-deep pattern of always feeling misunderstood. People see what they want to see, but do they ever really *see* me? My vision turns blurry, and I groan out loud, looking up as I try to blink back the tears. This is not the time nor the place for a meltdown. There might not be any paparazzi here, but influencers are just as rapacious.

If not worse.

I feel Oliver approach from the back as if my body still recognizes his energy. That feeling is just as confusing as having the familiar notes of his cologne waft around me when he places his coat around my shoulders.

"Who was that kid, anyway?" Oliver says, as if he still has rightful access to my personal life.

"He's not a kid," I say numbly, then swivel around, remembering who I'm talking to. "And it's none of your fucking business!" I spit. "Why are you even here in the first place?"

He slides his hands in his trouser pockets, the street light outlining the profile of his face. Even outside in the cold winter night, this asshole can easily find his light. He's the picture of glossy perfection. And I can't believe I once fell for it.

"I told you. I needed to see you," he drawls.

I stare at him in disbelief as his words pluck at my bruised heart. I repress the feeling and choose anger instead, a Hail Mary effort to protect myself against him. I rip his coat off my shoulders and throw it back to him.

"Too little, too late."

I try to storm back inside, but Oliver catches my wrist with his hand. I look down at where we connect, then slowly back up to his face. His brown eyes are full of an unsung plea, and a battle of contradicting emotions wages inside of me.

"Let me explain myself," he says quietly. "Please."

---

I BRING Oliver to an empty diner that Jamie and I frequented often when we were still in school. It's run by a couple who are well into their seventies. Most importantly, I knew they'd have no clue who or *how* famous Oliver was.

That includes the handful of senior regulars frequenting

this spot on a Friday night. It's the closest thing to anonymity I could think of without bringing Oliver back to my hotel.

And that was *not* going to happen.

Oliver pretends to peruse the sticky menu as if he'll find something that works with his keto diet. Even here, his demeanor is poised and practiced, always at the ready for an unexpected photo-op. Ruth, who's been working here for as long as I can remember, waddles her way to our table.

"Ready, doll?" she says, directing her question to me.

I smile and hand her my menu. "Can I please have the key lime pie and a coffee?"

She smiles and nods, jotting down my order.

"And you?" she asks, turning her attention to Oliver.

"What kind of herbal tea do you have?

Oliver's dazzling smile falls flat with Ruth.

"Regular," she replies dryly.

His eyes dart to me. "What does that —"

"He'll have herbal tea with lemon," I say as I rip the menu out of his hands and hand it over. "Thank you, Ruth."

She lets out a small grunt in response and walks away.

I can feel Oliver's eyes on me, and I reluctantly slide my gaze back to meet his. He's sporting an infuriatingly amused grin. I take a moment to imagine how good it'd feel to punch him in the face.

"What?" I snap.

He chuckles, and his levity has me clenching my jaw and crossing my arms as I lean into the booth.

"Come here often?"

I stare at him like he's the stupidest idiot on earth. Because he just might be.

"I grew up here, remember? Anyway —" I immediately want to change the subject. "Shouldn't you be in rehab? Or was that *also* a lie?"

His nonchalant facade wavers, and he sighs.

"I checked out this week, I was there almost three months." I catch the unspoken plea in his eyes as he leans his forearms on the table and clasps his hands together. "Look, Connie, I'm sorry ... I really, *really* am."

At the sound of his flimsy apology, I look away, laughing coldly as I tighten my arms across my chest.

"For what exactly? The cheating? You being a shitty boyfriend? The *public* humiliation?"

Oliver is about to reply when Ruth comes back with our order. He pushes himself off the table, and we both give her a thin-lipped smile, mumbling our thank yous, the tense silence particularly stifling. As soon as she leaves, he leans back toward me.

"For everything," he whispers harshly. "All of it."

He tries to reach for my hand, now resting close to my coffee cup, but I quickly take it away. Exhaling slowly, he leans back into the booth and stares at me.

"I know there's no excuse for what I did, but you have to believe me, Connie, I was *fucked up*. I didn't know what I was doing half of the time. I would never do anything to hurt you intentionally, you *have* to believe me."

I scoff and pull out a sugar packet from the basket just for something to do with my hands. I give the packet a few hard snaps as I pin Oliver with my stare.

"Charming." I rip the sugar packet open and dump it into my coffee. "A real fucking fairytale."

I catch his eyes dipping to my coffee, then back up.

"Refined sugar?" he comments as if he can't even help himself.

"Oh my god." The words roll slowly and deliberately off my tongue as I look up to the ceiling, then I slam him with a death glare. "That's rich coming from an addict."

He squirms in his seat as he sucks on his teeth. I've clearly touched a nerve.

"Ex-addict," he mumbles under his breath.

The conversation dies out as we both reach for our hot beverages. I add *whole* milk to my coffee, and he squeezes lemon into his tea. The clink of the spoons hitting the sides of our cups fills the tense silence until, finally, Oliver speaks again.

"I love you, Connie."

The words slice at my heart like a freshly sharpened scalpel. It feels like I'm bleeding out as I stare back at him, trying to keep my face as expressionless as possible.

When I speak, my voice is soft but shaky as I fight the familiar sting of unshed tears. "You have a cruel way of showing it."

Oliver's brown eyes turn mournful, and it's the first time I see real hurt splashed across his face since we started speaking.

"Let me make it up to you," he croaks.

My mind flashes to Huxley. And a pang of guilt hits me right in the chest.

*I need to talk to him.*

I worry at my bottom lip and look down at my uneaten key lime pie.

"I've moved on, Oliver."

---

It's just past midnight when I finally get back to my hotel. Oliver not-so-subtly tried to find out where I was staying. But I was not about to divulge such crucial information. The last thing I need is for him to transfer to my hotel, especially after telling me he was staying in Marsford Bay for at least a week.

I peel off my dress with a tired sigh as I replay the night in my head. It feels like that handful of hours lasted forever. A bone-deep exhaustion throbs throughout my limbs like I've just completed a marathon.

I feel wrung out; the emotions I've experienced tonight resting heavily on my skin like chainmail twice my weight. The night was going so well ... until it didn't. It felt so natural to have Huxley by my side. He looked so good on my arm, and my stomach would flutter anytime my gaze landed on the black hearts in his hair as if we shared a private moment, even in a crowd full of people.

I slump to the bathroom and start my night-time skincare routine, dying to just fall into bed. After taking off my makeup, I change into a silk set and *finally* crawl under the sheets, phone in hand.

I wasn't necessarily expecting some sign of life from Huxley after our fight—I know him well enough by now to expect the cold shoulder—but my heart still sinks when I see no messages from him.

Although it's getting late, I dial his number, hoping he'll pick up, but I'm not surprised when my call goes to voicemail. Letting out a loud sigh that feels like it's coming straight from my soul, I hang up. Chewing on my nail, I pull up our text conversation and start to type a message.

> I'm sorry about tonight.

I watch the blue cursor flash and flash and flash as I dwell on what to say next or if that sentence is even worth sending. I tsk under my breath and delete the whole thing. I'm too emotionally tired to come up with anything of substance. We can both sleep it off and talk tomorrow. My stomach twists when I remember that tomorrow is Valentine's Day.

*God ... What horrible timing.*

I slam my phone face down on the bedside table and turn

on the TV to some late-night rerun of *Futurama*, hoping it can quiet my mind enough for me to sleep.

"Some weed gummies would be great right about now," I grumble out loud as I sink deeper into the pillows.

I fall asleep not long after, the lights still on and the TV blaring.

# 35

# CONNIE

Sunday morning, I crack an eyelid and groan, the wine hangover making my mouth feel like cotton. I push myself up on my elbows, wincing at the rare sunny February morning filtering through the hotel curtains.

I feel awful.

Physically *and* emotionally.

I spent the entirety of yesterday—*Valentine's Day*—dodging Oliver's calls after he begged me to unblock him. He looked pitiful enough sitting in that diner on Friday that I did. I knew it would be a mistake, but I did it anyway. He wasn't deterred by silence either, text bombing me most of the day. I'm this fucking close to blocking him again.

Huxley, however, left me on read. Anytime my phone dinged, I'd lunged for it, hoping it was him, but it never was. The silent treatment stings far worse this time, and a small, hateful voice inside of me hisses that I deserve it all.

I should have stood up for Huxley in front of Oliver.

I should have at least done *something*.

Instead, I let him walk away.

I ended up drinking a whole bottle of wine last night and

spent hours online shopping in a vain attempt to numb it all out. I passed out with my laptop on my chest.

Finding my phone somewhere in the covers, I check the time. I still have hope I'll have a text from Huxley waiting for me, but instead it's just fucking Oliver begging to see me again. I'm about to throw myself into my pillows and loudly groan my heartache when an Instagram notification catches my eye.

It's from Sophia.

> Did you see this??

My stomach sinks even though I can only see the message and not what she's referring to. My heartbeat quickens as I straighten in bed and unlock my phone, now terrified of what I'll find.

It takes me a few seconds to realize she's sent me one of Huxley's Instagram stories.

*When the hell did he start using those in the first place?*

But when it finally dawns on me what I'm looking at, I feel sick.

It's a picture of Huxley, his arm wrapped around the shoulders of a twenty-something girl.

"What the fuck," I mutter out loud.

I deliberate if I should click on the picture and see if there are more pictures or videos like it, my pride not wanting him to see that I've been looking at his stories. I eventually cave, needing to study it closer.

The photo was taken last night at some bar. I don't recognize the girl, but she seems so pleased with herself, cozying up to Huxley. Something about his smirk feels mean and calculated. I can't tell if my hands are shaking because of the hangover or *this*.

It's when I notice his hair that my vision goes blurry. The black hearts in his hair are barely visible. It's as if he purposely shaved them all off. I click through his stories, and there are more of the same. I can only imagine what he did next just to get back at me.

*Why would he do this?*

This feels uncharacteristically cruel, the feeling of betrayal akin to what I experienced with Oliver. The only difference is that Huxley was never mine to begin with. But I at least thought that I meant more to him than this. It's as if he's purposefully trying to hurt me.

And it's working.

I stare at the picture, the knot in my throat threatening to choke me to death.

Maybe getting cheated on is all I deserve. I'm just a thing that men use, only to be discarded when they've had enough of me. I hold no real value. I mean nothing. Just a pretty little trophy and nothing else. The feeling of emptiness these thoughts summon is visceral, like tapping into a deep well I never knew existed inside of me.

I barely notice when the tears start to fall.

---

It's pushing midday when I arrive at the Remington the next day. I slept most of Sunday. When I wasn't blissfully unconscious, I spent my time eating Chinese takeout in bed, watching nineties romcoms and crying into my General Tso's.

I'm usually never the one to wallow—that's Jamie's field of expertise—but I just couldn't seem to snap myself out of it. It's as if I've opened the floodgates, and every bad feeling I've ever suppressed in the past decade came surging out of me.

I woke up with red and puffy eyes and booked a massage at the hotel spa to try to make myself feel better. It somehow made it worse, and I burst out crying on the massage table. I was mortified and apologized profusely to the masseuse. She reassured me in a soft, quiet voice that this was more common than I thought. Still, I made sure to fatten her tip before I left.

Now I'm scanning the theatre corridors dreading—but also hoping—to see Huxley after the shitty weekend I've had. He can't hide forever. Even if he and I are done, we still need to talk, or else the next McKenna family gathering will be especially awkward.

*See?*

I was right to think this was all a big mistake.

I get all the way to my office without spotting him, but I don't think I can withstand the painful anticipation, so I decide to just face the music and go looking for him.

Backstage. Dressing rooms. Lobby.

I can't find him anywhere.

Spotting Whit working in the auditorium, I stomp over and plaster a casual smile on my face, pretending that I'm not engulfed by anxiety.

"Hi Whit," I say, my voice cool, calm, and collected.

His head lifts from the chair he's working on.

"Connie." He flashes a smile. "Had a good weekend?"

I fight the nausea his question incites, knowing very well he's just making small talk.

I try to maintain my upbeat tone. "Great, thank you." I shift my weight from one foot to the other. "Actually, I'm looking for Hux, have you seen him?"

Whit's brows furrow in confusion, and my stomach sinks knowing I won't like what he's about to say.

"Huxley quit. Said he had a new construction contract starting up soon." He pauses. "He didn't tell you?"

I feel the floor sway under my feet, and my nose starts to sting. I'd rather die than cry in front of Whit, so I bite into my inner lip and will myself to turn on my survival skills. Be the actress I was born to be.

I slap my palm to my forehead and laugh. "Right, of course. Must have slipped my mind."

"Anything I can help you with?"

I smile and wave him off. "All good, thanks though."

He nods and shoots me a grin as he returns to fixing the chair. Turning on my heels, I bolt to my office and grab my purse. I get the hell out of the theatre without anyone seeing me. In the safety of my car, I let out a defeated screech and text Jamie.

> SOS. Where are you? I need to see you.

> I'm about to lose my fucking mind.

---

"I DON'T KNOW what's happening to me."

My voice is scratchy and hoarse as I sob into my hands, feeling completely unhinged and insane. Jamie tsks softly beside me on the hotel bed and scooches even closer, wrapping her arms around me from the side. She took the afternoon off from work just to come see me, and I'd be a lot more grateful if I weren't so consumed with unrelenting sorrow.

"Connie," she says quietly, "You never actually dealt with your breakup with Oliver." She pauses, rubbing my shoulder. "It was bound to come bubbling up."

My head pops up, and I look at her sideways.

"What do you mean?" I sniffle. "This is about Huxley."

Jamie tilts her head and narrows her eyes as if I'm being intentionally obtuse. "Connie, don't you think both are connected?"

I warily glare at my best friend as I wipe the tears out of my eye with the heel of my palm, most likely smearing my mascara in the process.

"How is me moving back to Marsford Bay and blocking Oliver, not me *dealing* with it?"

Jamie lets go of my shoulders to better look at me, straightening herself on the bed.

"You must be joking," she says teasingly, but her gaze is warm and caring. "Please tell me you're joking."

I sniffle, the tears still quietly rolling down my face.

"I'm *not* joking." My tone turns petulant, and I let myself fall backward into the mattress. I stare at the ceiling before adding, "You're acting as if this is the most obvious thing in the world."

Jamie snorts. "Because it is, you big weirdo." She presses her palm into the bed and leans closer to me so she can look me in the eyes. "All you did was *react* to the problem, you never actually processed anything. What Oliver did to you was horrible, Connie."

I look away. "Don't you think I know that?"

As soon as I say the words, another wave of sadness overtakes me, and I choke on a sob. I throw my arm over my eyes, trying to shield myself from the world as I cry with renewed vengeance, my body racked with sobs.

"Make it stop," I whine.

Jamie pats my free hand, then squeezes it.

"I know it sucks, babe," she says gently. "But you just have to let it happen. You have to *feel* it before you can finally release it. It's the only way to get to the other side. You'll feel a lot better afterward, promise."

<hr>

TWO HOURS later and after I've cried what feels like all the water in my body, Jamie and I head downstairs to the hotel restaurant for a bite to eat.

My eyes are swollen and puffy, and my hair could need some serious love, but I don't have the energy to care. Luckily, it's the lull period between lunch and dinner, so it's mostly just us and the staff.

I gingerly sip on some coffee as Jamie, fresh-faced and chipper, sips on some tea, watching me.

"Don't you feel better now?" she says with a pleased smile.

"I feel like shit."

She cocks an eyebrow as she settles her tea cup back on the saucer.

"Yeah, well, next time don't bottle up your emotions, and I won't need to witness an exorcism."

I snort out a laugh, feeling wrung out but grateful Jamie was there to weather the storm with me. "When did you become so wise?"

Her mouth falls open in mock shock, and more laughter bubbles up my throat. But Jamie surprises me by answering truthfully.

"Probably around the same time I broke up with Zachary."

My lip curls in disgust at the mention of her abusive ex. She was trapped in that relationship for almost four years. Thankfully, Ozzy eventually came along and made her realize she deserved the world.

"Not that fucking loser," I mutter under my breath.

Her smile is sad, as if she's connecting to her old self. She takes a dainty sip of tea before speaking again.

"All I mean is that I never realized back then how much that kind of toxic relationship could consume all of my thoughts, you know?" Her smile turns into a wistful grin. "You'd be surprised how much space you have left for self-reflection when you're not constantly in survival mode."

I narrow my eyes as I study her but keep the levity in my expression, my finger playing with the lip of my coffee cup.

"Are you implying I'm in survival mode?"

She smirks. "Would *you*?" She flattens her palms on the table and leans closer. "Look, I'm not saying that, in the grand scheme of things, moving back and buying the Remington wasn't a good idea. It was — It *really* was, but ..." She leans back into her chair and crosses her arms, hitting me with one of her all-knowing stares. "You can't tell me that those decisions were not hastily made as a counter-reaction to finding out Oliver cheated on you."

I say nothing for a few seconds, still toying with my mug.

"Ouch," I mutter.

Jamie's eyes turn rueful but loving, the care oozing out of her, and we exchange a few unspoken words before she says, "You know I'm right."

I hate to admit it, but ... she is.

"What am I supposed to do now?"

There's defeat in my voice, but it's paired with a silent plea, hoping that my best friend will swoop in and fix my life for me.

"What *do* you want to do now?"

Her question is ripe with a million and one unspoken questions I should also have an answer to. Namely, the ones about Huxley and Oliver.

My bottom lip starts to tremble, and I inhale deeply before answering. "I don't know," I whisper, the words stained with unshed tears.

Jamie leans across the table and places her hand over mine, her thumb caressing my skin.

"So let's start there, then."

**36**

## HUXLEY

"**A**nd what about your mother?"

I shift on the leather couch. My therapist, Dr. Frances, faces me in a chair, notepad balancing on her knee. She looks exactly like what I'd imagine a therapist would look like. Mid-forties, mousy with glasses, brown hair pulled into a tight bun, and an affinity with the color beige.

I drag a palm over my face, avoiding eye contact. It's my third session, and something about today makes me want to bolt out the door.

"What about her?"

I'm aware I'm being short with her, but I can't help it. Today just sucks. Like my skin is two sizes two small, and everything seems to hurt no matter what I do.

Dr. Frances adjusts her glasses up her nose.

"How would you describe your relationship?"

I sigh. I'm really in no mood to talk about my mother today —or any day. I thought I'd come in here and talk about my time in prison. But we haven't breached the subject in the three weeks I've been here. All she wants to talk about is my *fucking* childhood.

225

"Nonexistent."

Dr. Frances smiles, looking like she has all the patience in the world. Or until our fifty minutes are up. Only another fifteen left …

"Can you please elaborate?"

"She went to prison when I was around twelve years old," I say matter-of-factly, then shrug. "I think the last time I saw her, I was fifteen or sixteen."

"She's still in prison?"

"No, she got out a few years back."

Dr. Frances lifts her eyes up from her scribbling. "Have you been in contact?"

I scoff. "Why?"

"Because she's your mother."

Her calm voice grates on my nerves, and my knee starts to bounce. I hate where she's going with this, and I hate myself more for shutting down.

"She stopped being my mother a long time ago."

She tilts her head, eyes steady and receptive.

"And how does that make you feel?"

I laugh coldly, chewing on the raw skin of my thumb. "You want me to tell you a sob story?" I grit out, my teeth still gnashing on my thumb, knee bouncing up and down. "Is that what you want? You want me to tell you that I feel abandoned, and that I wish I had a mommy? What's the point, she's not the only one who fucking abandoned me."

I cringe, falling silent. I didn't mean to say the last part. It just … slipped out.

*She's going to have a field day with that one.*

I watch her jot down some notes, and I fight the urge to stand up and rip the notepad out of her hands. Shred the papers up like a feral dog and bark at her until she fires me as her patient.

Her gaze meets mine, and I feel my throat close up with dread. I hear her question before she even speaks it.

"Who else do you feel has abandoned you?" she asks.

I rip my thumb away from my mouth but continue the assault by picking at the skin with my fingers. Running my tongue over my teeth, I chew on my barbell, and I look everywhere but at her. I stare at a faded picture of flowers on the wall behind her chair. Then to her untidy desk near the window. Then at my feet. Finally, I meet her gaze.

When I speak, my voice sounds a lot younger than what I am now. "Who *hasn't* abandoned me?"

She slowly nods in thoughtful understanding like the good little therapist she is. Then checks her watch.

"I think this is a great place to stop. We can dive deeper into the topic of abandonment in our session next week." She looks up and smiles. "You did really great today, Huxley." I hate how her small praise affects me positively, but I keep my expression flat. "Anything else you wanted to discuss before we wrap up?"

My mind goes immediately to Connie and the horrible way we left off six days ago. Not to mention what I did over the weekend just so I could get back at her. A guilty pang slices through my gut, and I quickly push it all back down.

I'm sure Dr. Frances would froth at the mouth if I told her what happened and how I reacted. She'd no doubt relate everything back to my childhood somehow.

I shake my head, answering her question, "Nope, that's pretty much it."

I leave therapy like a bat out of hell, sucking in deep lungfuls of winter air as soon as I step outside. After expelling the excess anxious energy that the session brought up to the surface, and a much needed cigarette that I sucked down in record time, I check my phone.

It's still early evening.

I consider just taking the bus home, then remember Sophia's working tonight. The last thing I want to do when I feel this restless is go home and sit alone with my thoughts. I'll have to feed DK at some point tonight, but I still have a few hours to kill.

I sigh, considering my options and tapping a thumb on my thigh as I look up to the night sky.

My gaze is immediately pulled to the moon.

It's impossibly bright tonight, almost full but not quite, as if a giant came to shave some of its layers, making it lop-sided and oval. My stomach twists as I think of Connie. And I can't help but wonder if she's looking at the same moon tonight.

The thought hurts, and the memory of her telling me about her moon theory hurts even worse. I rip my gaze away, not able to bear another second thinking of her. Unlocking my phone, I quickly send out a text before I change my mind.

Up for a drink?

---

I MEET Ozzy outside of McCallum's, a neighborhood pub owned by one of his many friends in the industry. His face lights up when I approach him, like I'm somehow the best part of his day. There's that guilt again, bubbling up to the surface for treating my brother with such disdain for most of my adult life. I wish I weren't so full of bitterness and anger.

Maybe then I could let my brother in.

Ozzy grins, finishing his cigarette. "Charlie is starting to look just like you," he muses instead of the standard hello.

"Yeah?" I ask as I take his cigarette right out of his hands and steal the last drag. "So like a piece of shit?"

Ozzy barks out a laugh, and I smirk, stubbing the butt under my boot before we walk inside.

McCallum's looks like any standard Irish bar with faded

Guinness signs on the wall, countless beer taps, and a wide range of Scotch and Irish whiskey shelved behind the bar.

It's quiet tonight but just busy enough not to make it awkward. We pull out two high chairs at the bar and sit. Ozzy orders a Kilkenny, and I ask for a Jameson on ice.

As we wait for our drinks, Ozzy strums his fingers on the wood, staring at me with an amused look on his face. I sigh, already regretting asking him to hang out.

"What?" I ask with the same annoyed tone I used as a teenager. It only seems to come out when I'm talking to my older brother.

I avoid eye contact and start to shred my coaster to occupy my nervous fingers.

"So Connie, huh?"

My eyes practically roll into the back of my skull but luckily, my drink arrives, and I take a large gulp of whiskey to soothe the ache.

"It's not what you think," I answer flatly, staring at the TV above the bar.

I can tell Ozzy is still staring at me by the burn on my right cheek.

"You don't know what I think," he says.

There's no reproach in his tone, just endless patience. It reminds me of my therapist. I slide my gaze to meet his but don't move my head.

"Anyway, it's over, so it doesn't matter."

Ozzy's brows lift in surprise, but says nothing. He takes a sip of his beer, his attention swinging to the TV. The hair at my nape rises, suspicion prickling my skin.

"What?"

My brother looks back at me, licking foam off his lips and shaking his head.

"Nothing," he says.

But there's definitely *something*.

"What is it?" I probe, "It'd be a *little* too convenient for this to be the first time you don't have an opinion on my personal life, wouldn't it?"

Ozzy smirks as if caught. "It's nothing really, it's just that ..." He shrugs, looking down at his beer as he twists the base of his pint glass with a finger and a thumb, then glances back up. "It doesn't really sound over to me."

My heart sinks, and an overwhelming urge to beg for any scraps of information he has about Connie hijacks my thoughts.

I keep my face disinterested, bringing my glass up to my face, staring into the ice before saying, "Why? Did James say something?"

I drain the last bit of Jameson from the melting ice and order another round, even though Ozzy is only halfway done with his beer.

"I don't think it's my place to say ..."

"Fucking Christ," I mutter under my breath. "So why did you bring it up in the first place?"

Ozzy holds up his hand in mock surrender, and I want to slap that smirk off his face.

"Look, all I'm saying is that you two are a lot more similar than you might think." He settles back into his chair. "You both like to run away from your problems instead of fixing them."

"You can fuck right off," I spit, but there's no obvious ill intent in my threat, and Ozzy chuckles, taking a large pull of his beer.

"I have had enough of my therapist trying to psychoanalyze me. I don't need you on my case too."

Ozzy turns serious, and—Christ, why did I have to bring up therapy?

"How is that going?"

The coaster is now a giant pile of shredded cardboard.

"Annoying." I pause, then let out a long sigh, figuring I can give him a better answer. "It's, uh, harder than expected, I guess."

Ozzy smiles. "Yeah, it always is."

"What did you talk about when you went?"

He looks up at the ceiling as if recalling memories of his time in therapy before shifting his attention back to me.

"Mom and Dad mostly. Parentification of the eldest child. Neglect. I don't know, like, just normal stuff, I guess."

I scoff. "Yeah, normal stuff." I stare at the TV. "Parentification of the eldest child? What the hell does that mean?"

Ozzy laughs. "Don't worry about it."

I fall silent for a few seconds, trying to decide if I want to talk about my latest session or not.

I look at my brother from the corner of my eye.

"She wants to talk about my so-called abandonment issues next week."

Ozzy looks like he's holding in a laugh, and in a rare instance of camaraderie, I feel like laughing with him.

"What's so fucking funny?" I shoot back before taking a sip of whiskey, grinning into my glass.

Ozzy is now openly chuckling. "*So-called* abandonment issues, he says." I snicker but say nothing. "Forget therapy, you can just pay me, and I'll point out the obvious."

My smile doesn't wane. "Asshole."

We spend a few more hours together before we both have to leave. And a small piece of me feels like it's been stitched up by the time I fall into bed.

# 37

# CONNIE

I'm readying myself to leave the theatre, sliding my laptop into my purse when my phone buzzes on my office desk. After a week of silence, I don't expect it to be Huxley. Even though he hasn't posted any more incriminating pictures since Saturday, I'm now assuming he's moved on to the next flavor of the month.

And I pretend not to care.

I also pretend my meltdown on Monday never happened. It's so embarrassing to recall that I'm actively trying to gaslight myself into thinking I made the whole thing up.

That wasn't me. You've got the wrong girl.

Nothing to see here.

But the way my heart pinches when I see Oliver's name on my phone screen and not Huxley's proves that there's still a small piece of me holding on to hope. And it tastes bittersweet on my tongue.

Plans tonight? Let me take you out.

I sneer at his casual message. As if I haven't ignored him all week. The last time we spoke was at that diner last Friday. But it hasn't been without incessant effort to link up on his part.

Typically, I'd sigh loudly and move on with my day, but today, I hesitate. I'm not sure what about this specific moment has me reconsidering my usual M.O.

Maybe it's the confusing waft of loneliness stinking up my office. Or the lasso of nostalgia tugging on my bruised heart as I consider that *maybe, potentially,* I should let him plead his case again. My long exhale sounds like defeat as I finally decide to reply this time.

> Fine. Harvest. 8 pm

I DELIBERATELY ARRIVE at the restaurant fifteen minutes late. Oliver begged to pick me up at the hotel, but I still refuse to let him know where I'm staying.

Harvest is a Michelin-starred restaurant known for using only local ingredients, and I specifically chose it for its respect for their guests' privacy. There's far less of a chance for enamored fans to flock to our table than, say, at the Olive Garden. Not that Oliver would be caught dead eating in a chain restaurant—or eating carbs for that matter.

I spot his black sculpted hair and polished but casual outfit before I even walk up to the maître d'. I carefully watch him from across the room, busy flashing his Hollywood smile to the server as she tops off his water. He looks infuriatingly beautiful, even now when the memories of his affairs should make him look repulsive.

I quickly fix my expression from the bitterness currently burning my cheeks to effortlessly social as I smile at the maître d' and point towards my ex.

"Mr. Campisi is expecting me."

"Yes, of course, miss, come right in," he replies with a small nod and wide smile.

I thank him and give him my coat before walking into the dining room. Harvest has quite the industrial decor, with open ceilings and uncovered beams. It would feel impersonal if the food and service wasn't so damn impressive.

When Oliver finally sees me walk up to the table, he stands up to greet me. He tries to kiss my cheek, but I stop him with two manicured fingers to the chest. He steps back with a smile as if he thinks I'm just playing coy.

"You look drop-dead gorgeous, as always," he says while pulling out my chair. "Is that Prada?"

He's referring to my black long-sleeved dress.

"Yves Saint Laurent," I respond dryly. "Vintage."

He sits down in front of me and nods thoughtfully as if what I just said was some kind of philosophical musing that requires some further internal reflection.

"Well, it looks great on you — you've always had an eye for that kind of stuff."

Every word out of his mouth is already annoying me, and I feel my frustration and disdain for him spike.

*This was a bad idea.*

Luckily, our server reappears to fill my water glass, and I don't even give her a chance to ask if I'd like anything before I order some much-needed alcohol.

"We'll have a bottle of Louis Roederer Cristal, thank you." My tone is a bit too curt, but I try to save it with a wide, beaming smile.

She simply smiles back and nods. "Of course. I'll get that for you right away."

When my attention falls back on Oliver, his smile has turned slightly uncomfortable.

"What?" I say as I pick up the menu.

"I'm sober now ... remember?"

*Shit.* It did slip my mind. Guilt prickles my nape, but I don't let it show. I shrug.

"I'll drink it all myself then." My voice is dry and callous.

Unfortunately for me, my lingering feelings for him have my empathy for his very *real* addiction begin to filter through the cracks of the wall I've put up.

"Will it bother you?" My tone is much softer this time.

His smile is genuine as he shakes his head, and my heart thaws a thin layer of ice.

"Besides, I need to get used to it, especially in a place like LA."

"Yeah, well," I say before taking a sip of water. "You know you're not *legally* bound to attend every Hollywood party you're invited to."

He leans into his chair, his laugh smooth and velvety. "Touché." He pins me with his stare. "Might I remind you who I attended most of those parties with?"

Despite myself, I laugh at his slight dig, and he does too. There's a certain ease that settles between us, only possible because of all our shared memories.

The majority of them were good.

And that's what hurts the most.

My smile slowly fades as we stare at one another. His expression turns serious, too, seemingly guessing where my mind went. I hate that I can see real pain in his eyes. I hate that he's only human. With flaws, and addictions, and excuses, and propensity for fucking up. I hate that I once loved him. And I hate that I'm not sure if that love is entirely gone in the first place.

The server returns with the bottle of Louis Roederer and a champagne stand chilled with ice that she carefully places beside the table without a sound.

We fall silent, the tense moment not gone but lingering here with us, unwilling to dissipate. I wordlessly thank the server as she opens the bottle and then gently correct her when she places two flutes down.

"Just one, thank you."

She doesn't skip a beat and pours me a glass before swiping the second flute off the table and stepping away.

It's finally just us two again, and the tension has turned into this anthropomorphic entity with agency and a will all to itself. It sits between us on the table, cross-legged and patient, ready to wait all evening for us to speak what's actually on our minds.

It's Oliver who first takes pity on it.

"I'm so fucking sorry, Connie."

Melancholy turns to anger, and I cross my arms.

"You've said that already."

"I don't know how I'll ever forgive myself."

"So don't." I lift the flute to my lips but lash out a few more choice words before taking a sip. "You can carry that guilt for the rest of your life for all I care."

He says nothing. Just nods. It's barely visible, as if silently agreeing with what I've just said.

"You were the best thing that ever happened to me."

He says it so quietly, like it's meant for only him to hear. His words feel like swallowing razors.

I lean into the table and lower my voice.

"Is that supposed to make me feel better?" I hiss.

He shrugs and shakes his head.

"It's just the truth." He licks his lips as if he's deliberating on his next words. "You know ... I was planning to ask you to marry me."

"Okay well now you're just pissing me off." He opens his mouth to talk again, and I cut him off. "I don't want to talk about this anymore. If you don't want me to stand up and leave you alone at this table, change the fucking subject."

My heart is beating fast. I've lost my appetite, but I manage to stay seated. Somehow, I find a way to collect myself after downing all the champagne in my flute.

The server returns to take our order, and I can barely see straight, my heightened emotions wreaking havoc inside of me. Oliver orders for us both, his smile practiced and charismatic.

We spend the rest of our meal skirting around potential landmines. He catches me up on the latest Hollywood insider gossip. And I tell him about the Remington.

When the night is over, he offers to drive me home. I refuse *again*. And while we wait for my Uber, I let him press his lips to my cheek. It must be because of the entire bottle of champagne I just drank.

"I'm flying back to LA tomorrow for a meeting, but I'll be back next week."

"Don't come back next week," I reply dryly.

I avoid eye contact and pretend to look down the street for my ride. Oliver is unbothered by my attitude and grins.

"I'll be back next week," he repeats. "Maybe you can show me around the Remington? I can sit in on a rehearsal or something."

A car pulls up in front of us, and I look back over to my ex. He stares back, waiting for an answer, his expression genuine and expectant.

I give him a half-nod. "Maybe."

# 38

# CONNIE

I t must be past noon judging by how my stomach grumbles, but I'm steadfast in ignoring my hunger until I catch up on the emails I've been avoiding all week. Maybe I should make my life easier and hire a personal assistant.

A quick rap on the open door of my office plucks me out of my thoughts. I glance up distractedly. Then do a double-take when I land on blue hair and a heavy scowl. My body moves before I have time to think, springing up from my seat.

"Huxley." I say his name almost like a question. Or maybe closer to an accusation. Definitely not an invitation. "What are you doing here?"

His expression is cold and impassive, as if he wants to be anywhere but here. He takes one step inside, his hands stuffed deep inside his bomber jacket.

"I'm just here for my last paycheck. Thought I could get it from Whit but ..."

He shrugs, letting his words trail off while his gaze skates over me like I'm barely there. I bet he regrets not setting up his direct deposit right about now.

I thought I knew what I would say the next time I saw him,

but my mind blanks the longer I stare at him. All that's left is the conflicting ache of yearning, mixed with a heavy dose of white-hot anger.

"You could at least look at me."

My commanding words hold more power than I expect, hitting him like a bullet to the forehead, and we lock eyes almost immediately.

Although I'm nowhere near prepared for the animosity I find in his gaze. His jaw muscles are so tense, it's as if he's suffering just by sharing space with me.

His guard is up, and mine is too.

"You never gave us a chance," I say, keeping my voice calm and steady.

He gives his head a quick shake while his eyes narrow, shooting me a confused look. There's so much happening behind his eyes, but he doesn't say a word. He just glares at me until he chuckles so coldly that I feel the chill ripple down my spine.

He then turns around to close the office door as if seeking more privacy. Something about it makes the hair on my arms stand up. I feel the cold blade of apprehension press against my throat. Huxley turns back to face me, eyes hard.

"Or maybe I just knew you'd do something like that," he grits out.

"Something like that?" I repeat under my breath.

I don't even see the blinding anger coming; it just consumes me with no warning, like an old friend showing up unannounced.

"You know what?" My voice crescendoes, and I take a step toward him, my hands tightening into fists, nostrils flaring. "*Fuck you.*"

Huxley's hard expression wavers for a split second, and I relish in it, stepping even closer.

"You never actually trusted me or even deigned to give me

the benefit of the doubt. I'm sorry?!"—I level my hands with my shoulders and look around the office as if addressing an invisible audience—"Did we not have a breakthrough? Did we not share something that was actually fucking real? But as soon as there was a *whiff* of a threat,"—I stab him in the chest with two fingers—"you push me away without a second thought? Not just that but you go and fuck someone else?"

The hurt part of me hopes he'll object. Tell me he never did such a thing. That it's all in my head, but he only winces, lips sealed shut. My face is now inches from his, our eyes locked in a battle of wills. It only makes me more delirious with anger, so I go in for the kill.

"I guess you're just like him, aren't you?"

I don't need to say his name for Huxley to know exactly who I'm referring to. His nose flares with a sharp inhale. We're standing so close that I can feel his chest heave up and down as his cheeks turn red.

The silence that settles between us feels like falling into ice-cold water, painful and paralyzing. It's so quiet in here that we both hear my phone start to buzz on the desk behind me. Huxley is the first to move, his eyes slicing down to look over my shoulder.

His reaction is almost imperceptible. I can barely make it out, but when his green eyes crash back into mine, I suddenly know who's calling me.

*God, of course.*

That asshole's timing has always been perfect.

Huxley's voice is dangerously calm when he speaks.

"Answer the phone."

At first, I don't move, my mind racing. I know a dare when I hear one, especially coming from him. And the twisted part of me delights in it; the messy part of me that revels in this toxic back-and-forth cracks a smile, setting fire to my veins.

Huxley takes a step forward, making me stumble backward next to the desk.

"Pick. Up."

I don't break eye contact, and as soon as I reach for my phone, Huxley's hands are on me. His warm, seeking lips are on the curve of my throat, his fingers opening the button of my jeans. I feel utterly pulverized by his touch, but I clear my throat and answer Oliver's call.

"Hey," I say as innocently as possible.

I hear Oliver's voice answer, but I can barely think. Not while Huxley is pushing me against the desk, his deft fingers urgent and demanding as he slips his hand into my panties.

I concentrate just hard enough to hear Oliver say, "I'm heading to the airport, and I just wanted to call to tell you again how nice it was seeing you last night."

Huxley isn't being gentle when his fingers drag down my slit, pushing two fingers into me. No. He's staking his claim. But I'm so fucking wet that I invite the rough intrusion with a small hitch of my breath and a hand against his nape to steady myself.

I quickly reply to Oliver before he thinks the call has dropped. "I had a nice time too, I love that place."

I don't even know what I'm fucking saying. Only that it's riling Huxley up, and the urge to have him snap makes my mouth water. His free hand squeezes my breast, his body pushing me hard against the edge of the desk, making the legs screech on the floor. His fingers are soaked with my arousal as they pump hard into me while the heel of his palm grinds hard against my throbbing clit.

"Yeah," Oliver says with a warm laugh. "I loved the company even more."

I match his laugh, closing my eyes, but it sounds dangerously close to a breathy moan when it leaves my lips.

"When's your flight?" I ask casually, trying to move the conversation along.

Huxley lifts his head, his darkened gaze a storm of anger and need and desire. I can practically see the flames dancing behind his eyes.

"3:30," Oliver replies, "Should get to LAX by 7 or 8 tonight."

I keep my gaze locked with Huxley while Oliver drones on about time differences and flight schedules, my nails now digging into the base of his neck. Pleasure is shooting through me from every fucking direction, and I need to end this call before I get caught.

It's as if Huxley sees me plotting my next move because the next thing I know, he's flipped me around and bending me over. I let out a small *oomph* at the manhandling and cringe internally as I hear Oliver fall silent at my suspicious sound.

"What are you doing?"

I feel Huxley roughly tug my jeans down with two hands, and my skin turns electric like a deadly live wire.

"Oh ... uh ..."

I race through finding an excuse for my breathlessness as I turn my head around just far enough to watch Huxley. His eyes are stormy but unmistakably hungry as he pins me with his stare, pressing a hand against the small of my back and ripping the condom foil with his teeth with the other.

"I'm on the treadmill," I finally say. "I'm just about to hit five miles."

"Oh, I thought you'd be at the Remi," Oliver says, his voice still a little suspicious.

Like I give a fuck.

Not when I feel Huxley's cock push against my entrance, and I bite my lips on the moan surging up my throat.

"Just taking a late lunch," I squeak as I feel Huxley's strong hands grip my hips, his cock sinking even deeper. I let my head fall, my forehead now pressed on the desk. "Felt like expelling some nervous energy."

"Oh, that's good," Oliver says. "Exercise is always good."

As soon as Huxley starts pumping in and out with brute but steady force, I know I won't be able to keep this up for much longer.

"Anywaygottogohaveasafeflighttalksoonbye!" I blurt out the words as fast as I can and barely let Oliver say his goodbyes before ending the call and slamming my phone on the desk.

I slap my open palm on the desk.

"*Fuck*," I hiss in mind-numbing pleasure, then push myself up to look back at Huxley.

To my horror, I hear Oliver's muffled voice coming from my phone. "Hello? Are you okay?"

*Oh for fuck sakes.*

"I'm fine!" I squeak and hang up.

For *real* this time.

I swivel back to Huxley. His expression has turned arrogant, the curl of his lip utterly lethal. I think he's about to say something but instead, he pulls me up by fisting the back of my sweater. He meets me halfway, his body curling around mine as I keep my weight up with two flat palms against the desk.

He slows down his rhythm, sinking his cock to the hilt while his mouth hovers near my ear. Reaching his arm around me, he slips his hand down my center and finds my clit.

"Tell me again how I'm just like him."

His tone is vicious, but it only makes the pleasure ramp up inside of me. That and the deliriously slow slide of his cock now matching the teasing circles around my swollen clit. My mouth falls open, my moan so high-pitched it's almost silent.

"Did he ever fuck you like this, huh?" His voice is but a dark, threatening whisper, his body a looming force behind me. "Like he fucking hates you but can't get enough of you?"

The word *hate* echoes in my ear but it somehow just

heightens the raw sensation of his cock sinking deeper and stretching me wide.

I can't manage to form a single coherent thought. I'm a babbling mess, my orgasm rising, rising, rising. Huxley's teeth sink into my neck, the bite just hard enough for the invisible elastic band to finally snap, and I come on a long, keening moan.

Sliding his hand away from my clit, he grips my hips with two hands and fucks me with vengeance, like his life fucking depends on it. My orgasm drags on and on until I feel Huxley still behind me, his fingers digging into my ass as he comes.

In a blink, everything quiets. The small window of bliss we just experienced is still cracked open, still full of promise, as his forehead falls between my shoulder blades. While he catches his breath, hot against my back, his hands smooth over my skin near my hips. It feels like the most intimate of gestures compared to what we just did.

I sense the moment Huxley realizes the same thing, his hands suddenly falling still, his head lifting away from me, and the window slams shut.

As soon as he pulls out, I push myself up from the desk and turn to face him.

He's avoiding eye contact, throwing the condom in the trash, and zipping up his pants. I do the same, pulling up my jeans as the silence turns awkward. I hate it just as much as I hate how conflicted I feel right now.

We should be talking about this.

We should be squashing whatever is happening between us once and for all.

But my stubbornness keeps my lips tightly shut.

I expect Huxley to storm off, but he lingers near the closed door, and for a second, I think that maybe he'll be the first to address the elephant in the room.

He sighs as he runs a palm over his buzzed head, his eyes finally sliding to mine.

"My paycheck," he says.

I clear my throat. "Right."

*His stupid, fucking paycheck.*

Opening the top desk drawer, I riffle through a pile of loose papers until I find it and wordlessly hand it over.

He slowly pulls it out of my grasp and shoves it into his coat pocket.

"Thanks," he mutters.

He turns to leave but stops. He seems to deliberate before he takes a large step toward me and grabs me by the neck. Pulling me into him, he kisses me. It's hard and quick and over before I even realize he's done it.

He leaves without saying another word, leaving me standing there, breathless. I bring my fingers to my mouth, the force of the kiss still lingering on my lips.

What the hell was *that*?

# 39

# HUXLEY

"*Shit*," I say under my breath as I push open the theatre exit door and step outside. "*Fucking fuck*," I mutter again.

Dragging a clammy palm down my face, I stuff my hands in my bomber jacket and start walking as far away from the Remington—and Connie—as possible.

I'm trying to suck in the cold air to calm myself down, but my heart is beating so fast that I wonder if I should head to the nearest hospital and loudly declare that I'm having a heart attack.

What the fuck *was* that?

God, she makes me so fucking crazy. And *why* can't I use my words for once in my stupid fucking life?

Spotting a corner store, I dip inside to quickly buy a fresh pack of cigarettes. Before walking out, I unwrap the film from the new pack and throw it in the trash. I'm about to crumble my old pack and throw it out too, but stop myself at the very last second.

I look down.

Open the pack.

Pull out the one last cigarette in there.

It still has *Connie Broadbent* scrawled on it.

The cigarettes Connie wrote on didn't last long. I finished the pack that same weekend, but I couldn't bring myself to smoke the one with her name on it. Felt sacrilegious somehow. So I've transferred the offending cigarette into a new pack three times since last week.

I do it again now, popping one in between my lips, and replacing it with Connie's. I slide it upside down for good luck. It's a stupid thing we used to do as teenagers ... but I need all the luck I can get.

*God, I'm so fucked.*

---

WHEN I GET HOME, Sophia is standing in front of the microwave, one foot on top of the other, watching her bag of popcorn pop.

The relief I feel when I see her standing there is comparable to the first time I walked out of prison a free man. I don't bother saying hello. I just blurt out what's been on my mind since I left the theatre.

"I think I fucked things up with Connie," I say, toeing off my boots and flinging my coat on a hook.

"Oh, *now* you want to talk about it," she comments from the kitchen.

"I don't have time for your fucking shit right now, Soph," I groan as I circle the dining room table like a vulture, unable to sit or calm down. "This is really fucking serious."

"And it wasn't serious last weekend when you acted like a total asshole?" she asks casually as she strolls into the living area, shoving a whole hand of popcorn into her mouth.

"We just fucked in her office."

"Ew," Sophia mumbles, her mouth still full of popcorn. "Spare me."

She plops herself on the couch, settling the giant bowl beside her. I stalk up to her and she glances up without lifting her chin.

"It didn't end … great." I start walking in circles in front of her, mind racing. "We were fighting before it happened."

Sophia rolls her eyes and shakes her head. "God, you two."

I ignore her dig. "She's still talking to her ex." I look over to her. "Did you know that?"

She shoots me an irate look before bringing her finger up to her chin, tapping it while acting confused. "Now, now. I wonder why she'd feel pushed to even *entertain* the thought of her cheating ex?" She drops her hand and pins me with a deadpan stare. "It must have *nothing* to do with the pictures you posted on Instagram."

I stop pacing and fall silent, taking in the judgment on my sister's face, guilt gnawing at my insides.

"You didn't see them together, Soph. You would have walked out of there too, if you had been in my shoes."

She tosses some popcorn in her mouth and chuckles as if what I just said was anywhere close to amusing.

"What's so fucking funny?"

She furrows her brows, but as always, she's unfazed by my hostile tone.

"Did you even talk to her? Like *actually* talk to her before jumping to conclusions?"

Christ, she can be fucking annoying—especially when she's right. I reluctantly shake my head.

"You saw what you wanted to see, Hux. And you know?"— She brings a knee to her chest, circling her arms around it— "Your self-sabotaging tendencies are getting old."

Falling silent, we stare at each other, Sophia's eyes narrowing as if daring me to tell her she's wrong. I sigh, sitting on the coffee table in front of her, dragging both hands over my head before looking back at her.

"So what you're saying is this is all my fault," I say with defeat.

She shrugs. "At least some. Connie isn't all that innocent either." She presses her lips together before adding, "It's like you guys are allergic to talking."

I prop my chin in my palm, elbow on my thigh.

"Do you think there's still a chance?"

She studies me with those big, bright eyes of hers and then smiles warily. Leaning over, she pats me on the knee.

"Maybe stop being such an idiot, and things will work out for a change."

I puff out a laugh and swat her away.

"Thanks a lot, Soph."

She grins and opens her palm toward me.

"That will be a hundred bucks."

I shove her shoulder and scoff.

"Your advice isn't worth that much."

She crosses her arms and winks.

"We'll see."

***

I can't sleep.

I'm not even remotely trying to. I've just been lying in the dark for hours, staring at the ceiling, wondering if a lobotomy would feel better than this.

My bed has never felt this empty. I yearn to feel Connie next to me. Asleep and pressed against me, her skin warm and silky smooth against mine.

The fantasy is just as potent as a real memory. I ache for it. Ache for something simple but real. Ache for a domestic kind of life that I've never experienced before, even in childhood.

But who am I to think I even deserve that kind of life? Who am I to think I'd even know what to do with it if I ever *did* get it?

I sigh and turn to my side.

I unlock my phone and squint at the screen but don't adjust the brightness. I want Connie's face burned into my retinas. Burned so deep I see an imprint of her everywhere I look.

She posted pictures of the Hendrick's party to her profile the other day. I wonder if she was contractually obligated or if she posted them out of spite. Because I'm deliberately missing from all of them. It looks like she never had a date for the event in the first place.

I stare at them nonetheless.

*God, she's so fucking beautiful.*

Why did she even give me a chance?

Her earlier accusation comes back to haunt me.

*"You never gave us a chance."*

The regret is heavy and painful.

I fucking blew it.

I let out another long sigh through my nose and turn off my phone.

Sleep doesn't take pity on me.

I stare at the ceiling some more.

**40**

## CONNIE

"Yeah, the movers just left," I tell Jamie on the phone as I stroll through my new condo.

The moving company unpacked the bulk of it—furniture, dinnerware, etc.—but left less straightforward boxes for me to handle. Like my random little trinkets and my extensive nineties romcom DVD collection that I refuse to let go of.

"I still can't believe you didn't bother flying to LA to at least say farewell to your old place," Jamie replies.

I can tell she's at work by the bustle in the background.

Scoffing with amusement, I weave through boxes on the floor and head to the kitchen.

"Why? It's just a house."

"Just a house," Jamie repeats in subtle horror. "And what about LA? You're going to tell me that it's *just* a city? And not the place you called your home for almost a decade?"

I chuckle, tucking my phone between my shoulder and chin so I can open a cupboard and reach for a wine glass. The thought crosses my mind that all the dishes need a good wash, but it doesn't deter me from grabbing the bottle of Chablis in the fridge.

"It's really not that deep, Jamie," I tease. "You're just too sentimental for your own good."

She laughs warmly. "I truly cannot relate." I hear her fiancé call out to her in the background before she adds quickly, "Ozzy needs me, but I'll come over tonight and help you unpack, okay? Or wait — is that too sentimental for you?"

I snicker. "Bitch." I pour some wine into my glass. "Sounds great. I'll be here all day, so just come over when you're done."

James chirps her goodbyes, and we hang up.

The silence returns as I stand next to the kitchen island, the marble cool under my palms. I take a sip of wine, the taste tart and crisp, and inhale—slow and deep—as I casually survey my new place. It's understandably messy, with boxes and plastic bins everywhere, but at least my furniture is where it should be. It gives the place a sense of familiarity, as if I'm only a few steps away from calling this place my home.

I have a sudden urge to disregard unpacking for now and just sit in front of the living room windows overlooking the harbor.

My couch doesn't face the window, unlike how it was staged when I first came to visit. It faces the TV on the right-hand side of the living room. I drag a reading chair close to the windows for now, idly wondering if maybe I *should* just buy another couch for when this specific urge hits.

I add it to my mental to-do list and settle into the chair. Propping a foot up on the cushion so that my knee is close to my chest, I wrap my arm around my leg and take another sip of wine with my free hand.

Reality settles around me the longer I sit here in silence. It's like watching silt drift down onto the ocean floor. One instant, everything feels blurred, then, after a few patient blinks, a whole new world is revealed.

I might have fibbed to Jamie.

Of course, I'm sentimental. Just not for the same things she claims I should be for.

Sentimental for the person I was, even just a few months ago. Sentimental for the future she used to dream about. She feels like a ghost now. And her future looks nothing like my present.

And maybe, subconsciously, I've been grieving that version of myself while still continuing to move forward. Always forward.

Don't look back. Never look back.

Jamie could probably drone on about how beneficial it is to look to the past to better understand the future.

Pass.

*God, maybe I do need therapy.*

She'd probably drone on about that, too.

Then, there are the men in my life. They complicate everything. Although right now, it's hard to know if there's anyone left to begin with.

One man represents my past.

And the other ... well.

I once hoped he represented my future, but I'm not so sure about that anymore.

After Huxley left yesterday—and after I came down from the high of what we had just done—I was left more angry than confused.

I suddenly felt exhausted.

The game we had played for months suddenly felt vapid and unappealing. Childish and immature. Once again, I chide my impulsivity. Nine times out of ten it ends up biting me in the ass. And maybe I have to face the obvious: Huxley isn't ready for a relationship.

Maybe neither of us is.

I stare out the window, taking a slow sip of wine as the realization slowly dawns over me.

Has Huxley ever been in a committed relationship before?

*Shit.*

Why does it feel much too serious all of a sudden? For once, I'm grateful for Huxley's passive-aggressive methods of confrontation.

Ignore. Ignore. Ignore.

At least it gives me space to think.

Slow down and reflect on my past choices. I shake my head and laugh under my breath. Jamie would be so proud. She's right; running away from my problems just isn't sustainable anymore, especially at my age.

Sighing, I place my elbow on the cushioned armrest and plant my chin onto my palm, lost in thought. It really makes me wonder if my avoidant behavior stems from something deeper.

I snort out loud.

I'm not going down *that* path today.

*One thing at a time, Connie.*

I finish the last of my wine and set the glass on the floor next to the chair. I don't even realize what I'm doing until I'm already thumbing through the pictures on my phone.

I have to scroll through all the selfies I took of me and Huxley at the Hendrick's party to get to it ... as well as the ones Huxley took of me when I was giving him head earlier that day. Heat curls low in my stomach. I'm embarrassed to admit how often I've stared at those pictures. I didn't even realize he had taken them, I found them the next day when he had already started to ignore me. Given the circumstances, I hated how it made me feel. I even considered sending one to Huxley just to fuck with him.

Alas. I'm trying to act like an adult, and well ... I wouldn't risk that picture floating around unprotected. I'm just famous enough for it to turn into a scandal.

Finally, I find what I'm looking for.

It's the pictures I took of Huxley when we first visited this place together. The golden hour illuminated his face just right. The genuine curiosity in his eyes as he scanned the kitchen. I felt inspired to capture the moment.

I must be a masochist to want to look at these pictures. But the ache is just right. The memories attached to them speak of an easier time between us, even *if* that was less than a month ago. Nostalgia slowly turns into resentment, then into anger.

Why did he have to go and ruin it?

I sigh and shut my phone off, chucking it beside me.

Maybe the solution to all my problems is simple.

Stay as far away from Huxley as possible.

And stay single.

# 41

# CONNIE

Turns out that staying as far away as possible is improbable when my best friend and Huxley's brother are happily engaged and own a business together.

My silent protest lasts a measly seventy-two hours before I witness Huxley walk into the sandwich shop while I'm there visiting Jamie.

"*Shit*," I say under my breath as I crouch down in my chair trying to hide behind Jamie, who's sitting in front of me. It's a fruitless effort, to say the least when the shop is so damn tiny.

"What?" Jamie asks innocently.

I watch in horror as she swivels in her chair.

"No, wait!" I whisper harshly.

But it's too late.

Huxley is staring directly at us—at me.

I hear Jamie squeak a quiet *Oh* before waving at Huxley and turning back in her seat.

"Oops," she mouths my way, her gaze apologetic.

But I'm too busy being caught in Huxley's intense gaze to care about her small blunder. And by the stutter in his step, I can tell he doesn't know what to do. So I decide for the both of us. Standing up, I quickly shrug on my coat and grab my purse.

"I'll talk to you later — tell Ozzy bye for me." I kiss Jamie on the cheek. "Love you."

She nods in understanding, her eyes still wide. "Love you," she answers quietly.

There's no way for me to walk out the front door without having to pass directly in front of Huxley.

*Kill me.*

I keep my eyes down, holding my breath as I hug the row of tables to put as much distance as possible between him and me. But as soon as I walk past Huxley, he tries to grab my arm.

"Connie, wait."

My irritation spikes, and I shake him off, my eyes landing back to his. I'm surprised by how steadfast his gaze is, urgent and demanding, but I don't let it influence me.

"I'm not in the mood," I hiss before pushing the door open, the chime of the bell above the door bidding me farewell.

I've barely taken a few steps outside before I hear Huxley call after me.

"Connie, *please*," he says as he catches my shoulder and tries to swivel me around.

I turn on my heels and face him.

"What?" I bark, my anger rising by the second.

I can't pinpoint what exactly about this situation is making me so angry, just that I *am*.

Huxley lets out a small but exasperated sigh as if I'm the one being difficult.

"I wanted to talk."

His voice is soft but expectant, eyes mournful, but I refuse to fall for it. I narrow my eyes and cross my arms.

"How convenient."

"Convenient?" he repeats, looking confused by my response.

I feel a drop of cold rain land on my cheek. Reflexively, I look up to the gray February sky, another fat drop falling on my nose.

*Great.*

I glare back at Huxley.

"Now that you see me, all of a sudden it's *convenient* to talk when you've happily been ignoring me."

Huxley's expression turns sheepish, and I almost turn around and leave him standing there. But something has me rooted to the spot. Morbidly curious to see what he's going to say, my anxious breaths making my chest heave up and down.

"I've been —" He groans, eyes to the sky before dragging his hand over his face. It's as if he's already struggling to come up with something to say. His pleading gaze lands back on me as he takes a step forward. "Look, I've been meaning to, trust me, I have. It's just that —" He groans again, shaking his head. "I just couldn't find the words."

Unimpressed, I suck on my teeth and stare at him.

"You look like you're struggling now, too," I mutter. Tightening my arms across my chest, I try to ignore the cold rain now steadily falling on our heads. "Why don't I help you, okay?" Arrogance and contempt drip from my every word as I take a step closer in some subtle power play. "Why don't we start with I'm *so sorry* Connie that I'm a huge fucking asshole and fucked someone else the *first* chance I got." I cock my head to the side. "How about that?"

Huxley takes a step back as if I've physically struck him. It's a cheap thrill and only lasts a few seconds, but I smile devilishly nonetheless.

But his expression shifts from shock to outrage in a split second. He lets out an off-putting laugh as his lip curls, baring his teeth.

"Don't you fucking get it?" he spits, glaring at me sideways and tapping his temple aggressively.

The rain is falling even harder now, the water sluicing down both our faces, but we ignore it.

I roll my eyes, acting impatient. "Get what, Hux?"

He takes another step closer as he starts to answer me—or more like yell, his voice loud and angry.

"There's no one *else*, Connie." His nostrils flare, looking more riled up by the second. I don't move. I don't dare move. "I just went out with that girl to make you jealous. Do you not get that?" His eyes are wild, his face much too close to mine. "I didn't touch her. The thought of even kissing her made me fucking *sick*." His voice cracks, but he spits the last words with such venom that I wince.

For a few tense breaths, he falls silent. The raindrops cling to his long eyelashes, hugging his parted lips, dripping down his chin.

This moment feels bigger than us.

It feels like I'll remember this moment for as long as I am alive and breathing.

"Don't you get it?" he repeats, his tone softer now, laced with a visceral kind of hurt. "I fucking love you, Connie."

The earth shifts on its axis, my knees buckling under me. I'm split into two. One who wants nothing more than to fall into Huxley's arms and forget it all. Forget how we started. Forget how we got here. Forget everything. Except for us, standing in the rain.

To our dismay, she's not the one who decides to speak when I finally open my mouth.

"No." I shake my head. "You're the one who doesn't get it, Huxley." I pause, my bottom lip trembling. "You don't try to hurt someone you love."

Huxley barely moves, but his eyes widen as if he's just been shot. And maybe I've been hit too. It would explain the searing pain in my chest.

I walk away, leaving a trail of blood behind me.

THE NEXT DAY, in a measly effort to push the thought of Huxley as far away as possible from my mind, I decide to sit in on an early evening rehearsal with Virginia and Nacho. We have one more month of rehearsals before Hell Week begins, followed by opening night the second week of April, and things have gone surprisingly smoothly.

*At least one thing in my life is.*

It's also been quite the thrill to witness the play I've written come to life. If I were in a celebratory mood, I'd be gloating right about now.

I'm watching Mary-Beth monologue as Kate when I get a text from Oliver. I swallow down my groan, trying to be as silent as possible as I skim over his message.

He's back in town.

Even after I told him not to bother last week.

He thinks I was joking. I was not.

And I'm fairly certain that he believes that his flying here is this grand romantic gesture when it's anything but. It's so obvious that it's simply spurred on by guilt. I might have *some* sympathy for his addiction, but it's not as if he was being held at gunpoint when he cheated on me. He should stop trying to fix what's been slammed into a million pieces.

I sure have.

Leaning into Nacho's chair, I whisper, "Do you think we can have the actors take a quick break while I show my ex around the theatre? I wouldn't normally ask that, but he's close by."

Nacho gives me a double-take but keeps his voice low. "Your ex? As in *the* Oliver Campisi?"

I don't want to take away the sparkle in his eyes, but it's taking me everything not to tell him that Oliver is not worth the idolization. That he would have never even broken into the business if not for his mother, *the* Susan Renfort, a three-time Oscar winner in her own right.

I say nothing of the sort.

I simply give him a thin-lipped smile and nod.

"The one and only."

"Of course," Nacho says quickly. "And besides, I'm sure the cast would love to meet him."

I elbow his ribs and crack a real smile this time. "And by cast, you mean you."

He muffles his snicker and puts a finger to his lips as if playfully trying to shush me.

We return to watching the rehearsal, and I text Oliver. He answers back immediately.

"He'll be here in ten."

---

OLIVER IS EFFORTLESSLY CHARMING, as always. He takes the time to speak to everyone in the cast individually as they gush about his *superb* acting skills and *prolific* body of work. I drag him backstage before he starts signing autographs in the next ten seconds.

"Nice group of people you got there," Oliver notes as he follows me down a half-lit corridor.

"Please," I say as I shoot him an unimpressed look over my shoulder.

"What?"

I stop and turn around to face him, his face a picture of innocence.

"You're just saying that because they were showering you with praise."

Oliver cocks a grin but doesn't try to defend himself. He takes a casual step forward, his eyes dragging down my body, then back up.

"If memory serves, you enjoy praise just as much as I do."

A pleasurable shiver travels down my spine at the obvious innuendo. But it's more like a phantom reaction, a synapse fired by an old memory. It doesn't mean a damn thing.

I roll my eyes and cross my arms.

"This concludes your visit to the Remington," I say dryly. "You can leave now."

Oliver's laugh is dark and arrogant as if he's getting a kick out of me acting like a bitch.

"Oh, come on, babe, don't be like that," he coos. "I thought we could celebrate tonight."

My brows dip. "Celebrate what?"

"I'll tell you all about it at dinner," he says as he tries to place his hand on the small of my back.

Nothing about what he just said should leave me suspicious, but I get hit with a wave of apprehension nonetheless. The feeling is akin to tapping into a truth that I am not yet privy to but still recognize. I swing my hips to the side to avoid his hand and take a step away from him, my arms still crossed.

"Actually, I want you to tell me now."

There must be just enough defiance in my expression for Oliver to heed my demand, because he sighs but then smiles widely. His eyes shimmer as he slides his hands into his Moschino trench coat.

"Guess who just sold Love Lies Waiting to Universal."

My heart speeds up and sinks in one fell swoop.

"You're shitting me."

Too wrapped up in his narcissistic fairyland, Oliver doesn't pick up on my accusatory tone. Instead, he laughs in excitement, smoothing a hand over his pomaded hair.

"I know, can you believe it?"

He's too busy figuratively jerking himself off to see me coming. I shove him hard with two flat palms to the chest.

"What the hell?" he barks as he stumbles backward, trying to regain his balance.

"You mean *my* screenplay, asshole?!"

His expression sours instantly, his body turning guarded. "I mean, it was my idea."

"Your fucking idea," I repeat in disbelief. "You gave me one tiny plot point! I made it into a story and wrote the whole fucking thing and you know it," I hiss between clenched teeth.

I feel sick to my stomach, the walls closing in on me.

I can't fucking believe him. Can't believe he could stoop so low and do this, let alone think I would celebrate with him. And this time, he can't hide behind all his previous excuses. He's clean and sober. He did this with a clear fucking mind.

"I thought you were done with Hollywood. So what's the harm?" he asks with such snide arrogance that I think I just might be capable of murder tonight.

I stare back at him, completely dumbfounded.

I don't think I knew it was possible to feel this betrayed. Somehow, this hurts even worse than all the secrets and cheating. It's as if I'm finally, *finally,* seeing him for what he truly is.

A piece of shit who will always put himself first.

I take a step back and hold up a finger to him.

"Stay the *fuck* away from me."

I turn on my heels and storm off.

"Oh come on, Connie, don't be like that," he says half-heartedly from behind me, then raises his voice so it reaches me down the corridor. "I thought you'd at least be happy for me."

I don't bother turning around when I yell back at him.

"I'll be happy when you choke on your own spit and die!"

# 42

# HUXLEY

I put a movie on an hour ago, but I don't think I've listened to a single lick of dialogue since it started. I could very well be staring at the wall instead of the TV. I'm considering getting blackout drunk on cheap beer and whiskey just for a semblance of relief from my racing thoughts.

I jump when I hear the door buzzer go off. Sitting upright on the couch, I check the time on my phone. It's just past nine p.m.; maybe Sophia got cut from work and forgot her keys. Not thinking much of it, I stand up and push the button near the door that opens the front entrance downstairs. I have just enough time to grab another beer from the fridge and sit back down before I hear Sophia knock at the front door.

"It's open!" I say over my shoulder, my attention now back on the movie.

The door creaks open.

"Hey ..."

It's not Sophia's voice that I hear next, but Connie's. I jump from my seat and do a one-eighty to face her.

"Connie? Hey —" I look down, having an odd reflex to fix

myself now, suddenly hyper-aware of my bare chest and sweat-pants, then look back up. "I, uh — what are you doing here?"

My question isn't accusatory. It's more like a total and complete shock to see Connie standing in my apartment. It feels like my whole body has slowed down, waiting for an answer, rooted in place.

She looks wind-swept, as if she's been running from something. Then she shrugs, her eyes growing wide and watery. I'm hit with the realization that something is wrong.

Her voice cracks when she speaks. "I — I didn't know where else to go." She sniffs, fidgeting with the gold ring on her finger. "I just ... didn't want to see anyone else but you."

A few quick strides and I'm pulling her into me.

"What's wrong, baby? What happened?"

She sinks into my embrace. It's as if my arms around her were all she needed to feel safe, and my heart grows five times bigger. Wretched and used and ragged but beating, beating, beating. For her. Only for her.

"I don't want to talk about it right now, I just —"

She nestles her head into the crook of my neck and sighs deeply, never finishing her sentence as her hands snake around my bare waist.

"I'm here," I mutter before kissing the top of her head and hugging her even tighter. I gently caress her hair as we spend the next few moments just standing there, holding each other.

I patiently wait for her to unfurl herself out of my embrace. When she finally does, her eyes slowly slide up to meet mine, and my breath catches in my throat.

I don't know if I've ever seen so much vulnerability staring back at me. She silently searches my gaze. For what? I don't know. But it somehow feels right.

"Can I stay here tonight?" she asks quietly, her eyes still steadfast and thoughtful.

Her question has butterflies exploding in my stomach. I

can't help but grin as my hands travel over her shoulders and up to her face, cradling her still-cold cheeks.

"You don't even have to ask," I answer softly before pressing a soft but lingering kiss on her parted lips.

Her smile is delicate and dreamy when I pull away, and I struggle not to kiss her again and again so that smile can survive a lifetime on her perfect, freckled lips.

---

THE CREDITS ARE ALMOST FINISHED ROLLING, but I haven't moved from my spot on the couch. DK is curled up next to me, Connie on the other side. She's fallen asleep, her head resting on my lap.

A part of me still can't believe that she's here. That her guard is down and that we've spent a few peaceful hours watching a movie together. That she came to *me* for comfort. And that she even asked to stay the night.

It feels surreal after all our fighting.

But I'm not about to let our past ruin this for us.

Ruin this for me.

I gently rock her shoulder to wake her up.

"Hey," I whisper. "Let's go to bed."

I say it as if I've said it a thousand times before.

Casual. Familiar. Like, this isn't just the beginning.

Connie stirs awake and looks up at me with owlish eyes, her head still on my lap.

"Did I fall asleep?"

I chuckle, smoothing a hand over her forehead and into her hair.

"Yeah, sleepyhead, you fell asleep."

With her hand in mine, I lead her to my room. When I close the door behind us, I do my best not to act like this is the first time I've had someone in my room before.

But this isn't just anyone.

She's the girl I'm gonna fucking marry.

If she lets me.

We share little to no words, our eyes doing most of the talking. Connie stands near the foot of the bed, one hand clutching her upper arm, watching me rummage through my closet.

I pull a t-shirt off the hanger and walk over. Dropping the shirt on the bed, I kiss her delicately on the lips before I pull her knit sweater over her head.

Freed from the sweater, her hair tumbles back down, and she smiles, staring back at me. Her smile shouldn't crack me open like this. But it does. Oh, it fucking does.

I drop her sweater on the bed and smile back at her as I softly drag my hands over her cheeks, raking my fingers into her hair before pulling her into another kiss.

Unhurried. Chaste. But the intensity behind the kiss is life-shattering. Altering me the longer I keep my lips pressed to hers.

As I pull away, she reaches back and unhooks her bra. Then, she wordlessly tugs on her skirt so it falls to her feet, and steps out of it. I take a moment to soak her in, dragging a knuckle up her stomach and around the curve of her breast.

"You don't even feel real," I say under my breath, barely realizing I said the words out loud.

Her gaze is penetrating when I look up at her, watching me. Usually, I'd be embarrassed that she heard what I just said. But not this time.

This time, I don't want to hide behind deflection and prickly temperament.

I'm sick and tired of hiding.

She takes a step closer and skates her hands over my chest, my skin breaking into goosebumps under her touch. Her eyes are still steadfast and intense as she looks at me.

"Is *this* real?" she asks quietly.

I don't answer immediately, the silence nestling its way between us, warm and promising. Taking her hand in mine, I kiss her fingers.

"So fucking real."

She smiles again.

It's relief and affection and fucking unicorns and sunshine all rolled into one.

And I crack open even more.

While she puts on my t-shirt, I undress down to my briefs and slip under the covers. She follows me into bed, the cutest little grin on her lips, while she scooches into my open arm, pressing herself against me. I turn off the light and sigh back into her body, wrapping my arms around her.

The lack of tension between us right now is intoxicating, much more powerful than the head-spinning lust that we usually engage in.

Because this *is* real.

The realest thing I've ever fucking felt, that's for sure. Is this what it feels like to have luck on my side? No. This is much bigger than just dumb luck. It feels a lot closer to what Connie shared when we were snowed in at the theatre.

Fate.

"Thank you," Connie whispers, her nose pressed to my neck and tickling my skin.

"For what?" I ask casually, my fingers stroking up and down her arm.

"Just thank you," she says again.

I smile and kiss her forehead.

"Anytime, pretty girl."

## 43

# HUXLEY

I wake up the next morning to a trail of languid kisses up my neck. Busy hands explore down my stomach until one wraps around my cock over my briefs. I groan, eyes still closed, as I reach down and press her hand harder into my thickening shaft, lifting my hips with the pressure.

Opening my eyes, I flip Connie onto her back and pin her to the bed, letting out a long, pleased hum as I roll my hips into hers.

"Morning, baby," I rasp, smirking down at her.

She smiles, gaze soft, and sleep-mussed hair crowning her head on the pillow.

"Morning, baby," she parrots back as she pulls me into a kiss with a hand to the back of my neck.

She wraps a leg around my waist, her free hand traveling down my back, then slipping under my briefs to squeeze a handful of my ass. I moan into her mouth, pressing my hard cock between her legs. Biting her bottom lip, I pull on it before deepening the kiss once more.

It doesn't take long before the heat between us ramps up, our movements turning rushed and impatient. Pulling away, I

269

get on my knees and lean back onto my heels, my fingers hooking on the bottom of her t-shirt. But she beats me to it, ripping the shirt off in one quick swoop.

With her darkening bedroom eyes on me, she lifts her hips and quickly takes off her panties. I tug my briefs down, fisting my cock as I watch her slowly drop her knees open, baring herself to me.

*Goddamn.*

What a fucking sight.

I can tell by the way she's staring back at me and how her chest is heaving up and down that she's craving me as much as I am her. We wordlessly agree that we'll have time for foreplay another day but right now the need is a hunger that can only be satiated by me fucking her.

I reach over to the bedside table for a condom, but Connie stops me with a hand on my arm.

"I'm on the pill."

My gaze slides back to her, the implication of what she just said ringing loudly in my ears.

I'm choking on my own lust when I reply, "Are you sure?"

She smirks, and *god* it's so fucking sexy. "I'm good." She pauses, studying me. "Are *you*?"

I sit back on my heels, my gaze now devouring hers as my hands crawl up her open legs. Digging my fingers into the meat of her thighs, I drag her closer to me. Her laugh is dark and daring. She's enjoying every second of this.

I fall on one forearm, her face now close to mine as I run the head of my cock up and down her warm, wet slit, her back arching with the sensation.

"I've never fucked anyone bare before," I say with a teasing smirk.

I'm acting confident but *fuck*, the feel of her without any barrier is more than I can take. There's no way I can ever go back, and I'm not even inside her yet.

Connie's pleased hum turns into a moan as her eyes lock with mine. "Yeah?" she says with a curl of her lip.

Her hand slips between us, reaching for my shaft, making me circle her clit with the head of my cock, and we both moan with the feeling.

"Yeah," I answer, my voice chock-full with need.

She lifts her hips again while guiding me to her entrance, her mouth moving up close to my ear, running her tongue over my earlobe.

"What a good boy," she whispers.

I nearly lose myself as I sink deep into her cunt, her words heightening the feeling ten-fold. I whimper into the crook of her neck, my cock throbbing with mind-shattering pleasure.

"*Fuck baby*," I cry out as I rock my hips, pumping in and out of her perfect cunt with a steady rhythm.

She answers with a moan, her nails clawing at my back, then says breathlessly, "I love how perfect you fit me."

I lift my head and look into her eyes, knowing she's witnessing the awe written across my face. The complete rapture I'm experiencing of having her like this.

I fuck her hard.

And kiss her even harder.

While our lips and tongues clash together—desperate, starving—I feel her fingers glide through her arousal, slipping around the base of my cock, then back up to her clit.

Flinging one of her legs around my waist, I deepen the angle and break our kiss, needing to look at her. Needing to watch her come undone under me.

Hot breaths against parted lips. Sweat glistening on her bouncing breasts. Flush crawling up her chest and neck. Wide eyes filled with lust and pleasure.

I feel so fucking alive, it hurts. The good kind of hurt. The hurt that leaves me aching for more. That has my heart beating hard in my chest, demanding this never, *ever* ends.

The urge to blurt out to Connie that I'm in love with her, again, is on the tip of my tongue. It stings my tastebuds, demanding to be spoken. But I swallow it back down.

"Oh my god," Connie pants. The sound of her voice snaps me back to reality. She pushes her head into the pillow, eyes closed, and brows furrowed. "I'm so close."

I let out a pleased groan and slide my hand up her throat, wrapping it around her jaw. "I love witnessing you like this."

Her eyes snap open, breath puffing out in small, needy moans every time I sink back into her. I can feel her near the edge, her pussy squeezing my cock harder and harder the closer she gets.

Her voice is strained but dreamy when she speaks, as if lost between here and there. "You better come inside of me." She says it as a threat, her pupils blown wide as she stares back at me with unadulterated fire and desire.

Lust zips down my spine as I laugh low and dark.

"Oh, baby," I say with a wicked grin. "As if I were planning anything else." I kiss her like I want to eat her alive before pinning her with my stare. "I want you full of me."

My words trigger her orgasm, her mouth falling open on a moan so potent I feel it in my fucking bones. I follow right behind, pinning her down with my hips as I'm blinded by my climax, coming in hot, rapid spurts deep inside her.

Trying to keep most of my weight off her, I drop my head to her shoulder.

We fall silent, both catching our breaths.

"That was ..." I start to say, my head still in the crook of her neck.

"Fucking amazing," she says with a sigh, her hands caressing up and down my back.

## 44

## HUXLEY

We spend a slow, quiet morning together. Luckily, Sophia has class early on Thursdays, so we don't have to deal with her righteous smirks and leading questions.

For now.

After we both shower, I make us some scrambled eggs and roasted parmesan potatoes for breakfast. We sit in comfortable silence at the dining room table, sharing stolen glances and satiated smiles as we eat. DK is by Connie's feet, purring loudly. He seems just as smitten as I am with her as she idly bends down to scratch the top of his head.

I imagine every morning like this.

The thought feels so damn good that it makes me want to get on one knee and beg for Connie to be mine till death do us part.

I'm shocked when I don't.

I must have some restraint left after all.

"Shouldn't you be at your new job?" Connie asks out of the blue.

She studies me from over her cup of coffee as she takes a

273

long sip, her red hair in a ponytail, wearing another one of my t-shirts, tied in a knot, over her skirt.

I know immediately why she's asking. It was my excuse for quitting the theatre last week. I play innocent, not necessarily wanting to get into all my past—*and rash*—decisions right now.

I shake my head.

"Starts next week."

She hums, slowly nodding her head as she places her mug back on the table. She has this coy grin on her face as if she's holding herself back from saying something.

"Do you want to play hooky with me today then?" she asks, and my heart flutters as if she's flat-out proposing. "We can go to the movies or something. I just need to stop at the theatre to grab my laptop—" She stops herself, a shadow crossing her face. "I forgot it last night."

It occurs to me then that she still hasn't told me what happened yesterday. It must have been something big for her to show up at my door like that. And by the way she's avoiding my gaze, it must have something to do with her laptop still being at the theatre.

I decide not to beat around the bush.

"So what happened last night?"

Straightforward but devoid of accusation.

Still, she turns sheepish. Almost guilty. And, *shit*, maybe I shouldn't have asked.

"Promise you won't get mad?"

I puff out a half-scoff, half-laugh, but Connie stays serious, and we stare at each other for a quick loaded beat.

"I promise," I finally say.

She sighs softly. "Oliver is in town."

Fuck.

She's right.

I do get mad.

The rage I have for that loser ignites in my veins like a flame to gasoline. But I stay perfectly still. I'm not—I can't—I *won't* ruin it this time.

"You saw him?" I ask, desperately trying to keep my voice leveled.

She nods, watching me from under her lashes like she's studying my every reaction.

"He's been, uh … persistent." But then she shakes her head, waving her hands in front of her. "Nothing happened though," she starts to babble, "I was just giving him a tour of the Remington, and I didn't even really want him there, he's just kind of good at weaseling himself into situations,"—her eyes are everywhere but on me—"and then, well he said he had some good news and wanted to celebrate, and I was like, celebrate? For what? And he was like oh I'll tell you at dinner and I was like no tell me now,"—her gaze finally flicks to me—"and that's when I learned he stole my screenplay and sold it to Universal."

I let the flurry of her words settle between us while I piece everything she said together.

"You wrote a screenplay?" She nods, eyes wide. "And he stole it and sold it to Universal."

"I mean—" She lets out an exasperated sigh, and I can see the exhaustion in her hazel eyes. "He claims it was his idea, which okay, I guess he's right. But I *literally* wrote the whole thing myself. But it's his word over mine, and his mother is Susan Renfort, for god's sake."

I have no idea who that is, but I still understand the gravity of what she's implying. My heartbeat triples in rate, my nostrils flaring.

"That entitled piece of shit," I say, dragging my hand over the scruff on my cheeks. "I'm going to fucking kill him."

She laughs, but it's weak and defeated. "I wish." But then she smirks, her eyes on me. "I did tell him that I hoped he choked on his own spit and died, though."

I chuckle and drag my chair closer to hers. Lifting her hand to my lips, I kiss her knuckles, my lips lingering on the tattooed heart on her middle finger, before flashing her a grin.

"That's my girl."

She laughs softly as if a small puff of air is all the energy she has left. Leaning my elbows on my knees, I keep her hand enveloped between mine as I look up at her.

"So what are you going to do?"

Her expression turns slightly crestfallen.

"Nothing." She shrugs. "It's not worth the fight, I just want him out of my fucking life."

We fall silent, my hands still wrapped around hers. I chew on my words, deliberating if I should say what's on my mind. I can hear Sophia's voice in my head, taunting me.

*It's like you guys are allergic to talking.*

I do my best to climb over the boulder lodged in my throat and say the words out loud.

"So it's over between you two?"

Her gaze is pensive but comforting, her lips pressing together in a sad little smile. She places her free hand over top mine.

"It's *so* over."

---

FINALLY LEAVING MY APARTMENT, we head to the theatre. I walk inside with Connie to say hi to Whit while she gathers whatever things she left last night. Whit and I are catching up in the auditorium when I suddenly hear loud shouting.

Our conversation stutters to a stop, both our heads swiveling to the exit doors. It sounds like it's coming from the lobby.

Then I hear it again, but this time I recognize Connie's

voice, and I snap to full alertness. She shouts again, followed by a man's voice yelling back at her.

My body moves without me even having to think. My mind blanks as if suddenly on autopilot, my only urge is to get to Connie. *Now.* The feeling is eerily similar to when I used to shut down in prison. The lines blur, and I'm not sure if I'm here or back there as I stalk up the aisle of the auditorium.

When I slam the doors open, the threat becomes perfectly clear.

It's Oliver.

Like a fucking cockroach, he's slithered back, shouting at Connie as if he has every right to.

I feel like a bull charging after a matador, but neither of them sees me coming. I breezily step in front of Connie, and Oliver blinks in surprise, stuttering into silence.

I cock my head and grin arrogantly.

Then head butt him in his stupid fucking face.

The crack of my skull connecting with his nose echoes loudly in the empty lobby. I hear Connie gasp behind me, but she doesn't intervene. His head snaps back with the force as he groans loudly, bringing his hands up to his face. He stares back at me in horror, eyes wide. His shoulders curve inward as he bends slightly over, looking at his hands, blood all over them.

"You broke my fucking nose!" he whines, the words muffled behind his hands back on his face.

He snaps up straight, baring his teeth.

I see his swing coming a mile away. He could very well be moving in slow motion by the way I process his every move. I dodge his right hook easily and return his attack with a solid uppercut to the chin.

His body swings back like a rag doll, slamming down to the floor. I'm barely thinking. I just want him to pay. I have time to land a hard kick to his left thigh before I feel someone drag me away from him.

"Relax," Whit says into my ear. "Before you end up back in prison."

I blink back to reality, my heart battering in my chest, my breathing ragged and hollow. I look over to Connie, suddenly terrified to see her reaction to my violent outburst.

But there's nothing but pride in her gaze as she stares back, a subtle smirk on her lips. Relief washes over me like a powerful wave. Then, she breaks eye contact and turns to Oliver still moaning on the floor.

"And if you even *think* of pressing charges for what just happened," she barks, pointing a finger at him. "Know that I'll fucking sue for what you did." She steps closer, glaring down at him, her face set in hard resolve and spits on him. "Consider us even, asshole."

# CONNIE

Huxley is sitting on the couch in my office, facing me as I lean against the desk.

We haven't spoken a word since I dragged him in here a few minutes ago. After Whit pulled Huxley off of Oliver, he ushered us out of the lobby and told us he'd make sure Oliver left as promptly as possible.

Although Huxley split his eyebrow open with the force of the headbutt, and his knuckles are vaguely bruised, his body language is relaxed. There's a cocky smirk pulling at his lips as he rests back on the couch, his legs wide and his hands on his thighs.

"You shouldn't have done that," I finally say.

My statement is so half-hearted that Huxley's smirk never leaves his lips. I don't mean it. I know it. Huxley knows it. Hell, even Whit knows it.

I'm *glad* that Oliver got what was coming to him.

*Slimy piece of shit.*

"It's not funny," I say, but I can't stop smiling. "Given your record and all."

Huxley chuckles, resting his hands on the back of his head.

"Sometimes, you just gotta throw caution to the wind, baby." His smile widens, flashing his teeth, but he then falls serious, his gaze intensifying. "There was no way in hell I was letting him talk to you like that."

*God.*

I shouldn't find his casual attitude toward violence so attractive. Shaking my head, I shoot him an amused look.

"Just *try* not to let it happen again, okay?" I push myself off the desk. "We'd never hear the end of it from your brother."

I stroll over to him, and Huxley leans forward, giving me his hand to take. Slipping my palm into his, he tugs me onto his lap, and I giggle as I let myself be pulled down.

"It can be our little secret," he says with a teasing smile. Wrapping his arms around my waist, he gives me a quick kiss before adding, "Besides, he's not one to speak."

I snicker, my arms around his neck. "Very true."

When Ozzy first started dating Jamie, they had a run-in with her abusive ex at the restaurant where they used to work. Ozzy ended up dunking her ex's hand into the fryer. She didn't tell me until years later, after one too many glasses of rosé.

I guess we all have things to hide.

"So ..." I start, turning slightly nervous in Huxley's lap, chewing on my bottom lip.

"So ..." Huxley repeats, elongating the word as a way to coax me into continuing my sentence.

"I think we should start dating," I blurt out.

I can tell Huxley wasn't expecting me to say that by the furrow in his brow and his quirky little side-eye.

He playfully pats my ass before saying, "Isn't that what we're doing?" He kisses my nose. "Are you asking me to go steady, Connie Broadbent?"

I laugh a little too nervously for my taste. "I mean like *date* date. I feel like we've gone about this all wrong. What if we, like, I don't know ... *actually* get to know each other instead of just fucking and fighting."

Huxley's eyes turn hooded, his smile languid and confident. "I kind of like it when we fight."

I tongue my cheek, grinning back at him.

"Yeah, maybe a little too much."

He kisses me, smiling against my lips.

"So dating, huh?" he says in between kisses down my neck.

"Yes, dating," I breathe out as Huxley's fingers dance near my collar, pulling it down so he can trail his lips over my collarbone.

"Like flowers and shit?"

I chuckle under my breath, closing my eyes at the maddening sensation of Huxley's lips on my skin.

"Yeah, like, wine and dine me for once," I say teasingly.

His eyes glide up to meet mine, his side grin so refreshing to see on his face after countless scowls. Oddly, the fight between him and Oliver seems to have relaxed him. It's as if he's more confident about us than ever. It sends a thrill down my spine, giddiness tickling my heart.

"It'll be my absolute pleasure to wine and dine you, baby," he rasps. "I'll spoil you for the rest of your life if that's what you want."

My stomach flips with the way he phrases that last part ... I can't help but think of how our last fight ended, outside of Jamie's restaurant. How he told me he loved me. And how I so desperately wanted to say it back.

I wonder if he'll risk telling me again.

Or will he be waiting for me to say it?

Then, again—am I even ready for love?

I push my anxious thoughts to the side for now and smile down at him. Smoothing my thumb across his cheek, I kiss him.

For now, my heart is cautiously hopeful.

I think I just need a little bit more time to mend some of my broken parts. For once in my life, I don't want to rush into anything. Huxley means too much to me to ruin it with my old ways.

But the thought of Huxley and me finally dating feels like a warm beacon of light to my bruised heart. A sign that things are going to work out for us. Because if I am such a big believer in fate, then I also have to be an equally big believer in *us*.

***

THAT NIGHT, Huxley has his woodworking class, so I beg Jamie to come out with me for drinks since I don't want to be alone with my thoughts.

Baby steps.

I can sit in my feelings and reflect on it all tomorrow.

We meet up at a cute bistro uptown and choose to sit at the bar instead of a table. I catch her up with my new developments with Huxley, conveniently keeping out what happened this morning at the Remington.

"Then I told him I wanted to start dating."

Jamie gasps as if I've told her the hottest Hollywood gossip.

"And what did he say?"

I press my lips into a smirk.

"He said that he'd spoil me for the rest of my life if that's what I wanted."

Jamie looks like she's about to pass out, her eyes instantly watering.

"That's so romantic," she croaks.

Her reaction warms my heart, but I can't help but tease her.

"Please collect yourself, Jamie."

She snickers into her hand.

"Does that make us sisters now?" she says with stars in her eyes.

I snort into my wine glass. "Woah there, Jamie. As much as I love the idea, we *just* started dating like an hour ago."

She giggles and tucks a pink strand behind her ear.

"Well, a girl can dream."

We share a laugh, taking a sip of our respective wines.

Changing the subject, I look over to Jamie and quirk a smile. "Can you believe you're getting *married* in three months? God, time really does fly as we get older."

"I know, right?" she says breezily. "I swear the engagement party was, like, yesterday."

Hearing her mention her engagement party, I wince and shoot my best friend a guilty look.

She immediately turns suspicious, eyeing me with narrowed blue eyes.

"What did you do?"

I snort out a laugh. "Okay, wow, why do you immediately think I did something bad?"

She presses her lips together, clearly unimpressed.

"Because I've known you our whole twenties," she answers matter-of-factly. "You're allergic to impulse control."

I laugh, then sigh far too dramatically, moving my hair from one shoulder to the other. "*God*, you really do hate me."

Jamie smirks at my dig, her gaze shining with love and years of friendship.

"Go on," she presses, "Spill."

"So, uh ..." I chew on my inner cheek, toying with my wine stem, acting deliberately shifty. "I never told you that the first time I hooked up with Huxley was actually at your engagement party."

I brace myself, eyeing Jamie from the corner of my eye. Her mouth falls open, shock written clearly across her face. "Connie!"

I flash her a guilty smile, then hold up my hand. "Look,

please spare me the sermon," I whine. "I've already heard it all from Sophia."

"*Sophia* knew about it before me?!"

*Oops.*

I've known Jamie for long enough that I can tell she isn't mad *per se,* but I still feel guilty that I've kept that one secret for so long.

"I'm sorry I didn't tell you, I really am," I say with an apologetic pout. "It's just that Sophia had already guessed that something was going on between us, and I really needed advice from someone who knew Huxley personally, you know?"

She eyes me some more.

"I guess I can find it in my heart to forgive you," she finally says, reaching for her wine glass. "While we're here — any more secrets I should know about?"

I didn't plan to tell Jamie about the fight, but it comes out all in one go anyway.

"Huxley headbutted Oliver in the face today."

Her expression starts with shock and ends with concern. I can read exactly what's happening behind her worried gaze. I don't let her speak before pleading my case.

"*Please*, promise me you won't tell Ozzy. He'll just worry for nothing, I swear Huxley won't get in trouble. I handled it, I *swear.*"

I fill Jamie in with the last of my Oliver drama, and while I speak, she cycles through all the expected emotions: Shock. Concern. Disgust. Anger. Outrage.

"That *dick*," she spits when I finally finish my story, her body leaned into the bar toward me.

"To put it nicely," I reply with a snark.

Sitting up straight, she rolls her eyes. "Well, I can't blame Huxley for what he did then."

I lift an amused brow and take a sip of wine.

"Told you." I flag down the bartender and signal for another round. "*Anyway*, how's your online shop? Sold any paintings recently?"

Aside from owning a restaurant with her fiancé, Jamie is a prolific painter and has built up quite a following, selling her prints online.

"Good," she sighs happily. "Really good. I'm launching a new collection of prints at the end of the month."

"Oh! That reminds me," I reply with a coy wink. "I need a new James Ferdinand original for my place."

Jamie's face brightens, her mouth falling open into a wide smile. "Yeah?"

I return her excitement and smile. "Duh, I *am* your biggest fan after all."

She giggles. "Ozzy might fight you on that one."

I grin into my glass. "We'll see about that."

**46**

**HUXLEY**

The bus is late. I just came out of woodworking class, and I'm standing under the streetlight, scuffing the wet pavement with my boots, jumping in place and looking up to the night sky trying to expel some impatient energy.

*I really need a fucking car.*

"Hux?"

The voice is vaguely familiar and prickles in my ears.

Looking to my right, I find a blond man in his early thirties staring back at me.

*Shit.*

"Finn?"

Even though it sounds like casual disbelief, I'm actually experiencing existential dread, triggered by a ghost from my past.

Patrick Finnegan.

An infamous family name back in my old neighborhood, and one of three guys—including his older brother, Sean—who was involved in the liquor store robbery with me, six years ago.

It was his idea in the first place. And being the idiot that I am, I went along with it and almost ruined my whole life in the process.

Finn barks out a laugh and claps me on the shoulder. I try to hide my wince.

"Thought that was you." He takes a drag of his cigarette and waves it in my direction. "Always with that blue fucking hair."

I silently curse the late bus and return his comment with a dry laugh.

"Yeah, kind of my thing, I guess." I pause and decide not to beat around the bush. "When did you get out?"

Smoke billows from his lips before he answers. "Just a few months ago." He flashes me a crooked smile and looks around as if just realizing I'm standing at the bus stop. "You strapped for cash, brother? I can hook you up for old times' sake." He winks. "I've got a great connection."

I can only imagine what the hell that means. Knowing him, he's probably back to selling drugs. I try not to act disgusted, hoping he'll just leave me alone if I placate his small talk. Although I still let a small dig slip under the guise of camaraderie.

I grin. "Should have known you'd never go straight."

"Yeah." Finn laughs. "Trick is to not get caught this time."

I see the bus finally pull up from the corner of my eye. Relieved, I quickly say my farewells.

"Anyway, I've got to go. Good to see you."

*Fucking lie.*

"Good to see you too, brother," he replies with a wave. "And you know where to find me if you ever change your mind."

I shoot him a salute and jog up the steps of the bus. Inside, I sit near a window and watch Finn stroll down the street, hands deep in his coat pockets.

Our interaction has put me on edge, and I try to sift through my feelings before I get too lost in my own head. It's a layered mess of anxiety, discomfort, but also ... pride?

It's such an unfamiliar feeling that I hardly recognize it.

It's a growing pride in who I'm becoming.

Pride in the life I'm slowly building for myself.

Seeing Finn was like seeing a future that could have been; a parallel universe so close to mine it's only separated by one or two wrong choices.

I settle into my seat and pull out my book from my bag, but I'm still lost in thought. Connie must be rubbing off on me because I choose to take this chance encounter as a sign from the universe. A sign that maybe I *am* doing good. And that I'm finally on the right path for once.

---

"HUXLEY!"

Charlie jumps off the couch and barrels my way, practically knocking the wind out of me.

"Hey, little dude," I say, ruffling his brown curls and returning his hug.

Charlie might be a teenager now, but he doesn't seem to have lost his childlike glee. I was a walking cloud of anger and doom at fourteen, but not Charlie. Of all the siblings, he seems to have come out the least unscathed. Good for him. That makes one of us.

I look up to find Ozzy silently watching me from the couch, a subtle grin on his lips. His curious expression probably has to do with my unexpected visits lately. I've been coming around the house a lot more in the past month.

"Are you staying for a bit?" Charlie says, stars in his eyes. "Ozzy and I have been rewatching all the Fast & Furious movies, we're on Tokyo Drift right now." He smiles wide. "It's my favorite."

I chuckle as I take off my coat.

"Yeah, I'll stay a while. Tokyo Drift is my favorite too."

WHEN THE MOVIE is over and Charlie has gone to bed, Ozzy and I end up in the kitchen, having one last beer before I leave. I'm sitting on the counter while Ozzy leans against the stove, a comfortable silence accompanying us.

"Charlie loves it when you come around," Ozzy says with an easy smile before taking a swig of beer.

I can tell he's not trying to guilt-trip me. Just a simple observation from my older brother.

"Yeah, about that ..."

I look down at the floor and let out a heavy exhale, feeling apprehensive about what I'm about to say. This visit wasn't quite as out of the blue as I made it seem. As a nervous tick, I press my lips and rub them together, chewing on my barbell, while I slide my gaze back to Ozzy, who's waiting for me to continue.

"I've been meaning to talk to you about something."

Ozzy chuckles. "Should I be worried?"

I snort out a laugh. "No — no need. Just something that's been on my mind lately." But then my earlier encounter comes back to me. "Although I did bump into Finn earlier at the bus stop."

Ozzy's brows lift in surprise, then dip in what looks like anger. "Patrick Finnegan?"

"The one and only," I mutter before taking a sip of beer.

My brother rolls his eyes and scoffs as if the very thought of him is getting him riled up.

"What did that lowlife have to say?"

I shrug. "Not much. Asked me if I needed a job." Ozzy's eyes narrow as if shooting me an invisible threat. I crack a smile and snicker. "Stop looking at me like that, I got out of there as soon as I could."

"Good," Ozzy mutters.

"Anyway," I say, trying to get back on track. "That's irrelevant and not what I wanted to talk about." I place my beer beside me on the counter and rub my face with both hands before putting my weight on my palms on either side of my thighs. "I've been unpacking my childhood a lot in therapy."

The spark of pride in Ozzy's eyes has me groaning internally, and it takes me everything not to roll my eyes at him. I continue nonetheless.

"Part of me expected to talk about Dad a lot more than Mom, given she was absent for most of my childhood but ..." My chuckle sounds like a mixture of disbelief and sadness. "Apparently she's at the root of a lot of my issues." I shake my head, looking down at my feet before sharing a loaded stare with Ozzy. "It made me realize that it was unfair of me to have placed all my anger on you when you moved out. My therapist says that you leaving triggered my abandonment issues. And since Mom never cared to even notice me, well,"—I rub my palm over my scalp and shrug—"I transferred all that blame to you instead, and I'm sorry for that, I really am." There's a lump in my throat, and I'm having trouble keeping eye contact with Ozzy, but I stay steadfast and try not to berate myself for feeling so emotional. "And then that made me think of Charlie and how I disappeared on him, too, and how I *hate* the idea of being another person in his life that he can't depend on."

Ozzy hasn't moved, staring at me with wide, watery eyes, and my voice cracks when I finally speak the last of my thoughts.

"I want to be there for him like you were there for me — even when I didn't want you to be. And so, I guess what I'm trying to say is."—I swallow hard—"Thank you for never giving up on me."

We haven't stopped staring at each other. The silence thickens the longer Ozzy doesn't speak, but it doesn't make me uncomfortable. It simply appears like he's letting what I just told him sink in.

Finally, he moves, dragging his hand through his curls while placing his beer on the counter with the other. His smile is coy, but it's mixed with something I can't quite place.

When he eventually speaks, his words are slow and carefully chosen. "I didn't realize how much I needed to hear you say that until just now." His smile widens, and this time, I don't miss the love radiating through his facial expression. He takes a step toward me. "Come here," he says, waving me into an embrace.

I slide down from the counter and hug my brother tightly. This time, when the feeling bubbles up inside of me, I don't hesitate to voice it.

"I love you," I say, still hugging him. "I hope you know that."

Pulling away, Ozzy beams up at me and gives me a soft tap on the arm as if wordlessly reassuring me.

"Always," he says. "I never doubted it."

# 47

# CONNIE

"You can't count this as our first official date, you know," Huxley says matter-of-factly as he unfastens his seatbelt.

After having drinks on Thursday, Jamie insisted we both come for Sunday dinner. This would make tonight our first official outing as two people publicly dating.

I should feel nervous, but instead it just feels normal, especially when our outing is Sunday dinner at the McKennas. It's safe. It's family.

I smirk and open the car door.

"Oh?" I say innocently. "Already have something planned then?"

Huxley winks as he rounds the car, meeting me on the other side. "I'm working on it."

It's only been three days since we made up, and I know it's too early to declare that *this* time things feel different. But I can't help but think it. A lot.

Especially when I watch Huxley stroll up to me and slide his palm into mine. Leaning down, he presses a kiss to the back of my hand before smoothing a thumb over the skin, his gaze lifting to connect with mine under his lashes.

"Being a Libra and all, I should have known you were a secret loverboy," I say smoothly, although my heart keeps skipping a beat anytime he smiles at me like he is now.

He chuckles and pulls me into his body with an arm around my waist.

"You just never gave me the chance until now," he says softly before kissing me.

Giggling, I let my body fall onto his chest, wrapping my arms around his neck and returning the kiss before pulling away and heading inside.

As I walk in, I'm hit with the familiar scent of home cooking coming from the kitchen, and of another scent that is distinctly the McKenna household. It's warm and inviting, and my heart squeezes with affection. The first person to greet us is Sophia, who's sitting on the couch, one foot pulled up and propped on the cushion.

With her eyes still on her phone, she says, "I saw that."

"What?" I ask with a laugh as Huxley takes my coat.

"Whatever that was outside," she says, her attention still cast down. "Practically made me nauseous."

Her eyes lift after her last comment, a smirk on her lips. Huxley passes behind Sophia on his way to the kitchen, most likely looking for his older brother, and pats her head condescendingly.

"She's the cold-hearted one of the family," he says.

Sophia shrinks down as she tries to avoid her brother's hand. "Don't touch me!"

Her threat is playfully ignored as Huxley turns the corner and disappears. I laugh under my breath at the obvious sibling banter and sit on the couch next to Sophia.

"Where's Jamie?" I ask.

"Taking a shower, I think," she says, finally putting her phone down.

As her eyes slide to meet mine, her ominous smile widens. She stares for a few seconds too long before finally asking, "So?" She elongates the word as if the one-word question contains all the information I need to answer her.

I respond with a deadpan stare, narrowing my eyes, but don't say anything.

She puffs out a laugh. "You two *finally* saw the light. Took you long enough." Her smile turns saccharine. "Thank *god*, 'cause I was sick and tired of playing couples therapy."

I playfully shove her shoulder with my own. "Huxley's right, you are the cold-hearted one."

She giggles. "Well, *someone* needs to be rational in this family."

Looking over my shoulder, I make sure we're alone. "So what about you? Are you still seeing that bartender?"

Her body language turns a little squirrely, but she answers me anyway. "Nah, he started getting too clingy, so I broke things off. He's kind of ignoring me now."

I snort. "Too clingy?" Knowing her, she probably got turned off by something small and inconsequential. "Let me guess, he was just acting interested?"

"He was texting me too often." She smirks, then adds playfully, "Yuck."

I shake my head. "Classic Sophia," I chide.

Charlie appears out of nowhere in front of us and cuts in without even saying hi.

"Connie, have you watched the Fast & Furious movies? If yes, what are your rankings from worst to best?"

Sophia and I fall into a fit of giggles while Charlie stands in front of us, dead serious. Eventually, I do answer his question—of course, I've watched the franchise. I spend the rest of Sunday night surrounded by all my favorite people, Huxley now at the top of the list.

———

A FEW DAYS LATER, I meet Huxley outside my condo for our very first official date. He *insisted* on picking me up, and I find him standing beside Sophia's car, the late afternoon sun shining behind him, with a large bouquet of colorful gerbera daisies.

I giggle in shock at the sight of him. He looks so adorable, standing there, a hopeful smile on his face. His faithful bomber jacket is unzipped at the collar, distressed combat boots, and freshly dyed blue hair, while holding those dainty flowers. The urge is too strong—I *need* to document this.

"Don't move," I order while still a few feet away.

Pulling my phone out, I snap a few pictures, his smile turning sheepish the more he stands there—which just makes him look all the more charming. Finally, I skip over to meet him, my smile so big it's hurting my cheeks.

"For you," he says demurely, handing me the flowers with a soft kiss on the corner of my lips.

I play along, acting surprised as if I didn't know the bouquet was meant for me.

"That's so sweet of you." If I'm not careful, he'll notice the cartoon hearts floating out of my eyes. "Thank you."

Opening the car door, he ushers me in with a hand to the small of my back. The giddiness I'm feeling from just the first few minutes of our date is unprecedented, even after more than a decade of dating. First dates have never meant this much to me.

But if I'm being honest. It's because no one has meant this much to me. Huxley is all new territory, and I'm loving every minute of it. The feeling is reminiscent of a warm, effervescent wave gently rolling through my body.

He's kept the activity of our date a secret. When in the car, I —*again*—ask him where we're heading, but he simply sends me a mischievous wink before pulling out onto the street.

Fifteen minutes and a few neighbourhoods later, we park on a busy street, but I still don't know what I'm looking for. I vaguely know where we are, but nothing comes to mind until we walk up to the doors of an indie movie theatre.

It takes me a few seconds to put the context clues together, and when it finally clicks, my stomach explodes into a dozen butterflies.

Huxley has somehow managed to find what I'm assuming is the only movie theatre in Marsford Bay celebrating nineties romcoms with a special double-showing of *Can't Hardly Wait*, followed by my favorite—*10 Things I Hate About You*.

I turn on my heels and smile widely.

"You're kidding."

Even with my positive reaction, Huxley rubs his nape, looking nervous, then shrugs, his hand still up in the air.

"I knew you had a thing for the nineties and then heard about this place so ..." He smiles sheepishly, not fully finishing his sentence. "You like it?"

"Do I like it?" I parrot back, grabbing his forearm with both hands in pure excitement. "I *love* it."

Huxley's nervous expression fades into a shy smirk as if secretly celebrating his win. And my heart flutters when I think about the careful thought he put into seeing me happy.

"This is perfect, Hux. Literally perfect."

I kiss him, doing my best to convey all my affection through our parted lips and the touch of our tongues. Deepening the kiss with a tug to his coat collar, his hands smooth over my ass, pulling me into him. The moment slips into a place where time doesn't exist, and nothing else matters but us.

Eventually, Huxley breaks the kiss and chuckles softly against my lips. "If we don't hurry, we'll miss the first showing."

I pull away, grinning like a fool, and take his hand, leading us inside.

**48**

**HUXLEY**

The date is a hit, and I'm buzzing in my seat long after the lights go down and the first movie starts playing. By the time the second feature ends, the buzz has slumbered into a low hum of pure contentment. Especially when Connie spends the last half-hour of the movie with her head resting on my shoulder.

It's past eight and dark out by the time we leave the movie theatre. We slowly stroll out into the late winter night, Connie's arm tucked through mine.

The date is winding down, but I'm not ready to end it just yet.

"Dessert?" I ask, already subtly leading us down the street.

She beams at me, her body pressed close to mine as we walk. Her hazel eyes shimmer as if lit up from the inside out, and once again, she steals my breath away.

"Always," she answers with a small, sated sigh.

Unbeknownst to Connie, I scoped out the area before bringing her here and happen to know that there's a diner she might think is cute just around the corner.

As we walk inside, the bell chimes above our heads. We nod

298

at the server standing near the counter before we pick a booth in the far back, near the window. I slide in first, and Connie follows suit, sitting next to me.

For the first bit, in between ordering coffees and pie, we barely talk, our loaded glances doing all the talking for us. I think—or maybe hope—she's feeling a lot like me right now.

Content. Happy. Quietly satisfied.

When our slices of pie arrive—hers key lime and mine cherry—she takes a bite of mine before even tasting hers. She notices me staring and chuckles with her mouth full, the fork slipping past her lips.

"Sorry, was that rude?"

I grin and shake my head. I'd let her eat my whole damn plate if it meant I could stare at her like this forever.

"What's mine is yours, baby."

"Careful." She laughs, tucking a red strand of hair behind her ear while she takes a sip of coffee. "That sounded a lot like a proposal."

I turn my body so I can lean my back against the window pane to better stare at Connie some more.

"Don't tempt me," I answer casually.

She snorts. "God, you really are a romantic."

I kick her foot playfully under the table.

"And you're not? Miss lover of fate?" I tease.

Her laugh is much purer this time. And I burn to memory the hills and valleys of the sound, knowing I'll want to return to it again and again. Silence falls between us as I continue to stare at her, quietly drumming my fingers on the table.

"What is it?" she says, a crooked grin on her lips. "You look like you're lost in thought."

I respond with a smile before I speak. "Remember that question you asked me when we were snowed in?"

She casts her gaze down as if trying to recall, then looks up, eyes slightly narrowed. "About how everything happens for a reason?"

"Yeah," I say, slowly nodding my head. "Do you remember what I said?"

Her expression turns slightly suspicious, but it's paired with an amused smirk. "You said to ask again when something good actually happens in your life."

Wordlessly and with a small prompt of the hand, I tell her to ask again.

Her gaze turns soulful, and she stays silent for a few loaded beats.

"Do you believe that everything happens for a reason?" Her voice is quiet. Deliberate.

"Maybe." I laugh when her face falls. She was obviously expecting me to say yes outright. I take her hand and kiss her knuckles. "But right now? It sure does feel like it."

She presses her lips together as if trying to suppress her grin, her eyes sparkling like a starry night sky. But as she watches me, she gradually turns serious.

"Am I the good thing in your life?"

It's rare to see Connie looking so unsure of herself, as if she's nervous to even ask for fear she'll have assumed wrong. I reassure her with a stroke of my thumb over the top of her hand still in mine.

Something about the moment brings me back to the afternoon when I told her that I loved her. Feels like a lifetime ago. But it was just last week. It was the wrong time; I see it now. But it doesn't prevent me from thinking it again as she stares back at me.

For now, I'll settle for the silent declaration of my fingers leaving a slow caress on her skin. As well as telling her that she's the one good thing in my life right now. It's the closest thing I can say without flat-out telling her that I love her again.

"What do you think?" I finally say quietly.

Her smile is coy as she leans over. She plants a delicate kiss on my lips before settling back in her seat. "You are, too."

---

"Do you ever think about Mom?"

Sophia's fork full of scrambled eggs stops mid-way to her open mouth as she eyes me warily. By the way she's staring at me, it's as if I shouted the question across the busy restaurant. The eggs never make it to her mouth before she drops her fork back on her plate.

She crosses her arms before saying, "Is that why you took me out for breakfast this morning?"

I scrunch up my nose. "How is this me taking you out for breakfast?"

With her arms still crossed, she motions to her plate. "Well, I'm not paying for this."

I roll my eyes. "Fine, I'll pay. Can you answer my fucking question please?"

She widens her eyes and makes a face while looking to the side as if slightly appalled by my profanity. "Pushy," she comments while picking up her smoothie.

I know she's just antagonizing me on purpose but fucking hell, it's working and my knee starts to jump under the table as I try to keep my cool.

Sophia cracks a smile and takes a sip of her drink as if enjoying every second of my torture. I shoot daggers at her from across the table while she takes her time crunching on a piece of toast.

Finally, she answers my question, "Occasionally."

Her one-word answer irks me, but I press on. "Do you miss her?"

Sophia's upper lip curls ever so slightly as if the very thought repulses her.

"Do *you*?"

I shrug and take a sip of coffee. "I miss the concept of her, I think."

"The concept of her?" she repeats. Then laughs. "Okay, therapy."

"Yeah," I deadpan. Then, study her for a few seconds. "And given how fucking aloof you're acting, I think it might be your turn soon."

She points a finger at herself, mouth open in shock. "My turn?" She shakes her head profusely. "You got the wrong girl."

"Why the hell not?"

Never in my life did I think I'd be the poster child for therapy, but here we are.

She scoffs, shoving a piece of bacon into her mouth. She chews, which I can only describe as, *with attitude,* before swallowing and finally saying, "No therapist is going to tell me anything I haven't already figured out myself." Her voice is thick with annoyance. "Abandonment issues? Check."—she makes the motion with her hand—"Neglect? Check. Emotionally immature parents? Check."

Realizing the conversation is moot, I concede to her holier-than-thou attitude.

*For now.*

I hold my hands up as a sign of surrender. "Okay, fine. Whatever. Suit yourself."

I resume eating my blueberry pancakes in silence.

"Anyway," Sophia says pointedly, obviously wanting to change the subject.

She picks up her phone from beside her plate and starts tapping around on the screen.

"Oh my god!" she says a little too loudly.

Her mouth falls open as her body jerks forward in shock, wide eyes jumping up to meet mine. I can tell by her expression that her shock is out of excitement.

I don't have time to ask why she's gawking at her phone before she flips her screen around and shows it to me. For half a second, I can't tell why she's showing me a picture of me and Connie. Until I realize that the picture has been posted on *Connie's* Instagram profile.

It's been almost two weeks since we officially started dating. Best two weeks of my fucking life. But she had not once posted about us on her socials until now.

"That's a hard launch if I ever did see one," Sophia chuckles, grinning at her screen.

"Let me see." I grab my phone and pull up her profile. I study the picture some more. "She even tagged me in it," I mutter under my breath.

It's of us having coffee, sitting next to each other at her kitchen island. She's wearing one of my t-shirts and I think I might die of fucking bliss staring at us.

I look so happy. *She* looks so happy.

Maybe I should be embarrassed by how excited I feel about just a simple picture of us. But it's so much more than that. She's finally claimed me. For the whole world to see.

I lean back into my chair, feeling smug as I look back at my sister. Sophia's expression is one of quiet pride.

She smiles. "You deserve every second of this," she says softly.

Not long ago, that statement would have made me uncomfortable. Mad even. But not today.

Today, I receive it wholeheartedly.

Today, I believe it.

**49**

## CONNIE

I can barely stand still, bouncing on my toes while I wait for the elevator doors to open. I'm vibrating with excitement, counting down the seconds before Huxley appears. When the elevator finally dings, I leap in place, my smile widening when Huxley's gaze falls on me.

"Hi," I chirp, unable to hide my elation.

"Hi," he says, looking at me up and down as if trying to decipher what's going on with me.

He strolls in, the tell-tale sound of his keys jingling against his pants tickling my ear. Sliding both hands around my waist, he pulls me into him and smirks, his face now close to mine.

"Nice looking picture you posted earlier," he says smoothly, giving my ass a small, playful tap.

I giggle, circling my arms around his neck.

"Yeah? You liked that, did you?"

His smirk turns into a grin. "Does that mean I can start calling you my girlfriend now?"

The word girlfriend has my stomach doing a little swoop, and I pretend to act aloof when I answer, "I don't know ... Only if you want, I guess."

He gives my ass another little love tap and I let out another giggling laugh as he shuffles us backward until my thighs hit the couch behind me.

"Let me hear it," he orders, his mouth trailing down the slope of my neck.

"What?" I ask innocently as he nibbles my earlobe. "You want to hear me say that you're my boyfriend, is that it?"

His groan rumbles in his chest, and I can't stop smiling. His head pops up, eyes darkening as he stares at me.

"Say it again."

I smirk. "Boyfriend." I say it slowly and deliberately, a subtle tease in between the curves of the letters.

His lips claim mine, and I moan eagerly into his mouth, perfectly happy to spend the evening right here, making out with Huxley. Eventually, I do pull away, but not before I give him another quick kiss as I push him on his shoulder so he can release me.

"I have a surprise for you," I say giddily. "Sit, sit."

I motion to the loveseat I purchased especially for us to watch the sunsets. Just like I had envisioned when I first moved in. He looks at me with amused suspicion but still sits down and waits for me to join him.

I sit on my bent leg, facing him, and just blurt it out, my lack of impulse control getting the better of me.

"I bought us tickets to Brazil!"

I expect him to match my excitement, but his face drops instead. My stomach sinks along with his reaction; I'm not really sure *why* he's reacting the way he is.

"What just happened?" I ask slowly. "Why aren't you excited?"

Huxley's brows furrow, but he doesn't say anything, and with every passing second, my anxiety heightens.

Finally, he speaks. "Do you think I'm some kind of ... charity case?"

Nothing would have prepared me for what just came out of his mouth. Dumbfounded, I stare back at him. His tone isn't exactly defensive. But he said it much too quietly for me to dismiss the gravity of his statement.

"Wait, *what*? Charity case? Where is this even coming from?"

"Why else would you buy me something like that?" he asks.

*Literally, what the fuck is happening?*

I suddenly take offense. His weird aversion to me buying us these tickets is starting to piss me off. When I answer him, my tone is chock-full of pissy attitude.

"Oh, you can't think of *one* other reason I would buy something like that? Not a one?" I cross my arms and stare him down. Huxley blinks but doesn't say anything. "Because I love you, stupid."

Huxley's eyes widen, but he doesn't move. Aside from my heart slamming in my chest, I don't either. I keep my face flat, waiting for *some* kind of reaction from the man I just professed my love to. After what feels like an eternity of waiting, Huxley slowly smiles. It reaches all the way up to his sparkling eyes, and I suddenly have to remind myself how to breathe.

"Took you long enough," he says smugly.

Before I can react, he's on top of me, pushing me onto the couch. I let out a little shriek, Huxley's mouth on mine muffling the sound. He peppers me with kisses. On my lips, my cheeks, my forehead, and back to my lips.

Finally, he pushes himself up on his forearms and looks down at me, smiling.

"I love you, too, stupid."

I giggle, the rush of him saying it back thrumming through my veins.

"Hey, that's my line," I reply teasingly, unable to stop grinning.

His smile is just as radiant as mine feels, his eyes are steadfast and penetrating.

"So Brazil, huh?"

I nod with excitement.

"Thank you," he says warmly before kissing me again.

I slip my hand up his nape and smirk. "What's mine is yours, baby."

# EPILOGUE
## CONNIE

**One Month Later**

It's opening night at the Remington, and I'm so excited that I'm practically vibrating out of my skin. I'm just off stage, peeking through the heavy velvet curtains at the crowd gathering in the auditorium.

It's a full house, and the sounds of people chattering and laughing are like music to my ears, the sense of accomplishment tingling through my veins. I might not be the one on stage, but this is my moment nonetheless. It's my play. My words. And I couldn't be more proud of myself.

"Hey," I hear Huxley whisper from behind me.

His hands slide over my hips as I swivel around to look at him.

"Hux," I whisper back, acting surprised but still circling my arms around his waist. I kiss him before adding, "What are you doing backstage? I thought you were sitting with everyone else?"

He flashes me a crooked grin. "I am," he replies, followed by another quick kiss. "But I wanted to see you before it started." His smile turns coy. "I have a surprise for you in your office."

I lift my brows. "A surprise?" I smirk. "For me?"

"Yeah, for you, silly," Huxley says before taking my hand and pulling me toward the corridor leading to my office.

"What is it?" I ask playfully.

Huxley doesn't say a word but looks at me over his shoulder and winks. Butterflies flutter in my stomach at the sight. I'm still getting used to this side of Huxley. It's not as if his inclination to brood has magically disappeared since we got together, but there's a peacefulness to his demeanor now that I only caught glimpses of before. Aside from therapy, I like to believe I'm at least partly the cause of this new version of him.

Before getting to my office, Huxley turns to face me and takes hold of my other hand, now clutching both.

"Close your eyes," he says.

I tease him with a suspicious look, but close my eyes as instructed, squeezing both his hands when I do. Carefully, he guides me inside, positioning me in the room with gentle hands on my hips until he finally tells me to open my eyes.

My gaze lands on my desk. It takes me a few seconds to understand what I'm looking at, but when it finally dawns on me, my hands fly to my mouth.

"Oh my god," I say breathlessly, taking a step forward and bending down to have a closer look. "Is that ..."

On my desk sits a small wooden replica of the Remington stage. Carefully carved and painted, with miniature decor placed all across the stage as if still in the middle of renovation. Like the small ladder leaning against one of the walls. Or the small bucket of paint close by.

"Did you make that?" I say the words slowly, still in awe of all the details I continue to find as I study the model.

"Yeah," Huxley says behind me. "I made the bulk of it in woodworking class."

He pauses, and I turn around to face him. His smile is sheepish, and if I were prone to tears, I think I'd be fighting the deluge right about now.

"I worked on the rest of it at home as much as I could." He rubs his neck and shrugs. "I was really trying to get it done before opening night." His gaze softens, and I feel it warm against my skin. "Do you like it?"

"Oh, Hux," I say softly. I take his hands, prompting him to circle his arms around my waist. He pulls me closer as I slip my arms around his neck. "I *love* it." I kiss him tenderly. "This is the nicest thing anyone has ever done for me."

Huxley smiles against my lips, the kiss lingering and achingly sweet.

"Yeah?" he rasps.

"Yeah," I repeat in between kisses, then groan as if annoyed. "Ugh, I'm so in love, it's disgusting."

Huxley puffs out a laugh, trailing kisses up my neck before looking up at me. His green eyes scintillate as he squeezes me against him.

"I guess that means you're stuck with me forever, then," he answers teasingly.

I sigh, pretending to be bothered, and quirk a smile. "I guess I am."

# EPILOGUE
## HUXLEY

**One Week Later**

My palms keep getting clammy, and I wipe them on my jeans, my knee bouncing at hyper-speed. Connie's hand lands on my thigh, making me abruptly stop my nervous tick. Her gaze is comforting as she smiles.

"You good?" she asks quietly.

She's leaned across the small aisle between our seats, her thumb rubbing my thigh in a slow, soothing stroke. I rip my thumb out of my mouth, realizing I've been chewing on the skin.

"Yeah." I give her a sheepish smile. "Just a little nervous."

It's my first time on a plane. First time in First Class. First time at an *airport*.

When we first got to the airport a few hours ago, I was shocked to see how crowded it was.

"Is it always this busy?" I asked Connie.

She shrugged and said, "Pretty much."

The realization I then had was hard to explain. It's as if I'd never *truly* bothered to think how different people's lives could be from mine. Free to travel. Free to explore and roam the world.

Now, I'm twenty-five years old with a valid passport. And in a few minutes, I'll be in the air, flying to Brazil.

I can't believe my luck.

My luck.

Luck.

The word still feels so foreign on my tongue. If Huxley, freshly out of prison, could hear me now. He'd laugh in my face. But I refuse to feel embarrassed by a younger, more broken version of myself. I've earned this luck. I deserve this life.

"That's totally normal." She pats my knee. "Deep breaths, remember."

I nod and breathe deeply from my nose while Connie leans back into her seat.

"Who knows, maybe you'll love to fly — and besides," she says, smirking playfully. "Nothing a few glasses of champagne can't fix."

I snort. "Do they have beer at least?"

Connie laughs and nods. "Yeah, they have beer."

A few minutes later, we're ready for takeoff. Connie keeps her arm outstretched, holding my hand while the plane rumbles loudly under us. I swallow hard, my heart beating even harder, but it's mostly from excitement.

I can't believe this is happening.

I can't believe I'm heading to Brazil with my dream girl.

The love of my fucking life.

Our seats are in the middle aisle, and from over Connie's shoulder, I look out the window. I don't feel it when the wheels lift from the tarmac, but my eyes widen when the scenery starts to shrink.

*Holy shit.*

I'm flying.

I don't hide my reaction when I look back at Connie. I'm grinning like a fool. And she is, too. Something about this moment feels like an important turning point. Like I've finally left my old life behind. I still don't know if I believe in fate like Connie does.

But right now, I believe in myself.

And that's a powerful fucking thing.

# MORE FROM NAOMI LOUD

Don't miss out on the bestselling dark romance series "Was I Ever".

| | |
|---|---|
| Sunny and Byzantine | Was I Ever Here |
| Lenix and Connor | Was I Ever Real |
| Lucy and Bastian | Was I Ever Free |

# More from Naomi Loud

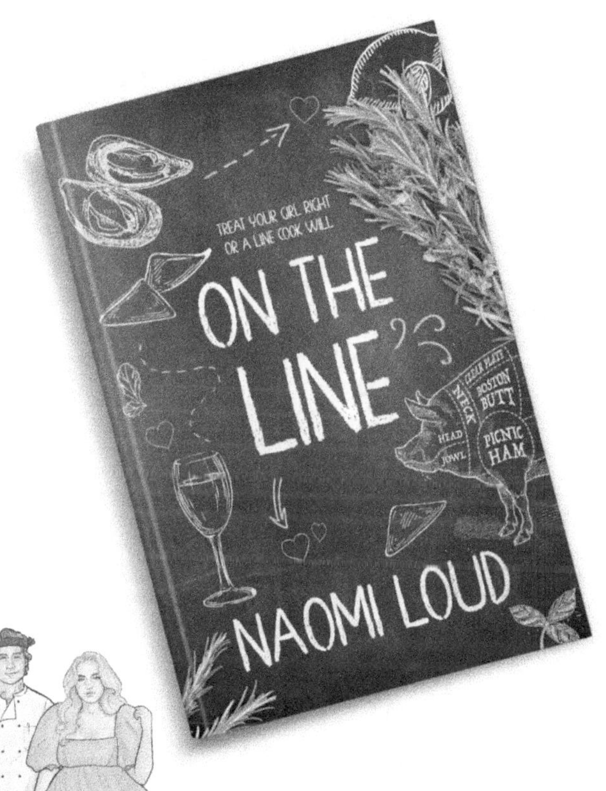


a line cook x
server romance

# Not ready to leave the Loudverse?

# Welcome to the Perverse City series ...

If you don't want to miss out on any future book announcements make sure to follow me on Instagram and Tiktok at naomi.loud or subscribe to my newsletter! You can find the link on my website: www.naomiloud.com

And if you loved Play the Part, I'd be forever grateful if you could leave a positive review on Amazon. Your support is why indie authors can continue doing what we love. Thank you!

# ACKNOWLEDGMENTS

Thank you to my alpha team (who've become *so* much more than that): Lotte, Cait, Shani, Bella, Meghan & Nouha. Y'all are my rock, my homies, my comic relief. I am the luckiest girl in the world. LOVE YOU SO MUCH.

FORMAL APOLOGY to my beta team: Mallory, Casadi, Jessy, Ada, Janine, and Aly. Who knew forgetting to add Huxley's tongue piercing would cause such an uproar? I am truly sorry. Please forgive me.

Thank you Ada (aka Archetype) for helping me so much with my branding and graphics for this book. You've made my life so much easier. I love your aesthetic so much!

Thank you to my editor Louise, this is our eighth book together!! And lastly, thank you to my cover designer Cat. Working with you gives me all the warm and fuzzies. You're so talented, I love you.

# ABOUT THE AUTHOR

Writer, occasional poet, and full-time witch, Naomi Loud is known for her angsty and heartfelt stories. Whether it be dark romance or contemporary, she loves to explore the complexities of the human condition and find the common thread that connects us all. Naomi lives in Montreal, Canada, with her husband and three cats, but secretly wishes she could live underwater.